HOW TO DITCH YOUR YOUR *Fairy*

JUSTINE LARBALESTIER

BLOOMSBURY

NEW YORK BERLIN LONDON

Published by Bloomsbury U.S.A. Children's Books
175 Fifth Avenue, New York, New York 10010

The Library of Congress has cataloged the hardcover edition as follows:
Larbalestier, Justine.
How to ditch your fairy / by Justine Larbalestier.—1st U.S. ed.
p.   cm.
Summary: In a world in which everyone has a personal fairy who tends to one aspect of daily life,
fourteen-year-old Charlie decides she does not want hers—a parking fairy—and embarks on a series
of misadventures designed to rid herself of the invisible sprite and replace it with a better one, like her
friend Rochelle's shopping fairy.
ISBN-13: 978-1-59990-301-9 • ISBN-10: 1-59990-301-6 (hardcover)
[1. Fairies—Fiction. 2. Magic—Fiction. 3. Interpersonal relations—Fiction.]
I. Title.
PZ7.L32073Ho 2008   [Fic]—dc22   2008002408

ISBN-13: 978-1-59990-379-8 • ISBN-10: 1-59990-379-2 (paperback)

Typeset by Westchester Book Composition
Printed in the U.S.A. by Worldcolor Fairfield, Pennsylvania
3 5 7 9 10 8 6 4 2

All papers used by Bloomsbury U.S.A. are natural, recyclable products
made from wood grown in well-managed forests. The manufacturing processes
conform to the environmental regulations of the country of origin.

Praise for

HOW TO DITCH YOUR *Fairy*

"*How to Ditch Your Fairy* is a stay-up-all-night read, full of clever twists, mature humor, and thoroughly believable characters. . . . Fast-paced and captivating, the storyline here never misses a beat."
—CurledUpKids.com

"Set in a futuristic fantasy city, this book puts a fun spin on fairy tales: fairies exist, but you may wish they did not. . . . This vividly imagined story will charm readers." —*Publishers Weekly*

"Charlie is totally likable, smart, and sarcastic, a perfectly self-involved, insecure teen. . . . This 'doos' (brilliant) fantasy will not be ditched." —*SLJ*

"This comic coming-of-age novel will entertain teen readers."
—*Kirkus Reviews*

"Larbalestier's inhabitation of Charlie's voice is crisp, funny, and wholly believable. . . . [The] well-drawn protagonist will easily carry teens captivated by the hysterical first page through to the finish."
—*VOYA*

"Thoroughly entertaining, totally enchanting, wickedly funny."
—Libba Bray, author of *A Great and Terrible Beauty*

"Welcome to your new obsession! Not only will you believe in fairies after reading this book, you will know what kind you have."
—Maureen Johnson, author of *13 Little Blue Envelopes*

Books by Justine Larbalestier

How to Ditch Your Fairy
Liar

For Stephen Gamble and Ron Serdiuk,
my two favorite fairies

NOTE TO READERS

How to Ditch Your Fairy isn't set in Australia or the United States of America but in an imaginary country, perhaps a little in the future, that might be an amalgam of the two. Like both those countries, it has an East Coast and a West Coast and there are islands too. But no one eats apple pie or Vegemite sandwiches and they play cricket as well as baseball.

CHAPTER 1
Killer Top

Days walking: 60
Demerits: 4
Conversations with Steffi: 5

My spoffs looked funny in the top, which is odd because my spoffs are tiny. I pulled the top up and tried to push them back where they belonged. Didn't work. Somehow the top was pushing my right spoff under my armpit and my left toward my neck.

I wasn't entirely used to having spoffs. I'm only fourteen and the lumps on my chest only started happening six months ago and, like I said, they're tiny. Mom says having any at all at my age is lucky. Except that all my friends have them. Anyway, up till now they'd shown no indication of straying far from my chest.

"Your fairy hates me," I said to my best friend, Rochelle.

"No, she doesn't," Rochelle said, admiring herself in the dressing room mirror. The little black dress she was trying on looked perfect; her spoffs were where they were supposed to be, not migrating to other parts of her body. The black brought out the gold in her eyes, which was strange seeing as how there's not any gold in black. Maybe her fairy was leaking dust.

"Your rentals won't let you wear that," I told her. Her parents were strict about Rochelle's clothes being suitably becoming. I pulled off the spoff-destroying top. I stared at it. It looked like a top: two sleeves, a sweetheart neckline, straight seams. The material wasn't even stretchy. How had it attacked me like that?

"It's not that short."

I looked at Rochelle in the dress. It managed to cover *most* of her thighs, but Rochelle is vastly tall, and dresses on her always seem shorter than they really are. "Yeah, but it's *that* low. You'll be shopping-grounded again."

"No, I won't." Rochelle hoicked up the top of her dress, disappearing all spoffage. "See? I'll wear it like this in front of the rentals and Dad'll think it doesn't reflect badly on him and won't say a word. Mom never notices what I'm wearing unless she thinks it's disgraceful." She struck a pose in front of the mirror, shoulders back, chest out (Rochelle is not spoffs-lacking), and fingers splayed like a fancy dancer. "Anyway, it's only twenty dollars."

"What?" I exclaimed, though it wholly figured. You'd think I'd've stopped being surprised years ago. "Those dresses are all two hundred dollars."

Rochelle reached around to dig out the tag hanging down her back and awkwardly held it out while turning so that I could see it. The tag was tattered and heavily

2

crossed out. I peered closer. The top crossed-out amount said $200, then $150, then $100, all the way down to the very edge of the ticket, where it said in teeny-tiny (dare I say fairy?) writing: *damaged, $20 only.*

I sighed. "Where's the damage, then?" The silk of the dress shone, exuding an aura of unwrinkled never-been-worn-before-ness. I couldn't even see a stray piece of thread. The top I'd just removed had several. The tag said $75. It was not reduced.

"Isn't any." Rochelle was staring at herself in the mirror, not smiling, but looking deeply satisfied.

"Your fairy never lets you down, does she?"

Rochelle nodded. "Yes, she does. She didn't do anything for that top of yours." She picked it up, turned it over, picked off another thread. "I was so sure this would look fantabulous on you . . . I like her best when she works for you too. You know I read in *Stars Weekly* that Our Tui says that fairies work best for virtuous people? That when she's been a bit naughty her fairy won't—"

"Oh! Did she finally say what kind of fairy she has? It's a charm fairy, isn't it?"

Rochelle shook her head. "Nope. She didn't. Anyway, I'm wondering if I've done something bad, and that's why she's only working for me today."

"That's silly. If fairies only worked for good people, then how do you explain Fi-or-en-ze Stupid-Name? Her fairy never takes days off and she's vastly up herself."

"You have a point," Rochelle said.

3

"Also I have four demerits, which indicates badness, right? But I'm certain my fairy's working as hard as ever."

"That's different! You got your demerits trying to *get rid* of your fairy!"

I sucked my teeth at her objections. "Anyway, Ro, you never do anything bad."

"I didn't let Joey come to practice."

"Your brother's a brat. He's almost as bad as Nettles."

"Nettles isn't a brat. Neither is Joey."

I allowed as how they weren't always that bad, which was true. Just a week earlier Nettles had baked me a lemon cake—my favorite. On the other hand she had "borrowed" one of my tennis rackets, broken all the strings, and stripped all the paint off it to use for one of her art projects. Instead of killing her, Mom and Dad had praised her creativity and then docked her pocket money to buy me a new racket.

"Are you girls finished in there?" the shop assistant asked, yanking the curtains open before we had a chance to respond. Just as well we were dressed already.

"Oh," she said, staring at Rochelle, "that looks lovely. Wow! It's like the dress was made for you."

Rochelle grinned, enjoying the new shop assistant. Suzy, her name tag said, though that most likely wasn't her real name. The owner of Best Dresses, Leatherbarrow, rarely got around to having new name tags made, so all the girls who worked there just swapped around the five old ones. As there were never more than three girls working at once, even on super-busy days, it worked out. But it meant that everyone was called Suzy, Ilian, Daisy, Rhani, or Lucinda.

The other girls knew Rochelle and her fairy and no longer bothered to compliment her. Too jealous, I reckoned. They were all standard boring pulchritudinous: big eyes, big mouth, little nose, and Rochelle wasn't, but she always looked better than them.

Rochelle, as you might have gathered, has a clothes-shopping fairy. Most people find it hard to like her because she has such a doos fairy, but they soon forgive her because a) she's a sugar, b) sometimes her fairy will work for her friends (though sadly not often), and c) her family is jaw-droppingly atrocious. Rochelle deserves her fairy.

Rochelle stripped off the dress and put on her own clothes (tartan skirt, white T-shirt, tailored black jacket with matching tartan cuffs and collar, which you'd think would look vile, but on her was far from it). She paid for the dress and we made our way out of Best Dresses, past Fairy World—where a stack of plastic Fairy Catchers were on sale (round hoops with sticky filaments attached that are supposed to catch fairies; I happened to know that they're useless)—and out of the shopping center.

I slipped my lucky cricket ball out of my pocket, rubbed my thumb over the seam, and started spinning it. "Time for ice cream?" I asked. "I haven't touched my fat allowance today."

"Me neither. Plus Dad's picking me up there."

"Fruit-flavored fat it is then."

5

CHAPTER 2

Rochelle

Days walking: 60
Demerits: 4
Conversations with Steffi: 5
Doos clothing acquired: 0

I had chocolate and strawberry in a crunchy nut and brioche cone, and Rochelle had lemon and lime in the vanilla cone. Neither of which put us over our fat or sugar limit for the day, though it did mean dinner was going to have to be lean. Worth it!

When I went to pay, Rochelle stopped me. "My shout. A little apology for my fairy not working for you."

"That's okay, Ro. She hardly ever does."

"Yeah, but she doesn't usually actively sabotage you . . ."

"No worries. I'm used to doxy fairies." I took a bite out of my ice cream and my brain went on the frizz. "Oh! Oh! Oh!" I clutched my right temple, trying not to drop the cone.

"Shouldn't take such big bites," Rochelle said, demurely licking her lemon and lime to demonstrate how ice cream *should* be eaten. "Small licks and nibbles, Charlie, not big bites."

I nodded even though stating the obvious is the most annoying thing in the entire world. Maybe her fairy did double duty as a saying-the-fragging-obvious fairy? The freezerization in my brain started to ebb away. "Steffi isn't—"

"Steffi?"

"The new boy. Stefan." His family had moved in just around the corner from my place, so we'd been hanging out.

"The wholly pulchritudinous one?" Rochelle said.

I felt my cheeks get hot. He *is* vastly pulchy—cheekbones so high they almost touch the sky, and glorious long black curls; not to mention his skin, which is the color of a chocolate kiss, my favorite candy.

"You still with me, Charlie?" She took another demure bite of her ice cream.

"Oh, sorry. Yes, that boy. He says where he comes from everyone calls him Steffi."

"He does, huh? Isn't that a girl's name?" Rochelle said, mock punching me.

"Ow!" Her mock punches are harder than most people's *actual* punches.

"Baby."

"Am not."

"Are."

"Not."

"Are. Infinity times a million." Rochelle punched me again, hard. "You lose, I win!"

"Don't tell anyone else about his nickname, okay?"

"Fairy's honor," Rochelle said solemnly. She always keeps her promises. "You been hanging out with him a lot, have you?"

"Um," I said. So far we'd had five conversations. Not that I was counting. "He's smart. Funny too."

"And pulchy."

My face got hot again. I took a small bite of my ice cream. "It's not just that. He's not like anyone I've ever met before. It's hard to explain." I thought I'd had crushes before. But this was different. As different as imagining summer on a cold winter's day. When your cheeks sting from the cold, it's hard to imagine being out in the waves under the sun, surfing. How I felt about Steffi was real; my other crushes had been vapor.

"You really like him, huh?" Rochelle said.

I nodded.

"And he likes you?"

"I think so. I mean, he likes me as a friend. He laughs at my jokes, but it's not like he has stacks of other friends. He only just got here." I shrugged. "It's hard to tell what kind of like it is."

"Well, at least you get to hang out, right? Remember Sandra's crush on Freedom Hazal?"

I nodded. He hadn't given Sandra the time of day.

8

There was much suffering before she realized that while Freedom was pulchy, there wasn't much more to him than clear skin, big eyes, and moppy hair.

"It could be that she's in a bad mood," Rochelle said.

"Who? Sandra?"

"No, my fairy. My aura's been kind of thick today. You know? Soupy, almost."

I pushed air through my teeth, mocking her. "Auras? Please!"

"Fiorenze says fairies create an aura around you. If your fairy's in a bad mood they make it all hazy around your head."

"You don't believe anything Stupid-Name says, do you?"

"Just because Fiorenze's vile," Rochelle said, "doesn't mean she doesn't know about fairies. Both her parents have PhDs in Fairy Studies."

"From an old-country university. That doesn't count! I bet they only have those degrees 'cause they paid for them. You know how rich her family is."

"But her mom teaches at UNA now. She wouldn't have a job *there* if her degree was dodgy."

"Oh." My mother studied biology at UNA. It's the best university in the city, which, naturally, makes it the best in the world. "Well, I heard they're only rich because they inherited the money."

"I heard that too. Apparently her grandmother invented some kind of computer thing." Rochelle shrugged. "That's not the point. Fiorenze's parents know about fairies, and fairy auras are her mom's pet theory. She has these special mirrors and you can see your fairy's aura floating all around your head. Mine's purple."

"You went to Fiorenze Stupid-Name's house! To our sworn enemy's home? You talked to her parents?" How could she?! We had a pact that neither of us would ever have anything to do with poxy boy-magnet Fiorenze Burnham-Stone, who's even more annoying and pretentious than her name.

"Basketball, Charlie. She's captain. Remember? It wasn't just me. The whole team was there! I *have* to socialize with her. Plus she was sick all last week and I agreed to fill her in on all the stuff that isn't in the notes."

"Stupid basketball team." Mention of it did not make me happy. I'm astral at sports—we're both at New Avalon Sports High, the best Sports high school in the city, probably in the world—but I'm not very tall. Okay, I'm not even slightly tall. I'm the opposite of tall. The shortest girl in my class and I always have been.

My mom says that makes me more environmentally sound than everyone else, because I take up less space and use less resources. But that is no comfort when you try out for the basketball team and everyone laughs at you. "Hey, shorty," they called. "You need a stepladder?"

Back at Bradman Sports Middle School I'd been the star point guard, averaging six assists a game. Six! And my ten points a game wasn't bad either. Tragically, none of that was on show at my high school basketball trial. I was one for twelve from the floor with only two assists. It was like there was Vaseline on the ball. And my strength, free throws? I didn't make a single one.

I wasn't even selected for D-stream basketball. All because of one poxy day.

As long as I could remember all I've ever wanted to do is play cricket and basketball. I couldn't wait for the New Avalon Sports High tryouts. It never occurred to me I wouldn't blitz in basketball. I'd actually worried that by the time I got to the final year of high school and had to pick one, I wouldn't know what to do. But I might not get to make that choice. My next chance to try out for basketball wasn't until the beginning of next year! So many months away . . . But I practiced whenever I could. Next time I was determined not to have a bad day.

"Our basketball team is not stupid," Rochelle said. "Anyway, none of us like her. But she *is* our captain. I can't avoid her!"

Fiorenze Burnham-Stone wasn't liked by any of the girls at school because she's stuck-up and won't talk to the rest of us, but mostly because of her every-boy-will-like-you fairy. Even though she's not that smart, or fun, or pulchy, or anything really—all the boys want to be with her.

"I wasn't at her house for fun, you know," Rochelle said. "It was pep-talky and strategy and you know."

"Is her house as big as everyone says?"

"Bigger," Rochelle said. "I only talked to her mom 'cause

there were all these books about fairies, but not supermarket-lite books, serious books, with not-fun covers and long titles. I was curious. You're the one who always wants to know about fairies. You should talk to her parents. Her dad has written books about fairies. Whole books! They're, like, world experts."

"Who believe in auras?"

"I saw mine in her mom's mirror. And this morning I had to blink and blink before I could see right, it was so thick."

"You don't think it was just sleep in your eyes?"

"That's what I used to think, but now I know better."

"Really?"

Rochelle nodded earnestly.

"Do you think fairies can read our minds?" I asked.

"No. They're not psychic or anything."

"So auras, yes; mind-reading, no?"

"Yup," Rochelle replied, ignoring my mockage.

"Hmmm, so how do they know if we're mean or not?"

"Don't you know *anything*, Charlie?"

I shrugged, not conceding ignorance, but not pretending I knew vast reams either.

"They can see what we do. That's all anyone needs to figure out if someone's mean and doesn't deserve a fairy. I mean, we can't read Fiorenze's mind, can we?"

I shuddered. "The horror. Can you imagine? Who wants to go into her malodorous mind?"

"Exactly," Rochelle said, finishing off her ice cream.

12

I wasn't sure what was *exactly* about it; our not reading Stupid-Name's mind didn't have anything to do with whether fairies could read our minds. "My mom reckons it's random—what fairy we have. No merit involved," I said. "Why can't we see them, anyway?"

"Because they're *in-vis-i-ble*. Why can't we see dust mites?"

"'Cause they're really, really small. But, Ro, we *can* see them. Through a microscope."

"That's cheating."

"Do you reckon we could see a fairy through a microscope?"

"Please!"

A car honked. Rochelle's dad rolled down his car window and yelled at her, even though she'd already stood up. "Sure you don't want a lift?"

I shook my head. Even if I hadn't been on my walking-only regimen, I wouldn't have taken a lift with Rochelle's horrendous father.

"Still walking everywhere?" Rochelle asked as her dad honked again. "You really think it's going to get rid of your fairy?"

"Hope so."

"See you at school tomorrow!"

CHAPTER 3

Parking Fairy

Days walking: 60
Demerits: 4
Conversations with Steffi: 5
Doos clothing acquired: 0

I have a parking fairy. I'm fourteen years old. I can't drive. I don't like cars and I have a parking fairy.

Rochelle gets a clothes-shopping fairy and is always well attired; I get a parking fairy and always smell faintly of gasoline. How fair is that? I love clothes and shopping too. Yes, I have a fine family (except for my sister, ace photographer Nettles, and even she's tolerable sometimes) and yes, Rochelle's family is malodorous. She does deserve some kind of compensation. But why couldn't I have, I don't know, a good-hair fairy? Or, not even that doos, a loose-change-finding fairy. Lots of people have that fairy. Rochelle's dad, Sandra's cousin, Mom's best friend's sister. I'd wholly settle for a loose-change fairy.

It can be arduous hanging out with Rochelle. She always looks doos in her perfect clothes. And sometimes I get bored going shopping with her all the time, even when her fairy is working for me. Sometimes I look forward to rainy days even though it means we have to play tennis indoors. Her fairy doesn't work on rainy days.

My fairy has no objection to rain. She just doesn't do anything useful except make sure that whatever car I'm in finds the perfect parking spot. That's why I'm walking home and not getting a lift from Rochelle's dad: it's all part of my campaign to get rid of my fairy. I'm starving her of opportunities to do her thing so she'll want to go and be someone else's fairy. Our Zora-Anne says this is the best method for getting rid of a fairy you don't want. It's how she got a charisma fairy after having been born with a never-getting-lost fairy. Our Z-A never went anywhere for five years so she couldn't get lost and then one morning she woke up with a brand-new fairy, and before she knew it she was a star.

It could happen to me too.

So I walk. I could take the bus or the ferry or the light-rail, 'cause it's not like they need to park, but somehow walking seems much more wearisome for a parking fairy. For two months now I have walked everywhere. I haven't even ridden my bike or board. For all I know my fairy may be gone already. But I can't be sure and there've been no signs of a new one.

I've read everything in the library about fairies, especially anything that touches on the question of how to get rid of one, which hardly any of them do! Talking to

Stupid-Pants Fiorenze's parents was tempting. But all they'd have would be theories. That's all anyone's got—even the Fairy Studies experts—but there aren't any that fit all the facts, and make sense, and can be proved.

No one has ever seen a fairy. There are lots of fake photo sites, but, well, they're clearly fake. Or they're so indistinct and smudgy it could be anything. Like Steffi said, some people don't think it's a fairy that makes sure that every car I'm in gets a parking spot. Some say they're ghosts or some kind of spirit, and some people, like my dad and Steffi, don't believe it's anything but luck.

My mom has many theories. She's the one who figured out what my fairy was. I was still a baby. She'd had to go into town every day for a week because she was giving evidence in a court case (she's a microbiologist) and Brianna, who used to look after me back then, was sick, so Mom had to bring me in and hand me to the lawyer's associate to mind while she was on the stand. Anyway, every single day I was with her she got a parking spot in front of the courthouse in the only spot without a parking meter. It didn't matter how late she was running or whether it was raining or anything. The only time it didn't work was when Dad took a day off work to mind me. Mom ended up having to park practically where we lived and catch a bus in.

"Bingo!" she thought. "My daughter has a parking fairy." After that she put it to the test and found parking spots outside the Opera House, in the ranges, and right near the

NACG on the first day of the Millennium Test. Incontrovertible proof that her first child had a parking fairy.

And the beginning of my life in cars. I'm always being borrowed by Mom, or one of her sisters, or her best friend, Jan, or Nana and Papa, or just about everyone in our neighborhood, whenever they're going to the doctor's, or grocery shopping, or anywhere that parking might be a problem. Every single day of my life someone asks me to get in their doxhead car.

I hate cars. I hate drivers. I hate their little squeals of joy when they find a parking spot.

But mostly I hate my benighted parking fairy.

CHAPTER 4

New Avalon the Brave

Days walking: 60
Demerits: 4
Conversations with Steffi: 5
Doos clothing acquired: 0

It was such a long walk home that I almost wished I'd accepted the lift from Rochelle. Then a bus got caught at the lights. There was hardly any traffic. I could cross against the lights, and if I ran flat out I'd make it to the next stop in time to catch it.

Two months of walking . . . I considered whether I was tired enough to give my fairy a sniff of parking possibilities.

Nope. I was not going to give in.

The lights changed and the bus zoomed away. I crossed the street at my own pace, walking by the baseball diamond, where littlies in uniform were doing catching drills and their coach was yelling encouragement. I walked past the bus stop and someone said *Charlie* in my ear. I dropped my lucky cricket ball.

"Gotcha!" It was Steffi, grinning. Black curls bouncing around his face.

I grinned back, wondering if it would be totally weird if I reached out and touched one of his curls.

He retrieved my ball, rubbed it on his shorts, though it was a long time since that ball had any shine, and then tossed it back to me.

"Thanks," I said, wishing I could think of something else to say, but all I could think of was his pulchiness.

"Saw you from the bus, so I thought I'd surprise you. How's it going?"

"Not too horrendous," I said, smiling. Especially not now that Steffi was here walking beside me.

"That sounds grim."

I smiled. In the five—five!—conversations I'd had with Steffi since he'd started school last week, he'd used a mountain of words like "grim." Words so injured your parents wouldn't even use them. But somehow because he was saying them, they didn't seem so torpid.

"You heading home?" Steffi and his family had moved into Bradman Court, just around the corner from my place. Convenient, yes?

"Yeah. Was shopping with Rochelle."

"Sounds like a ton of fun," Steffi said sarcastically.

One of our five conversations had covered the topic of how tedious shopping is, but I'd meant grocery shopping—not clothes shopping! He was still grinning, making his eyes even more intense than they already were.

I'd thought they were light brown, but now they seemed to have gold streaks in them. Like a tiger's or something. Not that I'd ever seen a tiger. Yum. (Steffi, not tigers— though I'm sure tigers are also a pleasure to look at as long as they're not trying to rip your throat out or anything.)

"So what does Rochelle need all those clothes for?" Steffi asked. "We have uniforms. Lots of uniforms! Ninety percent of the time we're at school or at a meet."

"She needs clothes to go shopping in." I shot a look at him; he was looking back at me.

"Of course!" Steffi bounced from his left foot to his right, then skip-hopped in front of me.

I giggled. "I tried on this top and it almost strangled me."

"Now that sounds more interesting. Did you kill it?" Steffi drew a finger across his throat. "You could have brained it with your cricket ball."

I spun the ball the other way. As if I would deliberately damage a cricket ball. I mean in a way that wouldn't enhance its spinning. "No, but I shoulda. It was vicious! It even mooshed my spoffs out of place."

Steffi stared at me. "Your spoffs?"

I gestured chestward, trying not to blush. "You know, spoffs." Why had I told him about the top?

"That's what you call them? Spoffs?" Steffi asked. "You people are crazy."

What else would you call them? "Anyway, I wrestled the top into submission. I think its strangling days are over."

20

"Excellent."

I giggled again. No one says "excellent." It's even more injured than "grim." And here was Steffi telling me "spoffs" was crazy. Hah!

"What?" Steffi asked.

He mock punched me (much lighter than Rochelle does) and I was so pleased he'd touched me, it was hard to keep from laughing. Then I worried that it was weird that I was happy that he'd just mock punched me. He'd probably do that with anyone he hung out with.

"What's so funny?" he asked again.

"Nothing."

"You people are always laughing at me," Steffi said.

"Sorry."

"I'm not mad. It's just so different here. It's hard to fit in when we don't even seem to talk the same, you know?"

"I guess," I said.

"Have you ever lived anywhere but here?" he asked, looking all serious, which made him even more pulchy.

"No. My family's been here for ages. My parents and my grandparents and their parents were all born here."

"Hmm," Steffi said. "Well, my city's a lot different."

I nodded sympathetically. There's no place in the world like New Avalon. It's one of the biggest cities in the world for one, and we have more sports, arts, design, and science stars than anywhere else. More of our politicians make it to the capital, and we have the strongest economy of any city in the world. It must be hard coming here from somewhere else and realizing how obscure your home is.

"And you Avaloids—"

"Avalon*ers*."

"Avalon*ers*," Steffi repeated. "Whatever. You act like I should know everything about your city and are suprised when I don't know who some supposedly famous person is. You don't believe me when I say that they're not famous anywhere but here."

"Like who?" I asked.

"Zora-Anne."

"You don't know Our Z-A?!"

"I do *now*, but I didn't. No one back home's ever heard of her. Also, what's with the *Our* thing? I never heard anyone say that before. Why is she always called *Our* Zora-Anne and not just Zora-Anne? Do you only use it for famous people? Does anyone call you Our Charlie?"

I laughed at the idea. "Maybe one day they will, but not quite yet."

"So only the famous people are *Ours*?"

"Uh-huh. What do you call the famous people from your city?"

"We just call them by their names. Stanislaw Leda is Stanislaw Leda, and Huntley du Sautoy is Huntley du Sautoy. No 'Our' in front."

"Aren't you proud of them?" I asked. I didn't have the heart to tell him that I didn't know who those people were.

"Well, sure. I mean, some. But others are lame. We don't worship them like you Avaloids do."

"Avaloners," I said. "We don't worship Ours. We're just proud of them."

Steffi looked like he was going to say something and then flicked his hands instead. I wondered if it was supposed to be like shrugging, or teeth sucking, or if it was more like eye cutting.

"Is that why you said everyone outside New Avalon hates us? Because we call famous Avaloners 'Ours'?"

Steffi laughed. His whole face changed and he looked even more pulchy. I started laughing too even though I wasn't sure what was so funny.

"Not everyone hates you. Believe it or not some people don't even think about New Avalon."

"But last week in Statistics you said that everybody hates us." The whole classroom had exploded.

"I did, didn't I?" he said, grinning. "Sure set everyone off."

He had. Everyone told him to go back to where he came from, and demanded to know what kind of a name *Stefan* was anyhow. (Just as well they didn't know about his nickname.)

Demerits had been handed out left, right, and center, but it had been a welcome distraction from calculating the shift in batting averages from the twenties to the present day. I have no love for statistics.

"It's true people hate New Avalon, but I mostly said it

23

to annoy Freedom Hazal. He doesn't seem to think any-one outside New Avalon has ever achieved anything."

"Freedom can be a bother." Which was an understate-ment. Freedom's good-skin fairy causes no amount of jealousy—fifteen years old and he's never had a pimple, or blackhead, or the faintest hint of heat rash. He gloats about it too.

But wasn't it true that most famous people were from New Avalon? I decided not to point that out.

"You still trying to get rid of your parking fairy?"

I nodded, pleased that he'd remembered. "It is my life's mission."

"I thought getting on the basketball team was your life's mission?"

"I have two life missions," I said. I wondered if I should ask him to sit with me and Rochelle and Sandra tomor-row. Or if that would be too pushy. He'd spent last week hanging out with his soccer teammates.

"So how will you know when your fairy's gone?"

"The new fairy will start doing new fairy stuff." I hoped so, anyway.

"What about vegetarianism?" he asked.

"Huh?"

"I read an article in the *New Avalon Times* that says sta-tistically vegetarians have better fairies than meat-eaters."

"Really?"

He nodded so solemnly that I wasn't sure if he was mocking me or not.

24

"But Rochelle's not a vegetarian," I pointed out. "Nor is Fiorenze, and they have the best fairies ever."

"Who's Fiorenze?"

"You don't know? She's in Fencing with us. Also Statistics and PR. She's vastly popular." *Sort of.* Not with the girls, she wasn't.

Steffi looked blank. How delicious was that? If he didn't know who Fiorenze was, that meant her fairy wasn't working on him. He was immune! I bit my bottom lip to keep the joy from bubbling out. "She has this fairy that . . ." I trailed off.

Steffi grunted, clearly unintrigued. "Anyway, the article said *statistically*. You need a bigger sample size than just two. Not that the article said where those statistics came from. Do you have any doubts about fairies?"

I stared at him. "What's to doubt? Every time I'm in a car, there's a parking spot waiting for it. Every single time."

"I'm sure. I don't doubt your parking abilities. But is it really tiny little invisible people with wings? When my grandparents were alive they talked about luck, not fairies."

"They were dumber in the olden days." I wondered again what Steffi's fairy was. Did he have one? Not everyone does. My little sister doesn't. (And, pox, do we hear about it!) My dad doesn't either, but he doesn't believe in fairies or luck. "I just want to be lucky at something other than cars finding parking spots. That's not too much to ask, is it?"

"Nope. I guess not. Wanna shoot some hoops?"

"Sure," I said. "Nothing I'd like better."

"You can show me how crazy they were not to pick you," Steffi said.

"I sure will," I said, slipping my lucky ball back into my pocket. I was starting to think Steffi might like me too. "Race you to my place?"

"You're on!"

CHAPTER 5
True Love. Grr!

Days walking: 61
Demerits: 4
Conversations with Steffi: 6
Doos clothing acquired: 0

Monday morning Steffi and Fiorenze were hand in hand walking past my locker. Steffi gazed up into Stupid-Name's eyes as if the answer to today's Public Relations quiz could be found there. It was only first recess! Yesterday afternoon he hadn't even known she existed.

"Fairy dung," I said under my breath.

"I hear you," Bluey Salazar replied. He has a dog fairy (all dogs like him even if they bite or pee on everyone else). I hadn't noticed him at his locker beside me. "She's not even my type, but whenever that fairy-fluffed Fiorenze is in the room I can't look anywhere else. It's so annoying. Gosh, she's . . . it was so much better last week when she was out sick."

"Oh," I said. That's why Steffi hadn't known about Stupid-Name. She'd been sick all of his first week at school. Why couldn't her illness have lasted, say, till the end of high school?

"You really think she's pulchy?"

Bluey sighed. "Only when she's around. There ought to be a law against a fairy like hers. Though I love what she's done with her hair."

Her hair was braided and the tips of the braids were dyed bronze—almost the same shade as her skin. Our standard uniform is a bronzey brown, so she was now bronze from head to toe with only her eyes and lips standing out. In no way did she look adorable, pulchy, or doos.

I grunted. "Must have cost a fortune."

"She's rich. I heard her grandfather was a king in one of the old countries."

"I heard he was a bank robber," I muttered, though I hadn't heard that at all.

"It's a pity she's so stuck-up," Bluey said. "You know, I think it's been weeks since she spoke to anyone other than a teacher. It's an even bigger pity she's already got the new boy." He sighed again.

"I thought you said you don't like girls?"

"I know. The whole thing is *so* annoying!"

We watched Steffi lean forward and bounce two of Stupid-Name's braids against each other.

Aaaarggh!

I was so ready to beat her about the head until her obnoxious, fragged, make-my-life-a-misery, doxhead fairy curled up and died. What was she doing with Steffi? *My*

Steffi! Had she had six conversations with him since he started school? No, she had not! Fiorenze had never shown interest in a boy before. Not one. Why Steffi!? Other than him being the pulchiest boy I'd ever seen.

"See you," Bluey said.

"Uh-huh," I replied, staring at Steffi and Stupid-Name. They were definitely holding hands, which is an infraction. Stupid-Name was looking coy and glancing at her feet while standing so close to Steffi their fairies must have locked wings. Until now she'd been way too up herself to be linked with any of the boys at school. Though she's always happy to let them carry her gear or buy her lunch or whatever. I'd never seen her holding hands with anyone before.

Steffi leaned forward and blocked Stupid-Name's face from view. I couldn't tell if he was kissing her or not, but it sure looked like it. But they couldn't be that insane, could they? Being caught kissing on campus or off meant instant expulsion.

My fencing coach, Van Dyck, came striding down the corridor in the gold and brown jacket all the coaches wore. Sandra claims that Coach Van Dyck's gaze is so intense she can set students ablaze. There are rumors that her fairy is a setting-students-on-fire fairy.

Adrenaline flooded through me. Steffi couldn't be expelled! I'd just met him!

Without thinking about demerits or injuries I threw myself at the lovebirds, catching Steffi at the knees in a tackle that sent him crashing to the ground and Stupid-Name with him.

"Whoa!" Steffi began.

"You okay?" I asked, standing up, offering him a hand.

Steffi nodded. Stupid-Name sat blinking with her back to the lockers.

"What was that about?" Steffi asked.

"Charlotte Adele Donna Seto Steele!" Coach Van Dyck said, rushing up beside us. "Did you just attack these students?"

"No, Coach. There was a, there was a—"

"Wasp," Stupid-Name finished for me, standing up. She started to describe the wasp's huge dimensions.

"A wasp?" Coach repeated. "Which has now vanished?"

We all looked around for the nonexistent wasp. I was grateful that there were so many windows, making the wasp's existence and disappearance slightly plausible.

"Apparently, Coach," Steffi said. He looked confused.

Coach Van Dyck ran her fiery gaze over Steffi, then Stupid-Name, before coming to a rest on me. "Perhaps in the future, Charlotte, you might want to call out instead of tackling people?"

"Yes, Coach," I said, waiting for the demerit.

Van Dyck held her gaze on me for several very long wordless seconds before walking away.

"Thank you," I breathed, "for the wasp thing." I couldn't believe I'd gotten away without a demerit. "I wholly appreciate it."

Fiorenze nodded, but didn't look at me.

"No worries," Steffi said. "But why did you tackle us?"

"Kissing," I said. "It's against the school rules. You could get expelled. If Van had seen you . . ."

"Really?" Steffi said, astonished.

Fiorenze stayed silent.

"Students aren't supposed to engage in any public displays of affection."

"How about that?" Steffi said, turning to Fiorenze. "A wasp, eh? Well done." He kissed her cheek, then said, "Oops."

Fiorenze looked down and then muttered something I couldn't hear, which made Steffi laugh. He shook his head as if he could not believe how funny she was. It was wrong. Stupid-Name does not tell jokes. She is without joy or humor. Yes, covering for me was good of her, but I doubt she was thinking about it that way. She knew that kissing was expulsion worthy.

Doxhead.

I opened up my locker, remembered that my tennis gear was in the change room locker, and closed it again. Fiorenze finally disentangled herself from Steffi. As she walked past, I looked up, and for less than a second we stared at each other. I started to say something—it seemed weird not to—but she had already turned away as if talking to me, or any other girl, might make her head explode.

Why was she so stuck-up?

I stomped off toward the changing rooms, where Rochelle greeted me with a sympathetic smile. She was wearing black satin matching bra and panties, reminding me of how great her fairy is and how torpid mine is. She opened her mouth to speak.

"Don't," I said, holding up my hand in the universal sign for seal-your-lips-I-don't-want-to-hear-it.

"She looks horr—"

I pushed my hand to within a fairy's wing of her cheek. "Which part of the hand are you not comprehending?"

"The little finger. Also the lower part of the palm."

I growled, opened my changing room locker, stared at my tennis gear, sweats, and tees in a crumpled stinking mess, and realized I hadn't remembered to take them home to wash, or to bring in fresh ones. If I wore the pongy clothes, I'd score a demerit. And if I burst into tears on account of the general decrepitude of my day, I'd earn another one. Crying is vastly frowned upon. "Dung."

"Erk," Rochelle agreed, stepping back. "Those are on the nose. You can borrow some of mine if you like."

As if. Rochelle is almost exactly twice my height. Okay, slight exaggeration. But to make it clearer: I am a teeny-tiny point guard; she is a correctly sized center. If I tried to play in her giant tentlike tennis uniform, it'd be a demerit. "Very funny."

"What about wearing your fencing whites? Or your cricket ones?"

"Or your swimmers," Sandra said, opening her own locker. Sandra Leigh Petaculo is my second-best friend at school. Her fairy is a serving fairy. No matter what, her tennis serves always go in. Coach Ntini predicts that with some real speed and power, she will be one of the best tennis players New Avalon has ever produced. She will certainly be one of the most sarcastic.

"Oh, yes," I said, "everyone is laced with humor today." Wearing incorrect attire is also an infraction.

"Except you, Charlie," Rochelle said, giving me her big-eyed, are-you-okay/can't-you-take-a-joke look.

"Fairy fragger," I muttered, pulling my fencing whites out. "Don't laugh."

✦ ✦ ✦

Coach Ntini levied my demerit and noted that I was only three away from a game suspension. He did this without saying a word: he looked at my fencing whites sorrowfully, turned on his tablet, noted the demerit next to my name, slipped the tablet back in his pocket, and held up three fingers.

I looked down at my clothing and mustered up an expression of shock, as if this were the first time I had noticed what I was wearing.

"I'm sorry, Coach."

"Your sorrow changes nothing; only your deeds can."

"Yes, Coach."

"Go." He looked in the direction of Rochelle, Sandra, and the rest of the B-stream tennis squad, who were warming up.

I slunk off toward them, wishing there was a way to execute my fairy, not merely make her go away. If I hadn't been stuck with her I wouldn't be walking everywhere, and I wouldn't have racked up demerits, nor would I be so knackered all the time that I kept forgetting to do all the stuff I was supposed to be doing. Like washing my clothes.

Doxhead fairy!

CHAPTER 6
Danders Anders

Days walking: 61
Demerits: 5
Conversations with Steffi: 6
Doos clothing acquired: 0

Just salad?" Rochelle said, peering at my lunch. She and Sandra were sitting at one of the tables overlooking the clay tennis courts. Big metal rollers were being run over each court, operated by a groundie sitting in the umpire's chair using a remote control. It looked like fun.

"That's nowhere near enough protein," Rochelle continued. "Do you want another demerit?"

"It's a *big* salad." I pushed the lettuce aside with my fork. "See? Tofu. A full protein portion."

"Heya, Charlie. You trying the vegetarian thing?" Steffi asked, putting his tray next to mine. "Okay if we join you?" he asked as Stupid-Name put her tray on his other side. She didn't say hello.

"Sure," I said. "Sandra? Ro? Meet Stefan."

"We're in Accounting together," Rochelle said, waving.

"Health," Sandra said.

"You all know Fiorenze, right?" Steffi asked.

We nodded and resisted saying "unfortunately." Fiorenze pulled a book out of her bag, resting it open between her electrolyte drink and her lunch. She turned a page and commenced reading.

"Well, yes, new boy," Sandra said, glaring at Stupid-Name. "But only since kindergarten."

Actually, Rochelle and I had only known her since middle school, which was long enough.

"Just you two," Sandra said loudly. "None of your other admirers, Fiorenze. It's crowded enough here."

Fiorenze kept reading, absently putting a forkful of food into her mouth. The three boys hovering behind her walked elsewhere with their trays, which they should have done anyway, seeing as how you get a demerit for stalking Stupid-Name. I glanced around the room. Dozens of boys watching her longingly. When I looked back, Steffi was taking Fiorenze's hand in his. She glanced down, but didn't say anything.

"Thanks," Steffi said, and smiled at me in a way that made me feel warm all over. How could he smile at me like that while holding her hand?

Sandra reached across and tapped Steffi's tie. "It's crooked. You don't want to get a demerit, do you?"

Steffi frowned and pulled at his tie, making it more of a mess. He still looked pulchy.

I itched to fix it.

"You get in trouble for not having your tie straight?" he asked.

"Yes," Sandra said. "Haven't you read the infractions list?"

Steffi did his West Coast hand-flicking thing. So doos! "I don't know. Maybe. There were so many documents. I concentrated on the ones that'd get me up to speed on classes."

Up to speed. Sandra and I giggled. Though she was laughing at him, whereas I thought it was adorable. Sandra never found anything adorable. Steffi was still holding Fiorenze's hand. Not adorable.

"You'd know if you'd read it," Sandra said. "It is vaster and wider than the ocean, full of infractions beyond number."

"I thought they were up to 811?" Rochelle said.

Sandra teeth-sucked. "For your immediate education, Stefan-the-new-boy: the top ten infractions are—"

"Wait a second. What's the difference between a demerit and an infraction?"

Sandra added an eye roll to her teeth suckage. "An infraction is the wrong thing you do; a demerit is what you get if you're caught committing an infraction. Right now you're committing an infraction—your tie, if a teacher sees, it gets you a demerit. Once you have eight, you get a game suspension, which means you have to miss your next game. Once you have four more

37

demerits—twelve altogether—you get another game suspension. Four more demerits brings you yet another. If you rack up five game suspensions they give you a school suspension. More than one of those and expulsion talk begins."

"How's anyone supposed to remember all of that? Plus—*harsh*," Steffi said. "Also—it doesn't make sense. You get a game suspension every *four* demerits but a school suspension every *five* game suspensions?"

"Because that's how it is," Sandra said. "It's not mathematics, it's punishment. Besides, you don't get a game suspension every four demerits until you've already gotten your first eight."

"*Okaaay*," Steffi said, sounding like he thought Sandra was crazy. "Then how do you make your demerits go away?"

"If your schoolwork is outstanding or you put in an exceptional performance, teachers and coaches can knock off a demerit or two."

Sadly, this had not happened to me since I took six wickets against Lower Devon a month ago.

"Or you can do public service," Rochelle said.

"So what are the top ten demerits?" Steffi asked.

"Infractions."

"Sorry?"

"The top ten infractions are cheating, drinking, smoking, doing drugs—other than those prescribed by a doctor or on the okay list: aspirin, yes; flyers, no—accepting paid sponsorship, gambling—"

"Gambling? But gambling's legal in New Avalon."

"Oh, sure, but if a student from New Avalon Sports High was allowed to gamble, what would stop them from betting on their own team? Or worse, *against* their team and then doing something to make sure they lost?"

"Huh," Steffi said.

"You need to read the list, Stefan," Sandra told him. "It's not just there to take up disk space."

Rochelle frowned, which meant she thought Sandra was being mean and it was time to change the subject. "How're you finding it here?" she asked.

"Which *here*?" Steffi asked, his eyebrows going up in a way that made me tingle. But he was with Fiorenze, not me. Even though that was because of her fairy. My head hurt.

"The school?" Steffi continued. "Or New Avalon? More intense than I imagined. Stricter too. The day is *so* long. Ten hours! And only Sundays off. Last week was the longest of my life. I hardly ever see my folks or my sister anymore."

"If you don't like it," Sandra said, "there's an enormous line of kids who'll take your place."

Steffi put his hands up, at long last letting go of Fiorenze. "I didn't say I don't like it. I'm just not used to it. There's no downtime. At my old school there were assemblies and pep days where you could goof off. There's nothing like that here."

"We're *goofing off* now, aren't we?" Sandra said.

"Um," Steffi said, "this is lunch."

"So NA Sports is stricter," Rochelle said, in case Sandra was starting a fight. "What else is different?"

"I've never seen the principal. I don't even know what she looks like."

"No one knows what the principal looks like," Sandra said. "Just how she is: velvet glove, iron fist. And if you find out what that means, you're in epic trouble."

"It's weird," Steffi said. "Aren't principals supposed to be visible? Go to games? Cheer us on?"

"The principal's not the public face of the school; that's the job of the alumni Ours."

"Alumni Ours?" Steffi asked.

"You know," Rochelle said. "Ex-students who are famous now. Like Our Makhaya and Our Darnelle. They do the fund-raising. Giving back to the school and inspiring us all."

"Weird," Steffi said. Fiorenze was still reading.

"How about your classes?" Rochelle asked. "I've only seen you in Accounting and Bio. What are your electives?"

"Soccer B. I was kind of disappointed. I thought I'd make A-stream soccer."

"The highest stream a first year can get into is B-stream," I told him.

"Really? I feel a lot better now. I'm also in Snooker C—"

"Fencing," I said. "He's in my fencing stream." Unfortunately, so was Fiorenze.

Steffi nodded. "Van Dyck's a great coach."

"You don't do any winter sports," Sandra noted with approval. "Winter sports are injured."

"Yeah, what is luge anyhow?" I asked. "And how come they have one of the biggest gyms on campus? Nobody cares about luge."

Steffi laughed. "What do you even call someone who does luge? A luger? Did you know—"

"So," Sandra said, with the emphasis that meant she was going to ask a question you're not supposed to, "are you and Fiorenze linked now, or what?"

I dropped my fork, then hastily retrieved it, hoping no one had noticed.

"Sandra!" Rochelle exclaimed.

"Linked?" Steffi asked, though I could tell he knew what it meant. He looked at Fiorenze, head buried in book, and then at me and smiled. I turned away. I liked Steffi, he seemed to like me, but then there was Fiorenze and her fairy.

"Are you and Fiorenze a couple now?" Sandra repeated.

Steffi blushed. Fiorenze turned a page and put another forkful of food into her mouth. I wished Sandra would shut up.

"We just met," Steffi said at last. "This morning."

"You were holding hands," Sandra said as if she were accusing him of ball tampering.

"Well, I guess we're friends." He looked at Fio again, smiled. "She's okay," he said, emphasizing the word so it meant something more than "okay."

"Yeah, yeah, all the boys like Fiorenze. Are you boyfriend-girlfriend friends or just friend friends?"

"We *just* met." He sounded confused. Was he struggling with feeling something just because a fairy made him feel it? I hoped so. Yesterday he'd liked *me*. If Sandra had seen, she'd've been asking Steffi these questions.

"Charlie," said Danders Anders, the star of the A-stream water polo team, looming over my shoulder. When he was playing, his team did not lose a match. Not a single one. No one in the school's history ever had such a record.

His fairy is a grip fairy. He has never lost his grip on a ball or anything else, for that matter. He's taller than Rochelle—another reason he's such an ace water polo player is that he barely needs to tread water—and has a neck that's wider than his head. Worse than the rugby majors even.

There was only one thing he could want: a parking spot. I've known Danders Anders since I was in fourth grade and he was in seventh. (I dubbed him that because at the time he was all dandruffy. He isn't anymore, but the name stuck.)

The only thing he has ever wanted from me is parking spots. He pays me, and (usually) warns me when he's

42

going to need my services. But he doesn't take kindly to my saying no. Not that he's violent or anything; it's more that he doesn't understand the word "no."

Danders Anders is the most direct person alive. He doesn't know how to do small talk, he doesn't listen to gossip. He's the biggest bully in school, yet he doesn't even know he is one. His Public Relations teachers have only allowed him to pass and become a senior because he is *such* a spectacular water polo player. Once he is an Our, his publicist will do all the talking for him, and when he retires he will *not* become a commentator.

Rochelle is the only one I know who likes him. Not that anyone *dis*likes him. He is what he is. Rochelle thinks he has a kind heart. I don't think he has an *un*kind heart, but he can be a trial.

"Hi, Andrew," I replied. (No one calls him Danders Anders to his face.) The last six weeks he'd not been driving on account of a broken arm, but since he'd gotten the all-clear, I'd been waiting for him.

"Tickets," he said, waving blue tickets in my face.

"She's not for rent anymore," Sandra said, cutting him off.

"What?" Blank, dazed expression.

"Charlie doesn't get in cars anymore."

"What?"

"Let me," I told Sandra, turning to face him. "It's like this, Andrew. I don't like my fairy. I don't like cars. I don't like parking. So now I walk."

"Everywhere?"

"Everywhere."

He held the tickets in my face. *Monkey Knife Fight*, I read. I thought they'd broken up.

"Parking hard," he said.

"Unless you can find me a doos fairy to replace the wholly injured one I have now, there's nothing you've got, Andrew, that I want."

"How long no cars?"

"Till the parking fairy goes away."

"Huh."

"See, Andrew," Sandra said, "paying attention to gossip is useful."

Danders looked down at the blue tickets in his hand. "Tickets."

"Walking, Andrew. That's all I do. Everywhere."

Danders grunted and walked back to his table.

"I can't believe that worked," Sandra said.

"We don't know if it has yet," I said.

"That was rude," Steffi said. "You two hardly let him talk at all."

"Explain, Ro," Sandra said.

Rochelle had just put a large piece of steak into her mouth. We waited as she finished chewing and swallowing. "I know it seemed mean, Stefan. But Danders doesn't think like we do. Did you notice the strange way he talks?"

44

Steffi nodded. "I just figured English was his second language."

Sandra laughed.

"English *is* his second language," Rochelle explained, "but not the way you think. He was born here, and his parents. Probably their parents too. But he has his own language because he doesn't think like everyone else."

"And here was me thinking he was just stupid," Sandra said.

Rochelle ignored her. "Also Danders thinks communication is a tube. One person puts meaning in the tube and another person takes meaning out of the tube and it's always the same thing. Nothing's changed."

"Okay," Steffi said, "now I'm really confused."

"We did it in PR. Wasn't that last week?" Rochelle looked at me. "You know. Language not being tubes or hubs, but webs?"

"Can't language be a hub too? Isn't it *just* the tube that's wrong?" Sandra asked.

"Still confused," Steffi said. "Also bewildered. What does any of this have to do with that big guy?"

"Danders thinks every statement has one meaning," Fiorenze said in a tone that made it clear that she thought we were all stupid. We turned to stare at her. "He doesn't understand indirection or wordplay. To communicate with him you must be direct, which seems rude to us, but isn't to him."

It was the most I'd heard her say outside of class. And if I counted the word "wasp," it meant she'd talked to me twice in one day. That was a record.

"Huh," Steffi said. For a microsecond he sounded like Danders Anders. "But what does that have to do with tubes or hubs or webs?"

CHAPTER 7

More Demerits

Days walking: 61
Demerits: 5
Conversations with Steffi: 7
Doos clothing acquired: 0

Danders Anders cornered me as I made my way to fencing. He didn't mean to corner me, but when you're as tall and wide as he is and I'm as little as I am, merely standing beside me constitutes menacement. He had Bluey Salazar and Freedom Hazal with him. They were sporting twin don't-look-at-me-it's-not-my-fault expressions.

"Hi, Bluey," I said. "Hi, Freedom."

They muttered their hellos and Bluey decided to be fascinated by the sticky linoleum flooring (they make it that way—it's meant to make it harder for us to run on) while Freedom's eyes were drawn to the lockers behind me. No one likes to be turned into Danders's minion.

"Tell," Danders commanded Bluey.

"This is Andrew's idea," Bluey began.

"Your motives are not mysterious," I replied, glancing at my watch. Being late for class is a demerit.

"You can get rid of your fairy if you don't wash for six weeks," Bluey blurted. "It worked for my sister's cousin's drama coach. And also for Our Tananarive. But it's got to be six weeks and you can't even wash your hands."

Freedom sucked his teeth in mockage. "No, you want to get rid of your fairy, then you have to fast. Starve her out. It's a hundred percent guaranteed and only takes five days."

"No," Danders said, counting to five on his fingers. "Too quick."

"What about using one of those sticky hoop things?" Bluey asked.

"A Fairy Catcher? They don't work!" I knew. I'd tried. They looked a bit like a butterfly catcher, though the net was sticky and had bigger holes. Mine had caught nothing but dust and insects.

Sholto Pak Sung, one of the legendary seniors, stopped in front of us. "Are you talking about how to get rid of a fairy? Velocity, doosers, got to be velocity. It's the only way. *Zoooom!* A friend of mine did 120 kilometers on his bike one time. After that his fairy was long gone. Though he also broke every bone in his body."

The speakers squeaked and popped and then let out a burping static sound, which meant an announcement was imminent. We all looked up, despite not being able to see it.

48

Due to an electrical fault, the speaker intoned, *B-stream fencing has been transferred from Fraser Hall to Merckx.*

"Fairy dung," I exclaimed, looking at my watch again. Merckx was on the far side of campus, on the other side of the A-stream football (all codes) ovals. I had eight minutes to get there. Without taking the shuttle, I wasn't sure it was possible.

"Another way to get rid of them," Freedom said, "is to—"

"Why are they telling me all this?" I asked Danders.

"Want Monkey Knife Fight."

"Danders thinks if you try a different fairy-removal method, then you can go with him to the concert and he'll get a parking spot. Because your fairy won't be gone yet but you can still go in a car."

"Gah!" I said, darting around Danders Anders and into the changing room and wishing I could just *give* him my parking fairy.

I hauled out my fencing gear, changed faster than lightning, slung my bag over my shoulder, and crossed the hallway at as close to a run as I could while always keeping one foot in contact with the ground (running in the halls is a demerit). When I got to the nearest exit I pushed through the door, hoicked my bag higher up my shoulder, sprinted down the steps, and along the narrow paths between courts, paddocks, and ovals.

Despite the purportedly world-class drainage system, mud and puddles were everywhere. The rain that hadn't been loud enough to wake me up last night had made a mess of everything. I jumped and skirted the puddles as best as I could off balance with a bag full of foils and sabers. Soiled sporting attire (before playing) is a demerit. I could wipe down my shoes and swap over my socks for clean ones, but could I do that *and* arrive on time? Looking at my watch again would just slow me down. I lifted my knees higher, digging for more speed.

In the distance, I could see the shuttle arriving at Merckx, disgorging its load of on-time B-stream fencers.

Frang, blast, and dung.

I ran even harder, skirting the rugby paddock, populated with big-necks doing tackling drills. Ouch. Then around the soccer field. By the time I arrived, warm-up had begun. I did what I could about my shoes and socks, then sprinted around the corner straight into Coach Van Dyck. We hit hard and went flying backward, neither of us falling. She grunted. I grunted. We both took another step back, semi-winded.

"Fairy dung," I breathed.

"Swearing is an infraction," Coach said. "So is running indoors. As is arriving late. That's three infractions, Charlie. Three. It could have been four—I've kindly not included your almost killing me as an infraction." Coach looked down at the tablet glowing in her hand. "Says here you showed up for tennis incorrectly attired. Four demerits in one day, Charlie." She shook her head. "You now have eight, which earns you a game suspension. You are aware of that, Charlie?"

"Yes, Coach," I said, biting my cheek so I wouldn't groan out loud. A game suspension. My first. I really hoped it wouldn't be cricket.

Steffi walked past us, his fencing gear slung over his shoulder, doos and loose-limbed, as if he were gliding rather than walking. I sighed. He winked at me and then nodded at Coach, who nodded back.

"But isn't he—," I began. He was later than me. Why wasn't he getting a demerit?

Coach wasn't listening. "A one-game suspension," she said, leafing through her pages. "No cricket meet for you Saturday."

I nodded. I'd never had a game suspension before. Why did it have to be cricket? I love cricket. Why not tennis?

"I am disappointed." She lowered her eyes and proceeded to bore holes in mine. I wholly believed in her setting-students-on-fire fairy. "I expect the absolute best from you today, Charlie. Beyond your best. Do you understand?"

I gulped, then nodded, trying not to squirm.

"I expect no further infractions of any kind."

"Yes, Coach."

"Your very best effort, Charlie."

I nodded and walked over to the warm-up area. The first person I saw was Fiorenze Stupid-Name stretching

51

out her quads. Our eyes met briefly. The word for how she looked at me: "disdainful." Rubbing it in that she had Steffi and I didn't.

Doxhead fairy.

I wasn't sure which one I meant: hers or mine.

CHAPTER 8

Best Dad Ever

Days walking: 61
Demerits: 8
Conversations with Steffi: 7
Doos clothing acquired: 0
Game suspensions: 1

Dad was waiting outside the main gates, sitting on a fire hydrant, sketching. He didn't notice me until I was standing right in front of him making a coughing noise.

"Hi, Charlie." He stood up, closed his sketchbook, slid his pencil down the spiral, and put the book in his back pocket.

"Hi, Dad," I said, a little nervous. There were precedents for Dad meeting me after school, but none of them boded well.

"I came to pick you up."

"But, Dad, you know I'm not—"

"Sorry. It's not being picked up, is it, if I'm walking with you? I've come to walk you home. I thought we could go the long way, by the river, grab a sundae. You haven't gone over your fat allowance today, have you?"

"No, I'm clean."

"Superb."

Although Dad didn't believe in fairies, he and Mom had been understanding about my not riding in cars. Concerned, but understanding. I wondered if that was about to change.

I said good-bye to Rochelle and Sandra. They were going to check out Our Zora-Anne's new shop in the city. Rochelle had tried to convince me to go, saying that her aura was sparkling and that she was sure her fairy would work for all three of us, despite that being almost entirely unprecedented. She was convinced too that Our Z-A's shop was going to be the best in the city. But by the time I'd walked there and then all the way home, I'd be too tired to any homework. Besides, I wasn't in the shopping mood.

"See you tomorrow," Steffi called, waving as he walked by. He and Stupid-Name had their arms linked like little kids.

"There's nothing I'd rather do than walk along the river, Dad." This was not true. There were many things I'd have rather done. Including go into the bathroom, lock the door, and lie fully clothed in the tub and stare at the cobwebs on the ceiling.

Why wasn't it me with Steffi? Still, taking a walk with my dad and eating a sundae wasn't anywhere near as loathsome as watching Steffi and Fiorenze goo-gaing all over each other.

◆　◆　◆

We walked for ages in silence. The path beside us was crowded with cyclists, skaters, and bladers, the rumble of their wheels almost drowning out the sound of boats on the river. There weren't many other walkers; most of the people using the footpath jogged or ran.

A blimp floated along the river with Our Z-A's name in the city colors of gold and green; trailing out behind was a green and gold banner that read: *Fairy Love Can Be Yours.* I watched the uneven reflections distort the letters till they looked like a green and gold jigsaw puzzle floating on water. Almost pulchritudinous. The blimp rose to go over the bridge and veered past the bright lights on the other side. The city, where Rochelle and Sandra were probably already trying on gorgeous clothes. A pack of skaters zoomed by, yelling out some wholly un-doos tauntage, just because I still had my uniform on. Probably Arts students.

On this side, once we'd left the school behind, it was parkland for as far as you could see, which in the dark wasn't very, even with all the fancy new lighting along the paths. Trees, bushes, flowers, climbing walls, skater ramps, restrooms, bubblers, more trees, bushes, and flowers. But no basketball courts or cricket ovals. I wished there was time for us to shoot some ball on the way home. I missed basketball so much it hurt.

I wondered what was up with Dad. Why the sudden need for alone time with me?

"Are you finally going to give Nettles a quokka?" Nettles had been nagging for one ever since she saw a quokka special on *World's Cutest Animals*. Little kangaroolike creatures about the size of a cat. They were pretty adorable. But Nettles did not have a good track record for pet maintenance: several dead fish, a lost cat, and two guinea pigs that Dad ended up looking after 'cause Nettles kept forgetting to feed them.

Dad laughed. "The no-small-marsupials-in-the-house rule still applies."

"Does that mean you'll be getting her a *big* marsupial then?" I said, with a smile that I hoped he'd think was mischievous and would distract him from whatever it was I was in trouble about.

"Very droll. How's school?" Dad asked, and I knew exactly what was up.

"Mom sent you, didn't she?"

Dad nodded. He didn't look fuming, but then he never did, which was why it was him coming to talk to me and not Mom. Dad's the enforcer. Mom says you have to be calm to enforce. Mom is not calm.

"She knows about my game suspension." I sighed. How could she not?

Mom has the quintessential mom fairy: a knowing-what-your-children-are-up-to fairy. It drives her nuts because she does not consider herself to be the kind of mom who would need such a fairy. But not as much as it drives us nuts (particularly Nettles).

"I was suspended from this weekend's cricket meet," I said at last.

"I'm sorry, Charlie. Your mother's upset. She thinks the whole not-going-in-the-car thing has gone on too long and gotten you in too much trouble. I agree. Do you want to wind up expelled? You love this school!"

"But, Dad . . . ," I trailed off. There was no point explaining yet again why it was so important. My dad doesn't believe in my parking fairy. He doesn't believe in *any* fairies, which many people believe is why he doesn't have one, which for him confirms that they don't exist. It's a whole circular reinforcement thing (that's what Mom calls it). Non-belief interferes with their fairy thing working. Or at least that's the theory.

Dad's disbelief is so strong that it cancels out *other people's* fairies. Well, almost everyone's. It doesn't have any effect on my fairy. Or Mom's. But one time Rochelle was shopping-grounded for weeks and weeks (she'd bought an extremely well-fitting cheongsam that her mom said was "immeasurably sexier" than it should have been for a twelve-year-old) and when the grounding was finally lifted, her parents decreed that she could only clothes shop with adult supervision and there were only four days until the school dance. But it had been raining solid for a week and it kept on raining until the day before the dance and Rochelle's fairy doesn't work when it's raining.

It was what Rochelle calls a VAST SHOPPING EMERGENCY because she *had* to have something new for the school dance (despite her wardrobe bursting at the seams), but neither of her parents could be her adult supervisor because they were working late and my mom was working late too (as usual), so Dad stepped in.

It was a disaster.

Everything Rochelle found that fit was ludicrously expensive, or if she *could* afford it, then it made her look like the most horrendous bug-eyed troll ever to live. She was so dirty on Dad I was amazed he didn't notice.

That's what comes from not believing in fairies. You rob people of a new dress for their school dance.

"Charlie? Are you listening?"

"Sorry, Dad."

"You're going to be suspended from all your games, which means you'll be off all your teams, which means you may wind up expelled. This is all you've ever wanted—to play cricket and basketball. I know basketball hasn't worked out. Is that what this is about? Are you acting out—"

"No, Dad!" Why did he have to bring up basketball? "I just wanted to get rid of my doxhead parking fairy! That's all!"

"For the sake of argument, let's just say fairies are real."

"Yes, Dad, everyone in the neighborhood has me ride in their cars because of my stellar conversational skills. Not because they always get the perfect parking spot if I'm in the car."

"I said I was pretending fairies are real."

"Big of you," I said, testing out the limits of dad tolerance.

He waved his arms as if to wipe away what I had said. "How does not taking the bus help get rid of your parking fairy? Buses don't need to park. Or your bicycle? There are bicycle hubs all over the city. And you don't park your skateboard, you carry it. You're making your life far more difficult than it has to be and most likely to no purpose at all. Why don't you limit your embargo to cars? If you'd just take the bus, or the light-rail, or a ferry, you wouldn't be late so much and you wouldn't be suspended from your cricket match on the weekend. Cricket B needs you!"

"But, Dad, I feel like the fairy's just about to leave. Like it could be gone tomorrow, or in the next hour, or the next minute." All day my fairy had been feeling somehow lighter. Like it was fading away.

"Charlie, Charlie, Charlie, Charlie, Charlie," Dad said, almost singing it. "You're putting your whole future in jeopardy for the sake of a nonexistent fairy."

"I thought we were pretending fairies were real?"

He let out a gust of air almost too violent to be a sigh. "We've spent a long time discussing the matter, Charlie. Your mother and I have decided that either you start riding the bus again, or you have to do enough public service to wipe out all your demerits."

"Public service!" I saw myself every Sunday picking up trash along the river, or worse *in* the river, or even more horrifying: stuck hours after school prying chewing gum from underneath every desk. "But that would mean no free time ever again. I'd be locked in epic servitude for the rest of my life!"

Dad smiled. "No, Charlie, just until your demerits are wiped out."

"But, Dad!"

"Why not start right now? We could catch a riverboat the rest of the way home."

"You promised me a sundae," I said to stall. We were minutes from the Ice Palace, the best café for sundaes in all of New Avalon.

"All right, how about after we've had the sundae?"

I thought about it. I looked at the inviting ferry stop, all lit up and shining. There were maybe twenty or twenty-five people waiting, so the next boat wouldn't be long. At this time of night most of the ferries had brass bands on board. You could pay for them to play whatever song you wanted. It was expensive, but . . . maybe if I caught the ferry I could con Dad into it?

But I was so close. Just a little bit longer . . .

"I'll do the public service," I said.

"A double sundae it is. Any flavors you want."

CHAPTER 9
An Intervention

Days walking: 62
Demerits: 8
Conversations with Steffi: 7
Doos clothing acquired: 0
Game suspensions: 1

On Tuesday at first recess, Sandra and Rochelle dragged me out onto the lawn overlooking the outdoor pool. Twelve swimmers were doing laps.

"Sit down," Sandra said. She and Rochelle remained standing. Sandra handed a protein bar to Rochelle, tossed one to me, then unwrapped her own and started munching.

"Why?" I peeled back the gold and green foil and took a bite. Chalky texture, unidentifiably disgusting flavor that was labeled *mangosteen*. "Yum. My favorite." Why couldn't someone invent a protein bar that wasn't foul?

"This is an intervention," Sandra said, sounding like a vastly grumpy coach. For a microsecond I could imagine her as just that: Coach Petaculo the Ruthless. I bet Sandra would even use a whistle. I hate whistles. "So you have to sit."

I sat down, but only because I was knackered and it was easier than standing. "A what?"

"We don't want you to get any more demerits. We love this school. You love this school. We don't want to graduate without you. We've already talked to her and she says yes. She's sure her parents will help," Rochelle said, looking at me triumphantly. "At least, she's sure her mom will. Her dad can be a bit weird. Anyway, it's all settled."

"What is? Who is?" I wondered if Rochelle and Sandra had gone insane. I finished off the protein bar and wiped my hands on the grass. A ladybug landed on my finger, tasted doxy protein bar crumbs, and flew away.

"You're going over to Fiorenze's tonight," Sandra said, "and her parents are going to teach you how to lose the parking fairy and get a new one."

"No, I'm not." Over my fairy-fragged body! Even if the world had ended and Stupid-Name's house was the only remaining shelter, I *still* wouldn't step foot in it. Even if ravening, rabid, rapid wolves were chasing me.

"It's the only way," Rochelle said firmly. "You've been walking everywhere for more than two months and you still haven't got a new fairy."

"That doesn't mean anything. I'm close. I can feel my fairy getting lighter."

Sandra sucked her teeth. "No one can feel their fairy."

"But if you go to Fiorenze's," Rochelle said, "you'll be

62

able to see your fairy's aura, whether it's lighter or not. They'll teach you how to get rid of it. They know everything there is to know about fairies!"

"I can't. I have to do public service at the cemetery."

"Which one?" Sandra asked.

"Hillside."

"Maybe you'll get to tend to Our Diviya or Our Lakeisha," Sandra said, rolling her eyes as if she were joking, forgetting that me and Ro had seen the shrine to Our Diviya and Our Lakeisha that is her bedroom.

"Maybe."

"Well, tomorrow night then," Rochelle said.

I shook my head. "Public service. I have to do public service every day after school until all my demerits are gone."

"C'mon, Charlie. Fiorenze's parents'll solve your problem. You won't accrue any more demerits, you won't have to do public service. Everything will be the way it should be, except that you'll have a brand-spanking-new fairy," Rochelle said. Then her eyes got wide. "Maybe even a clothes-shopping fairy—"

Sandra snorted. "You have the only known clothes-shopping fairy in the universe."

"I can't do it until Sunday," I said. "I've got public service every day till then."

"Fine," Rochelle said. "I'll organize it for Sunday then."

"But, Ro, that's my one day off. I was going to—"

"Visit Fiorenze's parents. Promise?"

63

I made a halfhearted movement of my head that could have been interpreted as a nod as soon as a shake.

Rochelle tsked. "Do you promise?"

"Mmpfyeh," I said, widening my eyes to their maximum earnestness.

"Say it again with your hands on your lap where we can see them," Rochelle said.

I uncrossed my fingers and put my hands in my lap. "I promise," I said heavily. "Ours' honor." I tried to think of something horrendous enough to be sufficient punishment for Rochelle and Sandra forcing me to spend my one day off at Stupid Fiorenze's. It called for something spectacular.

CHAPTER 10
Statistical Torpor

Days walking: 62
Demerits: 8
Conversations with Steffi: 7
Doos clothing acquired: 0
Game suspensions: 1

While I love this school more than anything, there are aspects of it that are less than doos. Like Statistics, my least favorite class. Hmmm, wait, that implies that it's on my list of favorites. It's not. If I had a choice between doing statistics or eating my body weight in empty calories—I'd take the ECs, thank you very much. I'd take amputation. Statistics is the worst thing in the known world. (Other than my parking fairy.)

And it's worse than it otherwise would be because Rochelle and Sandra aren't in my class. Vastly difficult to get through the worst class in the universe without the moral support of my best friends.

To add to my pain Steffi and Fiorenze are both in my Stats class. They sat side by side. Steffi passed her a note, which is an infraction, but Ms. Basu (we're all convinced she has a good-hair fairy since her hair is always shiny and never even slightly messy) didn't seem to notice, despite every boy in the class staring at them with jealous intensity, and every girl with the same. (Only the boys were wanting to be where Steffi was and the girls were wanting to be Stupid-Name.) Of course my pointing it out would only bring me a demerit. Dobbing is vastly frowned upon.

Besides, I would never do that, no matter how much the parties in question deserved it. I hoped Steffi wouldn't be at Fiorenze's on Sunday. Or Fiorenze, for that matter. No way could I stand to be around them all touchy-touchy love-love out of school. School was horrendous enough. It didn't help that Steffi was looking even more pulchy today than ever, even though his curly black hair was a mess. Or maybe that's why? Was messy hair pulchy? Or just Steffi's messy hair?

We were supposed to be reviewing strike rate calculations; I wasn't understanding it any better than I had the first time we learned it. I don't play cricket to improve my statistics. How many wickets I take and at what rate—it's immaterial to me. I don't care about my average (23.75), or my strike rate (51.61), or my economy rate (6.34), or my number of hat tricks (2). I just adore the feel of the ball between my splayed fingers, the little extra pressure I exert with my knuckles before it leaves my hand and is spinning just how I want it to, looking so innocuous that the batter lets it go only to hear the leather of the ball against the wood of the bails as they're sent sailing through the air. Sigh. Who cares if I manage that feat every twenty runs or thirty?

Steffi pushed another note to Fiorenze. I was too far away to have any hope of reading it, so I stared out the window, imagining that they were breaking up with each other: *I had no idea it was possible,* Steffi would write her, *for someone to be as stuck-up as you are. Furthermore, wearing brown with brown with brown does not work. If I weren't already unlinking with you because of your aforementioned stuckupedness, the brown thing would kill it for me. Plus you smell funny and aren't nearly as smart, witty, and overall doos as Charlie.*

I snuck another peek at the irksome twosome. He was smiling at her in a soft, wet, gooshy way and she was staring down shy and overwhelmed. It seemed unlikely they were merely hiding the pain of a breakup. If only Basu would give them multiple demerits.

I turned back to the window, and watched the B-stream volleyballers practicing spikes. Leaping, skidding, spiking. Volleyball is not my sport.

Don't get me wrong, I'm adequate, but I don't have the something extra you need to get into even D-stream volleyball at NA Sports. I thought I had that certain something for basketball. It hadn't occurred to me I wouldn't even make D-stream basketball. I thought I'd be in B with Rochelle. At Bradman I'd been the star point guard and now I only got to play ball in my own front yard.

"Charlotte Adele Donna Seto Steele?" Basu was looking

at me: the expression on her face was not kind. "Can you calculate career and season strike rates for the following batter?" The name K. S. Duleepsinhji appeared on the screen of my tablet with his entire career laid out in numbers. There was his cumulative runs: 995 scored from 19 innings. So 995 divided by 19. "52.37," I said.

"No, Ms. Steele. That is Mr. Duleepsinhji's average. I believe I asked you to calculate strike rates. The number of runs scored for every hundred balls faced."

I felt my cheeks heat up. Everyone knows the difference between averages and strike rates.

"Perhaps what is going on in class is of more assistance in the calculation of strike rates than what is going on outside the window?"

I looked down.

"Well, Steele?"

"Yes, Ms. Basu."

I glanced at the cloying couple. Another note went from Steffi to Fiorenze. I forced myself back to the calculations in front of me. Failing Statistics was not the extra little something I needed to add to my increasingly disastrous life.

CHAPTER 11

Public Service

Days walking: 62
Demerits: 8
Conversations with Steffi: 7
Doos clothing acquired: 0
Game suspensions: 1

Hillside cemetery is the biggest and oldest in the city. All the most famous Ours are buried there. It's surrounded by huge stone walls and all the entrances have wrought iron gates. It also has 360-degree views. On a clear day you can see the mountains to the west and all the way to the ocean in the east.

When I walked through the main entrance, I saw a light-skinned woman with canary yellow hair scrunched back tight in a bun, holding an official-looking tablet. I walked over to her. She looked me up and down, noting my NA Sports uniform, then turned to her tablet.

"Charlotte Adele Donna Seto Steele?"

"Yes." It occurred to me that until I started New Avalon Sports High I'd barely known what my full name was.

Even when my parents were mad at me they called me plain old Charlie.

"You're almost late. We expect those doing service to get here at least ten minutes early."

I started to apologize but she cut me off. "You will be punctual and you will attend every public service session you have agreed to do." She looked down at her excessively bright tablet. "Which is every evening except Sundays." She looked at me again. "You must be an exceedingly naughty girl."

"No, I—"

The look she shot me was poisonous. "For every hour's work you do, one demerit will be erased from your record."

A whole hour's work erased *one* demerit. How fair was that?! I wisely did not share this thought.

"This is your quadrant." She handed me a map. "Get rid of all garbage, weeds, and detritus. You are to make your quadrant beautiful. Your assigned partner hasn't arrived yet. So you will have to work even harder."

She indicated a pile of gloves, one of yellow fluoro vests, another of burlap sacks, and the last of gardening forks. "Take one of each of those and four sacks. One is for glass and plastic recyclables, one for paper and cardboard, one for compostable materials, and one for nonrecyclables."

"Right," I said. "Thanks." I tried on some gloves for size. None fit. I took the least ludicrously large ones. Two more people wandered in. Adults. The yellow-haired lady started barking the same instructions at them.

I picked up a sack. It was bigger than me. I stuffed one of the vests and a fork into it and then grabbed three more sacks.

"Put the vest on now!" the woman yelled. I turned around. She was staring right at me. "Do not take it off! Not until your work is finished! Go!"

"Sorry," I muttered, but she had turned back to her new offenders. I fished out its yellow splendiferousness and slipped it on, then stumbled away.

My quadrant was outlined in red. I looked around for a street sign. Diviya Street. My quadrant was bordered by Diviya, Eastern, Hillside, and Nelson. With my usual luck I'd been given a section that was about as far as you could be from the main gates. I headed off at a jog, passing the huge jacaranda, eucalyptus, and flame trees that surrounded Our Diviya's grave. She had wanted to be surrounded by the sound of birds. I wondered if she'd considered the possibility of bird droppings.

Two public service workers wearing the same brilliant yellow vests as me were on their knees scrubbing the marble monolith erected in her honor. I didn't recognize them, not from Sports. I hoped they were Our Diviya fans.

I didn't recognize any of the other workers in yellow vests. Most looked older than high school students. One of them resembled Our Little Jo, then I remembered that she'd been caught driving drunk. Maybe it was Our Little Jo. I looked away: vastly undoos to be caught staring at an Our.

As soon as I got to my quadrant, I started ripping up the weeds surrounding the nearest grave and hurling them into a sack. The stone was tilted and illegible. Most of the headstones around me were no better, their engravings worn down by wind and rain.

I visualized all the demerits peeling away as I dropped weeds into one sack, broken glass into another, and sodden paper cups into the third. Any minute, any day, any week now, my fairy was going to be gone.

The work wasn't that hard. There wasn't much rubbish and last night's rain made the weeds less stubborn than they might have been. I kept my back dead straight, bending from the waist, holding my abdominal muscles tight, and got into an easy, soothing rhythm. After a while I wasn't thinking about anything except weeds in first sack, plastic in second, soggy cardboard in third, nonrecyclables in fourth. No thoughts of basketball, or Stupid-Name, or my doxhead fairy. Except for the occasional used condom (touching one—even through thick gardening gloves—is erky!) interrupting my zenlike calm, it was delicious.

My partner showed up fifteen minutes late.

She went straight to the other end of the quadrant and started working without saying hello or even nodding.

Fiorenze Burnham-Stone.

Why? Just because we went to the same school didn't mean they had to put us together! And what had she gotten a demerit for? Holding hands with Steffi? I hoped so.

We worked silently for an hour. But I couldn't recapture

my zenlike weed and rubbish sorting. My mind kept spinning into unpleasant Steffi-and-Fiorenze-keeping-me-from-playing-basketball-with-their-evil-mind-control-over-my-fairy spirals. Even though that didn't make any sense. Why did she want Steffi? She'd never liked a boy before. Why start now?

Because he was the most pulchritudinous boy I had ever seen. Funny too. Talking with him was as fun as talking with Rochelle. Of course Fiorenze would like him too. Wouldn't anyone?

"Are you thirsty?" Stupid-Name asked.

I blinked. I hadn't realized she'd gotten so close. "What?"

"I brought some electrolytes."

I grunted and accepted the clear bottle she pulled out of her backpack. I'd stupidly forgotten to refill my own and had only half a bottle of plain water.

"Keep it," she said. No doubt she didn't want the bottle back after I'd infected it.

"Thanks."

"Gorgeous night," she said, standing up, stretching, and looking at the browny-yellow-gray sky. "What a view."

I stood up, rubbed my lower back, sore despite my abdomen-tightening precautions. She was right. I'd been so intent on demerit erasure I hadn't noticed how far up the hill we were. You could see all the way to our school with its spread-out buildings, ovals, cricket ground, nets, and courts, past the inky river with brilliantly lit boats, to the city lights with glowing blimps floating overhead, and the blackness of the ocean beyond. You could even see some stars.

"From up here even the traffic looks gorgeous."

I grunted again. Why was she telling me? Fiorenze didn't make conversation. I sucked down half the bottle. I was thirsty. "Thanks," I said.

"It was nothing."

It would probably be rude of me to agree with her.

"So, ah," I said. "I'm coming over to your place Sunday."

"Yes."

Neither of us said anything. I drank more of the electrolytes, put the bottle down, and picked up my gardening fork.

"Because you want to get rid of your fairy?" she said.

"Yup." If that was news to her, then not only did she not talk to anyone at school, she didn't listen either.

"Me too . . . ," she muttered.

"You what?" I asked, not sure I'd heard her right. She couldn't have said what I thought she said.

"Nothing," Fiorenze said, pulling her gloves back on. "I was just wondering how that was going."

"How what's going?" I bent down and picked up a shard of glass.

"Getting rid of your fairy."

"Slowly." But at least doing this service was making my mission easier. I'd be getting rid of my demerits as fast or faster than I accrued them.

"You should try to get a look at Tamsin's book," Fiorenze said.

"Who's Tamsin?"

"My mom."

Figured that her name would be as torpid as her daughter's. "She has a book about fairies?"

"*The Ultimate Fairy Book*. It has all her research and theories, everything she's learned."

"*The Ultimate Fairy Book?*" I repeated, wondering what kind of person would name their own book *Ultimate*. "I thought your dad was the one with all the books."

"Mmm," Fiorenze said, "but Tamsin's the one with the proper book. It has everything there is to know about fairies in it."

"Is there a copy in the library?" Maybe I could skip going to Stupid-Name's house.

Fiorenze looked at me as if I were insane. "Tamsin has never shown her book to anyone. She keeps it locked up in a metal box. She wrote it by hand."

I goggled. "She what?"

"Too easy to steal otherwise. This way there's only one copy in the world."

"But doesn't she want to publish it?"

"Yes. But not till it's finished."

Her mom sounded like a crazy person. "Why would she show it to me then?" I said.

"She won't. But if she leaves the room for a bit or the box is open, you should look at it."

"Okay," I said slowly. "You want me to pry into your mom's secret book?"

"I ... No. You're right. I was just ... Never mind. I guess we should get back to work."

She bent down to the weeding. I did the same, wondering why she was being so talkative. Why had she told me about her mom's book?

I wished I was anywhere but here. Preferably on a basketball court, shooting effortless three-pointers, while the basketball coaches looked on and realized their terrible, terrible mistake.

CHAPTER 12
Worst Sister Ever

Days walking: 62
Demerits: 8 − 3 = 5
Conversations with Steffi: 7
Doos clothing acquired: 0
Game suspensions: 1
Public service hours: 3
Hours spent enduring Fiorenze
    Stupid-Name's company: 2.75

By the time I got home the door to Nettles's room was closed and no light seeped out. Mom and Dad were in bed reading. They called out their hellos and good nights. I returned them trying not to sound as tired as I felt. I stumbled into my room, dumped my backpack, tried to feel pleased about the three demerits I'd just wiped out, then plugged my tablet into the big screen on my desk, and went straight to the PR homework, skipping my mail and all other temptations.

I had to come up with likely (and tough) questions (at least fifteen) at a press conference after a PR disaster and answer them with the most positive spin possible. I hadn't even read through the five scenarios yet. It'd be easiest to do the first one. But I was still burned from the test we'd been given back in middle school where it turned out the last question was an instruction not to do the test at all. Like most of the class I'd just started doing it and scribbled away until I was disturbed by the sound of giggling coming from all the smarty-pants (including Rochelle) who'd read it the whole way through.

In the first scenario you were captain of the New Avalon XI, who'd enforced the follow on and then lost. I checked the last scenario: a cyclist testing positive for enhancers after taking out the yellow jersey in the Tour. Ouch.

So okay, there was no *Do not do this test* trick. Deciding to stick with my strengths, I chose the cricket option: captain of the NA XI. I started searching for transcripts of follow-on loss press conferences and found several. I clicked on the oldest one.

"I can't believe that's homework."

I jumped. Or I would have if I'd been standing. When I turned to tell Nettles to quit it, a bright light went off in my eyes. Nettles capturing my soul. Again. She doesn't go anywhere without her camera.

"Nettles! You scared me. Put your camera away!"

Nettles grinned, her face matching that of the monkeys wielding knives emblazoned on her T-shirt. She peered at my tablet and the press conference I'd found. "You're just going to copy that, aren't you?" she asked, taking a photo. "Where's the creativity in that?" Nettles is very large on creativity.

"It's PR," I told her. "There's no creativity in PR. It's all spin, spin, spin. You just give it your all, take advantage of your opportunities, step up to the next level, make a 110 percent effort, and at the end of the day the best team wins because champions will out. Stop taking photos of me! It's late. The flash hurts my eyes."

Nettles teeth-sucked. "PR is also a compulsory at Arts, you know. And it's very creative. Much originality. Sports is entirely without originality. You're all learning to do something that's been done before over and over and over. Bounce the ball, hit the ball, throw the ball. I don't know how you can stand it."

"You're only twelve," I said just to annoy her. "What would you know?"

"Like fourteen's so old. And I know heaps about originality! More than you ever will!"

Originality is Nettles's other religion. I couldn't be bothered arguing with her about whether sports are worthwhile or not. I got bored with that conversation years ago. If my little sister couldn't understand the joy of your body in motion, of making a cricket ball do exactly what you wanted it to, of going under someone's guard and bending the point of your foil into their chest, of hearing the swish of a basket that is all net, then there was nothing I could say to explain it to her.

Nettles thought my school was an insanely strict nightmare run by sadistic uptight prison guards; I thought it was heaven.

"That's vastly doos for you, Nettles. Yay Arts and all of its *creativity* and *originality*." I yawned. Not to raz her, but because I was so exhausted I couldn't not. She snapped a photo. I'm sure my tonsils looked gorgeous.

"I won the Arts Junior PR special event promotion," she said in her it's-no-big-deal voice, which always means that it's a *huge* deal.

"You did?" I wasn't sure what she was talking about.

"Results were announced this morning."

I gave her a much-lighter-than-Rochelle punch. "Congratulations! What did you win?"

"Full credit. Family pass to the show. And my counselor says I should think about making PR one of my majors when I get to Arts High."

"Doos."

Nettles shrugged. "I don't want to be a PR hack, explaining why Our Vida uses elephant dung instead of clay to a room full of reporters who still think the word 'poo' is funny. Not joyous."

"The word 'poo' *is* funny." I yawned again. "I thought you said Arts PR was a vastness of creativity and originality?"

She shrugged again. "Anything can be creative and original."

"Even sports?"

"Except sports. Are you going to come?"

"Come?"

"To the show? It's a family pass."

"What show is it?"

Nettles teeth-sucked again. "Monkey Knife Fight. It's only their monstrous comeback. Sold out decades ago. They're fourth-row tickets. Right in the center."

"Doos seats," I said.

"So, you coming?"

"When is it?"

"Wednesday after next. Eight o'clock."

What would I be doing in two Wednesdays? Let's see . . . public service. And after that catching up on homework. Or, I could still be walking back from whatever oval I was playing on. Assuming I was playing. I might run up enough demerits to be off my teams and have my coaches hating me even more. I started to say I couldn't. Nettles was giving me her full-bore, eyes-cut, nostrils-flared, teeth-bared glare. I sighed. "I'll try."

"You'll *try*?" She was so cranky she wasn't even taking pictures.

"Well, I'm kind of—"

"If you weren't being so stupid about your fairy you could come. I don't even have a fairy! I'd love to have a parking fairy!"

This time I yawned so hard my jaw cracked. I winced and rubbed it. "Nettles, I'm tired. It's late, and I have lots more homework to do. Trying is the best I can give you."

"Don't then. I only wanted you to come for Mom and

Dad. But you're too selfish to ever think of anyone but yourself. Forget about it." She hissed and then left the room in an angry but quiet stomp (mustn't wake Mom and Dad). Her closing of the door was the quietest slam possible, but it rang in my ears as if it had been the loudest.

I turned back to my unoriginal and uncreative assignment. By the time I'd cut and pasted and reworded and reordered the questions off the transcript, my eyes were so tired the words on the screen blurred into each other.

By five a.m. I'd answered all the questions but had barely made word-count. I fell into bed bone-tired, brain-tired, fairy-tired, and sister-guilty.

Microseconds later my alarm went off: six a.m. I pried my eyes open with my fingers; they were glued shut with sleep. If the gunk in the corners of my eyes was bad fairy aura, then I was in for a vastly horrendous day. I rolled out of bed and into the shower before I realized I hadn't taken my pajamas off. I'd worked off three demerits last night at public service.

It was not enough.

CHAPTER 13
Steffi

Days walking: 63
Demerits: 5
Conversations with Steffi: 7
Doos clothing acquired: 0
Game suspensions: 1
Public service hours: 3
Hours spent enduring Fiorenze
    Stupid-Name's company: 2.75

Steffi was outside, sitting on my front steps, bouncing coins off the back of his hand as if they were jacks. I shut the front door behind me, my heart beating ridiculously fast. He pocketed the coins and stood up.

"Heya, Charlie. Okay if I walk to school with you?"

"Sure. Is something up? Where's Fiorenze?"

"Oh," he said, looking almost embarrassed, "we sort of broke up."

"Really?" I asked, having to dig my fingernails into my palms to keep from screaming with joy.

"Uh-huh."

"How about that?" I said, trying to think of something less torpid to say. I was smiling so big my cheeks were beginning to hurt, but Steffi was here, at my house.

"Shouldn't we get going?"

I looked at my watch. I was running late. "Yup. Sorry. Didn't get a lot of sleep." I wondered why he hadn't rung the doorbell to hurry me up.

Steffi slipped his backpack over both arms, jumped down the steps, and did three forward handsprings, then two backward, before landing on his feet with a big grin.

"Show-off," I said, cartwheeling across the lawn.

We smacked palms. Steffi shook out his arms. "That felt brilliant."

I grinned. It did. "Run to school?"

"You're on," he said, taking off.

I caught up with him at the lights. "Took your time," he said.

"Yeah, yeah. I'm not awake yet." I brought my foot up behind me to stretch out my quads. Steffi did the same.

"You know what I like best about school?" Steffi asked.

"There's something you like about school?" I asked, switching legs. "I thought it was all too weird for you."

"I love that everyone's into sports, that no one even talks about loving it 'cause it's too obvious. It's the air we breathe." He took in a deep breath. "At my old school there weren't that many sports types."

I hadn't realized he'd gone to a mixed school. In New Avalon mixed schools were only for the untalented. The light changed and we bolted across the street. His legs were longer than mine—whose aren't?—but my fast-twitch muscles are not too shabby. I passed him in the middle of the block.

"Hey!" he shouted. "It's not a race!"

"Yes it is," I shouted over my shoulder and sped up. This time it was him catching me at the light.

"You're fast," he said, breathing hard. We both were. I felt a trickle of sweat run down my back.

"Yup."

"Wanna keep pace the rest of the way?" he asked. "That way we could, you know, talk."

I grinned. The light changed and we jogged across together.

"It's hard to believe that all those things are really against the rules."

"You mean the infractions list?"

"Yeah," Steffi said. "Why does the school need to be so crazy strict?"

"Because it's a *sports* school, Steffi. Sports are all about rules. If you can't follow rules, you can't play sports. Discipline is the most important thing an athlete can learn, no matter what sport they play."

"Wow," Steffi said. "Do they make you learn that by heart?"

"Huh?" I said. Why did he always say such weird things? "No. It's just true. I like rules. They're why sports make sense. You don't have to guess what you're supposed to do, you just know. When I hit the middle stump and it goes cartwheeling, the batter's out. And the same rules apply to everyone. Like sports, the school is a rule-governed system that makes sense. If I follow the rules all's well, if I don't all's not."

"Well, sure, except for when someone cheats. Or when the referees make a bad call. Or when the rules don't apply to some people because they're so special. Like that Danders Anders guy."

"Danders gets demerits too, you know. He gets more than you do."

Steffi laughed. "You sound like my sister."

"What?" We were both jogging much slower now.

"She thinks I have a getting-out-of-trouble or never-getting-caught fairy—she calls it different things—but she's my big sister and is convinced that I get away with murder and always have. You know how big sisters are."

I stopped mid-stride. Steffi pulled up. "You okay?"

"Did you say a getting-out-of-trouble fairy?" That made *so* much sense.

"That's what she reckons."

"Hah!" I started jogging again. "Steffi, how many demerits have you gotten so far? How many times have teachers and coaches cited you for an infraction?"

"An infraction? Like what Sandra was explaining about? Would I know if a teacher or coach had given me one?"

"Oh, yes, you'd know." I started to run through the Steffi infractions I'd seen: kissing, holding hands, passing

86

notes to Stupid-Name, being sloppily and incorrectly dressed, arriving late, fighting in class (when he told us that everyone hated New Avaloners). I was sure there were more.

"Then none, I guess," he said.

"Hah!" I exclaimed. I *knew* it.

"What?"

"Your sister is spot on. At least two coaches saw you hand in hand with Stup—I mean, Fiorenze—that's an infraction; your tie was messed up all day yesterday—that's an infraction; you were later than me to Fencing and I got a demerit—you didn't."

"So?"

"So!? It means your sister's right! You definitely have a getting-out-of-trouble fairy. You can do whatever you like! And wholly get away with it! Oh, if I had your fairy . . ."

Steffi waved my words away. "All of that doesn't mean anything. I'm the new kid in school, they're just going easy on me."

"Ah, no, Mr. West Coast. They don't ever *go easy*. Not on anyone *ever*. Especially not on new kids. At the start of the year we were a class of 540. Now there's 403. You should have demerits up the wazoo."

Steffi shook his head and did his West Coast hand wave. "Doesn't add up—"

"Doesn't add up! I just thought of another one: you talked out of turn in PR when you were saying how everyone hates us. But you weren't given a demerit. Half the class was, but not you!" Why was he denying it when it was so obviously true?

"Whatever. Listen, Charlie, will you do me a favor? Don't mention this to anyone? Even though it's not true I don't want other people to be thinking it is."

I slowed my jog to a walk and spat on my pinkie, holding it out. "Fairy honor."

He did the same. "Ah, okay. Fairy honor." We pressed our pinkies together, then let go. I suppressed the shiver that contact with Steffi gave me.

"You can wholly trust me. I haven't even told anyone—except Ro and she's the queen of secret keeping—that you like to be called Steffi."

Steffi laughed. "I don't care about that. You do know it's mostly a girl's name on the West Coast too? I know how to handle the jerks who hassle me about it."

Jerks? "I'm sure you do. I'm glad you moved here. I never would've met you if you'd stayed back on the West Coast."

Steffi didn't say anything.

"Aren't you glad you moved?"

"Sometimes. A lot of the time I miss home. Ravenna seems so far away from here."

"What's Ravenna?" I asked

"That's my city. That's where I'm from. You never heard of Ravenna?" Steffi asked, sounding shocked.

"Well, I guess, um," I said, wondering if I should have heard of it. "Well, I haven't really studied geography. I was at a sports middle school too, so—"

"It's beautiful. Lots of hills."

New Avalon has lots of hills too, I wanted to tell him, but I had a feeling that wouldn't go down too well. "Are your friends back home proud of you for getting into NA Sports?" I asked instead.

Steffi sighed. "I don't suppose they've thought about it."

"Will they come visit you? Are you the first to move here?" I'd never met anyone from there before. I wondered if they were all like Steffi or if he was unique.

"Unbelievable. Do you only think about New Avalon?" Steffi's face darkened, like he was really mad. "All you ever ask me is what I think of your school, of your city, of you Avaloids, but you never ask me about where I come from, about my old school. Not a single person has asked me about home."

"Sorry," I said, not sure of what he wanted me to say. We couldn't help it that we came from the most important city in the world, could we? I patted his shoulder but he shrugged my hand off.

"Why aren't any of you curious?"

"Well—," I began. I didn't want him to be mad at me, but I didn't know what to say to make him happy again.

"Why don't any of you ever mention Stanislaw Leda? Or Huntley du Sautoy? Or Livio?" he asked, almost shouting. "They are only three of the most famous people in the world! But they're not from New Avalon, are they? They're not *Your* Stanislaw or *Your* Huntley or *Your* Livio so you just don't care!"

"But I love Livio!" I had reams and reams of Livio's music.

"You care more about *Your* Zora-Anne even though the only thing she's famous for is being charismatic because of some fairy you all believe she has. She doesn't *do* anything! She's not a sports star. She doesn't sing or write or dance or make scientific discoveries or design buildings. She's just popular and charming! What's the point of that?"

"She does do . . ." I stopped. I couldn't think of a single thing Our Z-A did.

Steffi flicked both his hands. "And you, Charlie, you say you want to travel, see more of the world, but you're not interested in anywhere but here. If it doesn't have to do with New Avalon, or more specifically, with New Avalon Sports High, you're not interested."

Was that true? Then I remembered. "I *have* asked you about the West Coast. You said they think we're stuck-up, that they hate us, and I asked—"

"You asked me what they think about *you*. That's not curiosity about the world, that's more of being obsessed with New Avalon." Steffi was waving his arms around and walking faster. I'd never seen him so cranky before. He still managed to look pulchy. His lips were so soft-looking. So gorgeously shaped. I wondered if he'd be mad at me if he knew that's what I was thinking. "You do know this isn't the only city in the world, don't you? It's not even the biggest."

"But I . . ." That was hardly fair. "It's not the biggest? That doesn't sound right. Are you sure?"

Steffi let out a loud sigh. "I'm not mad at you, Charlie. It's not just you anyway. It's the whole city. Sometimes I feel like the West Coast has disappeared and that Ravenna and all my friends there have vanished into thin air. That I'm just imagining the mail I get."

We turned the corner onto Mallett, the steepest street in New Avalon, and thus in the world (though Steffi now had me wondering if that was true) and got a sweeping view all the way out past the river and the city to the ocean. NA Sports lay at the bottom of the hill. I looked at my watch. "Oops. We've only got five minutes."

Steffi looked at me and grinned. I smiled back. He really wasn't mad at me. "Want to sprint it?"

"Sure," I said. Did I mention that Mallett is steep? At least if I had a broken ankle I'd be off school and couldn't rack up any more demerits. Well, not as many.

"You ready?" he asked, looking at me sideways. When he looked at me like that I was sure he liked me close to how much I liked him.

I nodded. I would probably do anything he suggested.

"Let's *goooo!*" He took off.

I ran as hard as I could, caught him, then momentum took over and it wasn't so much running as keeping from toppling over. We screamed all the way down the hill.

CHAPTER 14

Doctor Tahn

Days walking: 63
Demerits: 5
Conversations with Steffi: 8
Doos clothing acquired: 0
Game suspensions: 1
Public service hours: 3
Hours spent enduring Fiorenze
    Stupid-Name's company: 2.75

We should have been given several demerits. We arrived less than a minute before the bell (that's one), our ties crooked (two), our hair messy (three), shirts untucked (four), the echo of our yelling (five), only just faded away. We were laughing and panting and then Steffi hugged me and the sensation of him being so close, of inhaling his sweat, feeling the heat rising from our bodies, drove all thoughts from my head. It was so intensely sublime that when he let go of me I almost fainted. But hugging like that should have been our sixth demerit. (It's only okay if you've just scored a goal or your team's just won.)

There were oceans of coaches and teachers around. A sea of brown and gold coaching jackets, and the brown suits of the teachers. They must've seen and heard us. It should've been at least six demerits each, and another game suspension for me, but they didn't say a word.

Steffi's getting-out-of-trouble fairy had covered me too. What a stellarly doos fairy. How could he not believe?

Rochelle was waiting for me. "Hello, Stefan," she said, straightening my tie.

"Hey," he said. "See you later."

"Later," I repeated, watching him walk away. He was the doosest boy in the world. Much dooser than Sholto Pak Sung or any of the other crush-inducing seniors.

He turned back to wave. "See you in Fencing!"

"Fencing," I repeated.

Rochelle snapped her fingers in front of my eyes. I jumped.

"Do I have your attention? Have you forgotten it's our physical today?"

"Oops." I'd completely forgotten. All students have to have a monthly physical examination on account of the school having to make sure we are in tip-top condition at all times. It is wholly tedious and you have to make up the missed class in your own time either at lunch or after school. Given that I had public service after school, that meant lunch was now gone. I sighed. Rochelle grabbed my hand and pulled me at great speed down the hall to testing without breaking into an actual run (one foot on the ground at all times). I tucked in my shirt as best as I could with my other hand. We made it through the door just as the bell rang. Phew.

Before I could even sit down, one of the nurses handed us both a container and led us to the bathroom, neither smiling nor saying anything to us. Nurses are under strict instructions not to fraternize with students. She stood outside to wait until we were done.

Despite having completely forgotten I was due for a physical, I did, in fact, need to pee. Had I remembered, I'd have drunk liters to make sure of it. Nothing worse than sitting in testing, drinking and drinking and drinking, then waiting and waiting and waiting until you need to go, then going back and forth to the bathroom with the nurse through several false alarms. When you can't pee, having a nurse standing outside waiting makes your bladder even more nervous.

Fortunately this time it wasn't an issue for either of us. We handed the nurse our containers. I for one am always happy to relinquish a container full of pee. I'm repulsed by how warm it is. You'd think after so many years of giving urine samples I'd've learned not to be a baby about it. You'd be wrong.

We washed our hands thoroughly, waiting till the door swung shut behind the nurse, before talking.

"So you and Stefan . . . ," Rochelle began.

My cheeks got hot.

"Woo-hoo! I knew it! He does like you! And without a

94

stupid fairy making him! I mean, why else would he come sit at our table when he and Fiorenze just got together?"

"They broke up."

"I knew it!"

My cheeks felt even hotter. "He didn't say anything about linking." I hoped the heat on my face didn't show. "I think he just wanted to see what it was like walking to school."

"That's right, Charlie, he just wanted to walk to school with you even though it takes so much longer than taking the bus." Rochelle finished drying her hands. "We should go back in. You don't want to accrue any more demerits."

We returned to the waiting room and sat in the two remaining empty chairs—unfortunately, not next to each other, not that we were allowed to talk. None of the other students bent over their tablets were in my year or streams so I didn't know them, though some I knew by sight, and obviously everyone knew Cassie-Ann Zahour.

Cassie-Ann was in final year A-stream basketball. It was rumored she'd already been offered five endorsements, not to mention contracts for several top teams. A book was being run on which ones she'd take. She was wholly destined to be an Our. I'd had many daydreams of feeding the ball to her under the post while she scored and scored and scored. Back when I'd thought I'd be in a basketball stream.

Rochelle'd had a crush on her for as long as I could remember and was mournful that the odds of being promoted from B-stream to A-stream basketball while still only a first year were vastly low, in the vicinity of zero, in fact. She would have to wait until she graduated and hope that some day they wound up on the same team.

I turned to the med form on my tablet, wishing, once again, there was a same-as-last-time button you could press, but no, you had to start from scratch, giving them your name, DOB, ID, class, electives, etc., etc. all over again before you even got to your diet, sleep patterns, and all the other health questions. Wholly maddening; vastly numbing.

I was last to transmit my form and so was last to be called in for a physical. I had plenty of time to think about Steffi. Was he interested in me in more than a friend way? I had no idea. That hug had seemed way more than friendly. But maybe it was just the exhilaration of having conquered Mallett.

He always seemed pleased to see me. But he hadn't tried to hold my hand or kiss me like he had with Fiorenze Stupid-Name. Not that I'd let him kiss me—I was against being expelled. But maybe her all-boys-will-worship-the-ground-you-tread-on fairy had made him rush things?

I wondered what it would be like having Steffi's fairy. I wouldn't use it for evil like, say, kidnapping Fiorenze and dumping her on an island far, far, far away. All I wanted was to stop racking up endless demerits. Not to mention it being the perfect antidote to my mom's knowing-what-her-kids-are-up-to fairy. How wondrous would that be?

Did Steffi like me? Was it a friend thing waiting outside

96

my house to walk to school with me? Or a boyfriend thing?

"Charlie Steele?"

I followed the nurse into the windowless testing room, rolled up my sleeve, and presented my arm for puncturing. A vial of blood and a skin swab later, I was ushered into Dr. Tahn's office.

Frang, blast, and dung.

Tahn is my least favorite doctor. I call her Dr. Ha Ha. She thinks she has a humor fairy so everything she says is hilarious. It's best to laugh at her jokes no matter how unfunny. She acts like she's your friend, and always, always wants to know how you're feeling, how you're *really* feeling. At my last physical I'd only been walking everywhere for a month, so I hadn't yet racked up that many demerits, plus I'd gotten the businesslike Dr. Baranova.

I sighed and sat down.

"We're quite the walking cloud of gloom, aren't we, Charlie?"

I never know how I'm supposed to respond. Should I agree and get the heart-to-heart over and done with? Or should I disagree, in the forlorn hope that the heart-to-heart can be avoided?

I grunted noncommittally.

"I see you've been accruing many demerits. You're a regular demerit queen, aren't you?"

I smiled to demonstrate that I was amused, even though I wasn't.

"So what's going on, Charlie? Trouble at home? Are your parents beating you? Ha ha!"

"No, Doctor, no beatings."

"Well, whatever it is, Charlie, if you keep accruing demerits at this rate you could end up in the principal's office."

I shuddered. The principal's office was practically a synonym for "expelled." I didn't want to find out exactly what *velvet glove, iron fist* meant.

"We need to work together to keep you out of her office."

"Yes, Doctor." I failed to suppress a yawn.

Tahn's eyebrows shot up. She looked down at her screen. "Says here you've been sleeping well."

"Yes, Doctor, when I get to bed I fall asleep right away."

"And yet you're yawning?" She poked at the screen. "You're doing public service?"

"Yes, Doctor."

"You were logged out of your session last night at five a.m."

"Yes, Doctor."

"Perhaps that is why you're yawning?" she said. "You're not getting to bed early enough for a sufficient night's sleep."

"Yes, Doctor."

"Charlie, lots of students in their first year at Sports have difficulty adjusting. It's nothing to be ashamed of. If there's something going on at home you should let me know. We want to work with you to solve your problems."

Her screen beeped.

"Your blood work is excellent. Your physical adjustment to Sports High is going very well indeed. Now we only have to help with your mental adjustment. I've scheduled an appointment with one of the counselors at lunch today."

I nodded, trying not to let my dismay show. Now I'd have to make up the class (Accounting) this physical had replaced during my dinner break. I'd been hoping to do as much homework as possible during lunch and dinner so I wouldn't have a repeat of last night's disaster and resulting five a.m. bedtime. Sigh.

"You'd better hurry along to your next class if you don't want to get another demerit."

"Thank you, Doctor."

I jumped up and without actually running got out of there as fast as I could. I had five minutes to make my next class. Piece of cake. I glanced at my timetable. Fencing. And it was still in Merckx.

Dung.

No way was I going to make it on time. Yet another demerit to be worked off. On the other hand, Steffi seemed to like me and I was positive that my fairy was getting lighter.

But at first recess Steffi and Fiorenze were side by side, dangling their feet in the pond and feeding the ducks (though both taking off your shoes and feeding the ducks are infractions). I had to blink to keep from crying. Crying is also an infraction.

For just a second I thought about transferring to another school. Or killing them both.

I didn't know what I'd expected. Stupid-Name's fairy had worked on him yesterday. Why not today? As long as Fiorenze and her fairy were around it didn't matter whether Steffi liked me or not.

"I'm sorry, Charlie," Rochelle said, handing me a protein bar—mangosteen again, erk!—and pulling me away. "C'mon, let's shoot some hoops. I can show you some new drills."

CHAPTER 15

Rochelle's Lucky Day

Days walking: 66
Demerits: 4
Conversations with Steffi: 8
Doos clothing acquired: 0
Game suspensions: 1
Public service hours: 16
Hours spent enduring Fiorenze
    Stupid-Name's company: 2.75

By Saturday I had racked up eleven (eleven!) additional demerits, bringing my grand total to seventeen, or it would have except that ten more hours of public service got me down to seven and kept me from getting any more game suspensions. Missing my cricket match on Saturday had been malodorous in the extreme, but at least I'd been able to do another three hours of public service and thus end with only four demerits.

It was still my worst week ever. On top of my inevitable lateness demerits, I managed to forget to recharge my tablet so that I had to borrow a crappy one from tech support, as well as forgetting my Statistics and Health homework. According to the counselor, Ms. Wilkinson, whom I now had to see twice a week (frang, blast, and dung), it was one of the worst weeks for a first year student ever. And had thus been *duly noted*.

On the bright side, I got through the rest of the week without encountering Danders Anders again. If only I could say the same about Steffi and Fiorenze. Them I saw every day, holding hands, giggling, staring into each other's eyes. Yet Steffi walked to school with me in the mornings as if Fiorenze and her fairy didn't exist. When I asked about her he'd shrug or say they'd broken up. By recess they'd be back together again.

It hurt so much it was hard to think about anything else. Why hadn't Steffi stayed in Ravenna where he belonged?

Despite us never issuing an invitation, they sat with me, Rochelle, and Sandra at both recesses, lunch, and dinner. Or, rather, mostly not me because I was in the library doing homework, which was preferable to watching the two of them.

I no longer believed in their breakups. They would be together forever.

+ + +

It was seven a.m. on Sunday, the one day of the week I get to sleep in, and there I was waiting for Rochelle. She had continued not to take *no* for an answer. So even without ravening, rabid, rapid wolves chasing me, I was going to Fiorenze Stupid-Name's house to learn how to get rid of my fairy.

I really hoped Stupid-Name's mom would find me a better one. I wondered if I'd get to look at her mysterious book. The one Fiorenze had told me about. What was it called? That's right, *The Ultimate Fairy Book*. It better be.

Nettles and Mom and Dad were still asleep. Except for that one awkward walk home with Dad, I'd barely seen my parents all week. I missed them. I even missed Nettles. I couldn't remember the last time we'd cooked together or she'd done my hair. Nettles is vastly gifted at hair. I even missed her yelling at me about my lack of creativity and originality.

There was a loud knock. I grabbed my backpack, slung it over my shoulder, and opened the door.

The early-morning sunlight made Rochelle's skin gleam and her dress golden. I closed the door behind me and saw that the dress was gray, not gold. It floated, making her look just how I imagined a fairy would.

"Wow!" I picked up the hem, discovering layers. The top few slid through my fingers. "So soft. Like it's made of clouds or something."

"Just silk." Rochelle twirled. The layers flared out and floated softly through the air. I'd never seen such a beautiful dress before.

"So I'm guessing the designer fair was a success."

Rochelle grinned. "It's vintage, by Our Diviya, would

you believe! From before she died, so not only did she *really* design this one, I found pictures of her wearing it!"

"No!"

"Yes! Guess how much it cost?"

"I can't. Knowing your fairy—ten cents! Seems like the better the clothes she finds you, the cheaper they are."

Rochelle smiled hugely. "Five dollars. The woman was convinced it was a mistake. She checked through the inventory list, then the master list, and finally rang Our Diviya's headquarters. And five dollars it was! I *love* my fairy. This is the best dress ever! And you should see the black leather coat my fairy found for Sandra!"

I sighed. While they'd been finding the best clothes of all time, I'd been clearing another quadrant of weeds and glass.

"How about the boots?"

I looked down. "Is that suede?"

"Blue suede."

"Blue suede shoes."

"Boots," Rochelle said.

"Were they courtesy of your fairy?"

"Oh, no. They were a regular bargain. My fairy doesn't do shoes. You know that. Sandra got a green pair. But don't worry," Rochelle said, squeezing my hand. "My fairy found something for you as well."

"No!"

"Yes." She opened up her backpack and pulled out a plastic bag. "Here," she said, handing it to me.

I took it and pulled out a dress. Emerald green and slinky. "No way!" I said, staring at it in wonder. The dress seemed to have been made out of fairy dust. "It's gorgeous."

"Also Our Diviya. See? It's bias cut. That's her trademark. Go hang it up. You have to treat it gently. It's vintage."

"Thank you, Ro. You're the doosest!" I dashed upstairs, hung it up carefully, and then dashed back down again.

Rochelle grinned. "Can't wait to see you wear it."

I shut the front door behind us. "Off to the witch's place."

"Fio's not *that* bad."

"Yes she is."

"I have vastly pleasing news for you on that front. Are you ready?"

"Sure. Tell all." We walked to the end of the street and then headed downhill toward the river. It felt weird following the route to school on a Sunday. But Fiorenze's house was in the poshest neighborhood, on the other side of the river, overlooking the ocean. It would take us at least two hours to walk there. Lots of time for catching up on gossip.

"Fiorenze and Stefan have broken up."

A tiny electric spurt of happiness went through me and then just as quickly disappeared. "Again. How many times is that now? They'll be back together within nanoseconds."

"I don't think so." Rochelle screwed up her nose. "Fiorenze was at the fair too."

"No. She was out in public? On her own?"

Rochelle teeth-sucked. "Not on her own. She was with Tamsin. Her mother. Gosh, that woman has a talent for scaring the boys away. Anyway, Fiorenze came up to us, said hi, how goes it, what have you bought, burble, burble."

"She came up to you? Volunteered conversational openings? She burbled? Did she seem entirely healthful? No sign of fever?"

"I know! It was odd in the extreme. She asked some questions about you."

"She did? About me? Maybe it was just because she knows you and me are friends. She *is* in your basketball stream." It amazed me that just saying the word "basketball" sent a ping of sadness through me.

"Oh!" Rochelle's face brightened. "That's my other piece of news. We're not in the same stream anymore!"

"We're not?" I repeated, not understanding.

"No. I'm A-stream now!"

I screamed and hugged her and she squeezed me back, lifting me a little way off the ground. "No! No! No!" I shouted.

"Yes! Yes! Yes!" she shouted back at me.

"How is that even possible?!"

"You know Elena shredded her ACL Friday—"

"Yup." I touched my knee superstitiously. We were all afraid of blowing out our knees. "Oh, of course!" Why hadn't I thought of it? Elena out meant they'd need a backup for her backup. Elena is a center. Rochelle is a center. I smacked my forehead. "I'm so slow!"

Or rather so caught up in my own troubles. Selfish, selfish, selfish. I hugged her again. "Congratulations! Wow! They picked a lowly first year! You're in A-stream *already*! Beyond-words doos! You'll be in the starting lineup by the end of the year!" And basketball still won't even be one of my electives. "Stop thinking bad thoughts, Charlie," I told myself sternly. "Stop being selfish and sorry for yourself."

"Don't be silly," Rochelle said. "I'll just be happy if I get some minutes coming off the bench!"

"I always knew you'd be the first of us to make A-stream. I'm so happy for you!"

"Thanks. I'm wholly happy for me too! And, you know, I just bet they'll be holding new basketball tryouts soon. Elena's out for months. They've lost so many players, they'll have to get at least a couple of new ones."

"That's right!" I wouldn't have to wait till next year to get into basketball!

Rochelle's grin widened. "We'll be playing together again. Soon, I bet. Now, I believe I was revealing some doos Fiorenze gossip."

I nodded. "She was asking you many questions."

"So, I asked Fiorenze where Stefan was, and she said, and I quote, 'I don't know.'" Rochelle looked at me expectantly.

"That's it?" I said. That didn't mean anything. "She doesn't have to know where he is all the time." I didn't know that.

"But she said it with a shrug in her voice as if she didn't *care* where he was and then she changed the subject. Trust me. They are well and truly broken up."

I tried to imagine what a shrug in a person's voice would sound like and failed. "If you say so." But I didn't believe it. I'd had enough of Steffi's on-again off-again linking with Fiorenze. I didn't believe a word either one of them said.

"I say so."

We turned the corner onto Mallett, the steepest street in New Avalon. Below us the river glittered and there were already two blimps floating over the skyscrapers of the city.

CHAPTER 16

Attack of Danders Anders

Days walking: 67
Demerits: 7 − 3 = 4
Conversations with Steffi: 8
Doos clothing acquired: 1
Game suspensions: 1
Public service hours: 16
Hours spent enduring Fiorenze
    Stupid-Name's company: 2.75

Walking through the city even at eight thirty a.m. on a Sunday, there were cars everywhere. Horns honking. Drivers being hateful to every pedestrian who exercised their legally supported right of way. Drivers exceeding the speed limit, not caring whether they lost points or not.

And then, worst of all, Danders Anders pulling up his car and rolling down his window.

"Get in."

"No." I kept walking.

"Andrew, she doesn't get in cars anymore," Rochelle

explained, following me. "Besides we have somewhere we have to be."

Danders kept his car at a slow crawl beside us, causing an instant traffic jam, filling the air with profanities, and more horns honking. What is it about cars that turns everyone into a doxhead?

"Emergency."

"Me too, Andrew."

"No parks."

"We don't have time," Rochelle said.

I sped up. There was no reasoning with Danders Anders. Up ahead was a pedestrian-only street. We could lose him there.

Danders stopped his car. Right in the middle of the street! He got out and caught up with me in a few easy paces. Then he picked me up as if I weighed no more than a bag of cotton candy and headed back to his car.

I screamed as loud as I could and kicked with all my might. "Let me go! Let me go!"

"Can't," Danders said. "Emergency."

Rochelle grabbed his shirt, trying to slow him down. She is tall and strong. But he is taller and stronger.

"Andrew! Let her down!"

Rochelle put her body between him and his beloved car. "Let her go, Andrew. She doesn't want to get in your car."

"Need her," Danders replied, as if that was reasonable. Behind him the traffic built up even more, the horns louder and angrier.

Danders pushed Rochelle aside with one hand while keeping me from escaping with the other. I screamed so loud it hurt.

He winced. "Stop," he said, reaching for the door handle. I screamed again, aiming at his ears.

"Ow," Danders said as Rochelle tried to stop him from opening the door. He swatted her away, while I screamed again so loud I thought my voice would break. Danders yelped and fell, taking me with him on account of his grip fairy. I landed on top of Danders, who was still yelping. I looked up.

Two police officers. One of them holding a stun gun. *That* was what had caused Danders's yelp.

"Andrew Khassian Rogers?" the one with the stun gun asked, but I could tell it wasn't really a question. They knew who he was.

Danders blinked.

"Let go of the girl."

Danders let go of me. I pushed off him. How many demerits did you get for being arrested?

"Are you all right?" the non-stun-gun-wielding officer asked.

I nodded. "He didn't hurt me." I doubted he'd used even a tenth of his strength.

"And you?" the officer asked Rochelle. She had what looked like the beginnings of a bruise on her cheek.

She touched it gently. "He hurt my face."

"Accident," Danders said, rubbing his butt. "I hurt too."

The officer stood on tippy toes to look at Rochelle's injury. "There's no broken skin. Can you touch it?"

Rochelle put her fingers to her cheekbone. "It's not too bad."

"Probably not broken."

"No thanks to him," Rochelle said. "How could you?"

"Accident," Danders repeated.

"Would you like to press charges?" the officer asked. She was not serious. Nobody pressed charges against stars of A-stream teams, especially ones like Danders Anders who were in their final year and on the brink of superlative careers.

"I'd *love* to press charges," Rochelle answered. "That would be joyous."

The officer grinned. "Wouldn't it?"

"Come on, Ro," I said, grabbing her arm. "We're still an hour away from Fiorenze's."

"Okay, okay," Rochelle said. She turned to the officer. "I don't suppose you could rough him up a bit?"

"I thought you *liked* Danders?" I asked.

"Less now than I did."

The officer laughed. "Stun gun's all we can do and it's done. You can comfort yourself knowing that Mr. Khassian Rogers won't be comfortable for several hours. Do get your face checked out, though."

"I will," Rochelle said. "Thanks for rescuing us."

The officer tipped her hat. We waved as we walked away.

"Something's up with Danders," Rochelle said.

"You think?" Sandra's not the only one who can be sarcastic.

"I've heard rumors."

"Really? Like what? Is he going to run away and join the circus?"

Rochelle laughed. "No, someone saw him with people he shouldn't be with."

"Like who?" I tried to think who he shouldn't be with. "Arts students?"

"Hah! No, more like criminals."

"Criminals!"

"I mean, they didn't say, but that was the impression I got."

"Who said?"

"Freedom Hazal. He said that a friend of his cousin's had seen Danders at a temp nightclub in the produce district. It sounded like Danders was using flyers."

"Drugs? Danders? Freedom's a gossip."

"Doesn't mean there's not something to the gossip. Danders is acting vastly out of character." She touched her cheek and winced. "He never used to be violent. Flyers can make you violent."

"I guess." Though Ro's cheek was kind of an accident. We continued our trek toward Fiorenze's house, putting the malodorous Danders Anders out of our thoughts.

113

CHAPTER 17

Tamsin Burnham-Stone

Days walking: 67
Demerits: 4
Conversations with Steffi: 8
Game suspensions: 1
Public service hours: 16
Hours spent enduring Fiorenze
    Stupid-Name's company: 2.75
Kidnappings thwarted: 1

Fiorenze Burnham-Stone's house was ginormous.

I'd heard the rumors, obviously. After her foul-and-grossly-unfair fairy, and the fact that her parents had made no effort to lose their accent, the hugeness of their house was the most talked-about thing about the Burnham-Stone family. But I hadn't realized quite how big.

As we walked up the long drive under an archway of flame trees, the house that came into view wasn't simply big, it took up the whole block. It was five stories high, made of pink marble, and surrounded by an ornate garden with columns and arches and fountains. The whole thing sat at the top of the cliff with ocean views on one side and city views on the other.

"Fairy dung!"

"Come on, Charlie, I told you she had a big place."

"This is not a *big* place. This is a castle, a coliseum, a cathedral. The Sports Museum isn't as big as this place. It's the same size as school! I say again: fairy dung! Are her family insane?"

"Possibly." Rochelle grinned. "But they know a plenitude about fairies and they're going to help you."

I wondered if they really could.

I caught the smell of salt. The smell brought a rush of memories: days surfing, snorkeling, doing laps in the bars, sand castles, beach volleyball. I tried to remember the last time I'd been to the beach. Definitely not since I'd started at Sports. That made me a little sad.

"Can you smell the ocean?" I asked.

"Yeah, isn't it fantabulous? When's the last time we went to the beach?"

"I was just thinking that! Let's go next school break. After my fairy's gone."

"That's the spirit!" Rochelle punched me. I winced. She ran up the front steps and rang the bell. The door opened instantly.

It was Fiorenze. "Hi, Rochelle. Hi, Charlie," she said. "I saw you coming up the drive."

We both said hi back. Then we all stood there awkwardly for what felt like hours.

"Oh," Fiorenze said at last, "come in." She opened the door wider, revealing the biggest foyer I'd ever seen. The floor was made of swirling marble. There were two giant curving staircases and the biggest chandelier I'd ever seen.

"Oh," Fiorenze said again. "It is kind of big, isn't it?" She made it sound like that was a really bad thing.

"Sure is. You must have like five rooms of your own!"

"She has two," said a strange-accented woman, walking toward me and holding out her hand.

She was pulchritudinous. No, not pulchy exactly, stylish. She was the same height as her daughter. Her skin color was a little darker, with more red. She had the biggest eyes I'd ever seen. Her hair was close cropped, making them look even bigger. And New Avalon is full of big-eyed pulchies. It was hard to believe she wasn't an Our.

But to be an Our requires not just fame—you have to be a proper New Avaloner. She'd only lived here ten years or so. Not long enough to lose her accent. Not that a Fairy Studies professor would ever become famous, not unless they captured a fairy or something.

"I'm Tamsin," she said. "You must be Charlotte."

I shook her hand and didn't tell her that I hate being called Charlotte. I couldn't quite imagine her calling me *Charlie*.

"Hello, Rochelle. How are you?"

"Fine, thanks, Tamsin." Rochelle spoke as if calling her by her first name was perfectly natural. No way could I call this goddess by her first name.

"Are you girls hungry? Thirsty?"

"No, thank you," Rochelle said. I shook my head. I was feeling too awe-full to speak.

"Well, then to business it is. Darling, show Rochelle the new additions to the basketball court. Didn't you say she's an A-streamer now?"

I tried not to think jealous thoughts. Even if I'd made B-stream I couldn't have replaced Elena; I'm just a little point guard.

Fiorenze looked down. "Oh, I thought we—"

"See you later, darling." She turned to me, swiveling elegantly. I wondered if she'd ever been a dancer. "This way," she said as if her words were part of the same movement.

Following her, I was convinced that if anyone could get rid of my loathsome fairy, it was Tamsin Burnham-Stone.

CHAPTER 18

Two Fairies

Days walking: 67
Demerits: 4
Conversations with Steffi: 8
Game suspensions: 1
Public service hours: 16
Hours spent enduring Fiorenze
   Stupid-Name's company: 2.75
Kidnappings thwarted: 1

Dr. Burnham-Stone led me up the right-hand curving marble staircase and down a long corridor that wasn't lined with family portraits, though I could imagine them.

"Have you considered that you might have the fairy you have for a reason?"

"Um," I said. To make sure my blood is full of carbon monoxide? Stupid cars.

"Some people believe that everyone gets the fairy they deserve. And that changing your fairy will create chaos."

"I hadn't heard that," I said. I did not *deserve* my fairy! "How do you mean chaos?"

"I mean what I say," she said grimly. "Chaos."

That wasn't any answer. "Yes, but what do you mean by chaos?"

She opened a door and led me into a large room. I was startled to see myself a hundred times over. The walls were lined with mirrors. I automatically straightened, pulling my shoulders back, and flattened my core muscles. The result of years of fencing lessons in front of mirrors.

Dr. Burnham-Stone put her finger over her lips and gestured for me to sit down. But there weren't any chairs, only cushions and loads of books in precarious piles. At the other end of the room was a metal box with a huge padlock on it.

I wondered if that was her secret fairy manifesto! Fiorenze hadn't been kidding about it being locked up. The padlock was the biggest, most unbreakable in the universe. How on earth did Fiorenze expect me to get a peek at the book?

I sank cross-legged onto the nearest cushion, keeping my stomach muscles tight and my back straight. Fiorenze's mom sat down opposite me with a notebook in hand. She stared at me as if I were a bug she was figuring out how to kill.

I wasn't sure what to do. Should I stare back? That seemed rude. I rested the backs of my hands on my knees like I was going to start meditating. Hardly! I hate meditating.

Dr. Burnham-Stone kept staring at me. I wondered if

Fiorenze was adopted. Fiorenze's eyes were smaller, her nose bigger, and her hair had tighter curls (when it wasn't braided, that is). Maybe she favored her father. I wondered where he was. Wasn't he a fairy expert too?

I felt a trickle of sweat roll down my spine, which was crazy because the room wasn't hot. Wasn't cold either. I wished she'd say something.

I shifted position just a hair because my calves were aching. Her eyes narrowed.

"Must not move," I told myself, which made me want to move.

She hadn't moved a muscle (except the glaring ones). I couldn't even tell if she was breathing. I wondered what she was seeing when she stared at me. Could she actually see my fairy? Did she have a fairy that let you see other people's fairies? Surely if that was true she'd be famous. I mean, how doos would that be? Everyone would want her to stare at them and at their newborn babies. Maybe she could even tell what fairy they had in the womb.

"Why are you staring at me?" I asked, even though I knew I shouldn't, but she was hardly going to give me a demerit, was she? "Are you trying to scare the fairy away?"

Dr. Burnham-Stone snorted.

My legs started to go numb. I am not a fan of staying in one position for more than a few seconds. Hence the not liking of meditating. Another trickle of sweat ran down my spine.

My left cheek was itchy.

And my shoulder.

Since when did shoulders get itchy?

"Can you see my fairy, then?" I asked. "Are you memorizing it?"

"Something like that," she said, opening up her notebook and scribbling in it.

I crossed my legs the other way and shook out my arms. Dr. Burnham-Stone kept scribbling, glancing up at me and frowning, and then scribbling and scribbling and scribbling some more.

I wondered what time it was. I hoped it wasn't too late. I had a vast amount of homework to get through and it was going to take a couple of hours to get home. Unless her scribbling was her figuring out how to get rid of my fairy, in which case I could go by bus and it wouldn't take more than twenty minutes or so (traffic depending).

She closed her notebook and stood up. "Come here," she said, leading me to the corner of the room, where there were mirrors on two sides. I stood up and followed her. "Stand there," she said, pointing to the corner of the room.

I stood with mirrors on two sides of me while she dragged two portable ones to make a third and fourth wall around me. Millions of reflections of myself over and over and over again.

"What do you see?"

"Um, me?"

"Look closer."

I looked closer, staring at myself multiplied into infinity. But I couldn't see anything unusual. I just looked like me.

"Can you see your fairy's aura?"

"Um."

"Do you see anything hovering around your edges?"

"I can see *you*."

"Look closer."

I did. I could see the tiny faint hairs on my face. Were teeny little hairs fairies? Or did she mean the freckles on my nose? How come no one else in my family had freckles? Not even Nettles, who's a shade or two lighter than me. Not fair. There didn't seem to be any fairy aura caught in any of my freckles.

"Relax your eyes. Let yourself see!"

I tried. But I just saw even more Charlies.

"Um," I said.

Dr. Burnham-Stone frowned. "You need to relax your eyes. Stare at one point. Stare at your nose until your vision blurs."

I stared. My nose blurred. My head started to ache and then something shifted, my nose unblurred. And there was an arc of smudgy light around me. As well as a brilliant one around Dr. Burnham-Stone.

"See?"

I did see. "Yours is golden; mine is blue and white."

"Yes. Except that you have two auras, not one."

"So one of them's mine and the other is my fairy's?"

"No," she said, as if I were a little dense. "They both belong to fairies. One is your original fairy's. See the thicker white aura? The thin blue one belongs to your proto-fairy. It's waiting for the parking fairy to leave before it emerges fully."

"Two fairies?" Was that even possible?

"Yes, two. Though it's more like one and a fraction. Your parking fairy is definitely weakening. See how much less bright it is than mine?"

I nodded.

"Continue walking. Your parking fairy is almost gone. But you must also encourage the proto-fairy. Do things that will strengthen it."

"Really?" I said, staring at the white aura. It wasn't nearly as bright as her fairy's aura, but it was still considerably thicker and brighter than the proto-fairy's blue smudge. "But isn't there something you can do to snuff out the parking fairy right now?"

"It's better to finish the work you've begun," she said, sounding a bit like Coach Ntini.

Dr. Burnham-Stone, I decided, was excellent at not answering questions.

"What's my proto-fairy, then?"

Dr. Burnham-Stone shook her head. "That you must discover for yourself."

"How?"

She smiled. "You will find out."

"Can you give me something to read about proto-fairies?

Will I get a hint about what it is? What if it's worse than the parking fairy?" I didn't really think she'd hand over the *Ultimate Fairy Book*, but it was worth a shot.

She shook her head. "Little is known about them."

"What do *you* know, then?"

Dr. Burnham-Stone cut her eyes at me.

"I'm just asking," I protested. "How can I encourage it if I don't know what it is?"

"A proto-fairy is exactly what it sounds like. A fairy that isn't fully formed yet. You don't need to know any more than that."

I disagreed. I thought I needed to know *heaps* more than that. What kind of a scholar didn't want to teach you stuff?

CHAPTER 19
A Surprise

Days walking: 67
Demerits: 4
Conversations with Steffi: 8
Game suspensions: 1
Public service hours: 16
Hours spent enduring Fiorenze
    Stupid-Name's company: 2.75
Kidnappings thwarted: 1

When I finally got home I was so wrapped up in my thoughts about fairies—why couldn't Dr. Burnham-Stone tell me how to get rid of the parking fairy right away? Why was she so vague? What was my proto-fairy?—that I didn't notice Steffi sitting on the front steps of my house, grinning at me, until I was almost treading on him.

"What are you doing here?" I asked, even though I couldn't help being pleased to see him. "Fiorenze didn't want to hang out with you?"

Steffi waved his arms about in a most undoos way. Almost like he felt guilty for the way he kept mucking me around. Always with Fiorenze and her stupid fairy at school, but running after me otherwise. It wasn't fair.

"Let's not talk about that," he said. "So how'd it go?" he asked. "Is the fairy gone?"

"How'd you know where I was?" I sat down beside him, but not so close we were touching. I didn't trust him. I knew he'd be back with Stupid-Name the minute he saw her at school. "Stup—I mean, Fiorenze told you?" I hated to think about them together, talking about stuff— about me.

"Uh-huh," he said, looking down. "She mentioned it. What did Tamsin say?"

He called her Tamsin too? "That I have two fairies now."

"Two? Double the fun, eh?"

I looked at him. He was smiling. The warmth of it made me smile too. I wished I could stop liking him. "Yup. One of them's the parking fairy. She says it's getting weaker. Isn't that doos? But she also says I have to keep walking everywhere to make it go away fully."

"Bummer."

I nodded, though I wasn't wholly sure what "bummer" meant.

"So what's your other fairy, then?" He shifted a little closer to me and I got this weird sensation like I could feel where he was even though we weren't actually touching. Tingly. I told myself to shift away, but my body didn't listen.

"I don't know. Tamsin says it's a proto-fairy." If I moved a tiny fraction of a millimeter closer we would be touching, which would be bad.

"Proto-fairy? What's a proto-fairy?"

"A fairy that isn't a whole fairy yet. I think."

"Do you have any idea what yours might be?"

"No." My body felt like it was somehow leaning toward Steffi's even though I was holding myself so rigid and still my muscles were starting to twitch. It was the opposite of how I'd felt holding still to keep Dr. Burnham-Stone from glaring at me. That was on purpose holding still; this was not.

"Do you have any ideas? Anything you've gotten better at lately? Any luck increases?"

I snorted. "Hah! Luck increases! Try the opposite. My life is all demerits and public service." And liking a boy who acts as if he likes me except when he's with the girl I hate most in the whole world.

"Grim."

"She says that I have to do stuff that will encourage the proto-fairy to become an actual fairy."

"Makes sense," Steffi said. "But how can you do that if you don't know what it is?"

"I see you've spotted the problem." I sighed.

"Maybe your other fairy is a worry fairy?"

"A worry fairy?"

"Your forehead's all scrunched up." Steffi touched his thumb to my forehead to smooth my frown. I held my breath. "Too much worry. Must be your new fairy messing with you." He moved his hand away, but I felt warmth where his thumb had been. Almost like it was still there.

"Worry fairies would take worries away, not add them," I said softly.

"Let me be your worry fairy, then." Steffi grabbed at the air just in front of my face. "This is me removing a worry. And here's another one. And another. And . . ."

Steffi's face was so close to mine that I felt his breath against my cheeks. I could smell the coconutty soap he'd used and the faint salt of his sweat.

Then I felt his lips against mine. Warm and soft. My lips buzzed, a tingle shot all the way down to my toes.

Steffi shifted, but he was still so close I could see the almost invisible hairs on his cheeks and the tiny half-moon scar in his left eyebrow. I'd never noticed it before.

"Oh," I whispered.

Steffi kissed me again.

"Oh," I thought. "More kisses. Bubbly warm kisses."

"Kisses," I said, then my brain spasmed. "Kisses!"

I jumped up. "Steffi! You can't do that!"

He stared up at me as if I'd spontaneously combusted. "You don't like kissing?"

"No! I mean yes. I mean, aargh!" How could he be kissing Fiorenze one minute and me the next? "Kissing is wholly against the rules."

"But we're not at school."

"Steffi! It doesn't matter. It means instant expulsion.

EXPULSION. Doesn't matter where or when you get caught. Anyone could see us here!"

"I saw you. Heard you too," Nettles said, sticking her head out of the living room window. She waved her camera. "And I've got photos!"

"You did not take photos!" I yelled. My cheeks were so hot they burned.

She took another photo. "Did too! Several kissy shots."

"I'll kill you!" I screamed, even though I knew she would never use the photos against me. I really wanted to kill Steffi. Or Fiorenze. Or her fairy. Or possibly all three.

"Won't that get you expelled too?" Nettles asked, clicking away.

"Shut up!" I said.

She just laughed. "If you went to Arts you could kiss as much as you want. Though why anyone would want to . . ." She made a mock kissing sound. It sounded like a frog drowning.

"Let's go, Steffi," I said, grabbing his hand, pulling him up, so he was standing practically on top of me, which only made me wish we would kiss again. I stepped back.

"Don't you have homework to do?!" Nettles yelled as I practically sprinted away. My muscles hurt. I'd had to skip my massages for the last few weeks. Too much homework to do on account of I'd lost so much time from all the walking around. And so on times a bazillion million zasquillion.

Steffi trotted along beside me, laughing.

"What's so funny?" I asked.

"Your sister and her camera. You."

"Me?"

"The way you take all those rules so seriously. I mean, me and Fio were kissing at school and no one said a word. Ntini walked by. I'm sure he saw us. Didn't bat an eye."

My brain split in two. One half was thinking, "He's not even embarrassed that he was KISSING Stupid-Name?! And now he's kissing me?! Is that what they do on the West Coast? Kiss each other all day long?!"

The other half yelled at him: "That's because you have a never-getting-into-trouble fairy! You could stand on the table in the cafeteria with the wrong uniform on and your tie crooked and shout out that New Avalon was torpid and self-obsessed, and in the ensuing riot you would be the only one *not* to get double demerits."

Steffi grinned, untroubled by my accusation. I wanted to punch him. "I'm not sure you can call a city 'self-obsessed,' but if there is a city that fits that description, it's New Avalon."

"If you like Fiorenze so much why did you kiss me?"

"I . . . ," Steffi began, his grin finally going away. "It's hard to explain. I don't like Fiorenze. Not really—"

It was too much. "She has a fairy! It *makes* you like her! Why can't you resist it?"

"It's not like that," he said. "When she's around—"

"It's *exactly* like that!" I yelled, turning back to the house, but Steffi grabbed my arm. "Don't touch me! Don't speak to me! I don't ever want to see you again!" I screamed as loud as I could, shaking off his hold, and I sprinted back to my place, up the stairs, and into my room, slamming the door loudly and satisfyingly behind me. The whole world was conspiring against me. I hated it and everyone in it, but especially the kissy-kissy boy Steffi. He didn't like *me*; he just liked kissing.

There was a gentle knock on the door.

"What?" I growled.

My dad opened the door. He was holding the laundry basket. "Hope you don't mind, but I did your laundry. Well, as much of it as I could find." He put the laundry basket down. "Thought you might be running out. Folded it too."

"Thanks, Dad," I said, biting my lip to keep from crying. Why did I have to like a boy who was bewitched by a fairy?

"I'm impressed by all the public service you've been doing. As long as you keep up this getting-rid-of-your-fairy campaign I'll do your laundry. All I ask is that you leave it somewhere I can find it. Under the bed and crumpled up in your school bag is not the most convenient—"

There was another knock on the door. Mom slipped in holding a plate loaded with food. "Dinner, love. We weren't sure if you'd eaten or not." She put it down on my chair, there not being any space on the desk.

I burst into tears, and my parents kissed the top of my head, hugged me, and told me everything was going to be okay. Sometimes parents are more than tolerable.

CHAPTER 20
A Revelation

Days walking: 68
Demerits: 4
Conversations with Steffi: 9
Game suspensions: 1
Public service hours: 16
Hours spent enduring Fiorenze
   Stupid-Name's company: 2.75
Kidnappings thwarted: 1
Number of Steffi kisses: 2
Fights with Steffi: 1

I was not surprised to see Steffi and Stupid-Name together the next day. Hurt, but not surprised. When you like a boy who can't resist an every-boy-will-like-you fairy, you have to expect it. I wondered if this was what the rest of my life would be like. Liking someone who only liked me part of the time.

Nor was it a shock that he didn't say hello, or look at me—I had told him not to, but I *was* surprised when Stupid-Name came up to talk to me at the end of Fencing (to which, of course, I'd been late. But at least I had clean whites on account of my dad's mercy laundry run).

"Hi, Charlie," Fiorenze said.

"Hi," I replied, continuing to wipe down my practice foils and put them in my fencing bag. Why was she talking to me? She had Steffi. Why did she have to come and gloat about it?

Steffi was deliberately looking vastly pulchy. I'd had to bout with him too. And even though I couldn't really see his lips behind the mask, it was like I could feel them there. I kept remembering what kissing him was like. Naturally I lost.

Stupid Steffi.

"Are you doing more public service on Wednesday?" Fiorenze asked. Why wouldn't she leave me alone and go back to her kiss-anyone boyfriend?

"Yes." And why couldn't Steffi resist her stupid fairy? Why didn't I have her fairy?

"Me too," she said.

I zipped up my bag and hoisted it over my shoulder, heading out the door.

Fiorenze trotted along beside me. "Do you think they'll pair us again?" she asked.

I grunted. I had no idea. Nor did I care.

"Coincidence us both doing Wednesdays, isn't it?"

I stopped and stared at her. "I do it *every* night." That wasn't strictly true—I didn't do public service on Sundays—but close enough.

"Oh," Stupid-Name said. "Sorry."

"Fio!" Steffi called from the steps of the bus. "You coming?"

"You'd better go," I pointed out.

"Oh," she said again, turning to where Steffi was waving at her, his hair falling into his face, his fencing jacket askew. "You're right." She turned back to me. "Um . . ."

"What? I have to go. I'll be late." I stalked off across the football fields (all codes), wishing my fencing bag wasn't quite so heavy, or my locker so far away.

The grounds had dried up considerably since last week. I knew the city needed more rain, but I was feeling selfish enough to be grateful that I wouldn't have to waste time scraping mud off. At least something was going my way.

"Gorgeous day, isn't it?" Stupid-Name said.

"What?!" I exclaimed. "I thought you took the bus."

"Um."

"Why aren't you with Stefan?"

"I just, um, felt like a walk."

What was up with her? We'd known each other for years without her saying a word and now, all of a sudden, she was stalking me.

"And, um, I wanted to ask—"

"Oh, no!" Up ahead Danders Anders was walking toward us. His hulking frame was impossible to mistake for anyone else's. I thought about running, but I had the fencing bag over my shoulder, plus running would put me farther away from where I wanted to be, not closer, which would mean more demerits.

"What? Oh. He wants you to get in his car, doesn't he?"

"Seems like."

"He moves very quickly, doesn't he?"

"It's those long legs," I said.

Danders lurched to a stop in front of us. "You car later," he said without bothering with any prepositions or a *hi* or *how goes it* or *I'm really sorry I attempted to kidnap you.*

"No," I said.

"Stung," Danders said. "Hurt."

"They stung you because you attacked me."

"Car, six. Emergency."

"I don't *have* to do anything, Andrew," I said, my voice starting to break. "I said no. I mean no. You can ask me a million, bazillion, kajillion times. You can offer me all the gold on the planet, the keys to the land of Ourdom, and I would still say no. So stop asking!"

The muscles in his forehead twitched as if he was trying to make sense of my words even though such computing powers were beyond him. I wondered which one of us would blow a gasket first.

"Car."

"No!" I began. "You can't—"

"She doesn't have a parking fairy anymore," Fiorenze said.

I closed my mouth.

"My mother got rid of it for her."

Danders swiveled to stare at Stupid-Name. "What?"

135

"She doesn't have a parking fairy."

"No parking fairy?" His forehead was convulsing. "Fairy gone?"

Fiorenze nodded. "Fairy gone."

"No fairy?" Danders asked again. "Charlie good fairy gone?"

"Charlie's good fairy gone."

"Where go?"

"We don't know."

"Don't know?" Danders asked.

"Don't know," Fiorenze confirmed.

"Really?"

"*Really*," Fiorenze said firmly, sounding almost like her mother.

"Sad," Danders said and then slouched away without another word.

"Wow," I said, watching him disappear. "I can't believe he bought it." Danders isn't great at grasping change.

"I know," Fiorenze said. "He is the strangest boy. I wonder what goes on in his head. Do you think he even realizes that we're human beings the way he is?"

"Hey, you lied!" Being caught lying is vastly serious. Depending on the circumstances you can be expelled. Why had Fiorenze lied for me?

She nodded. "Sometimes you have to."

"He probably only believed you on account of your boy-attracting fairy," I said without thinking. I blushed.

She didn't seem to notice. "Doesn't work on seniors."

"What?"

"It only works on guys around the same age as me."

"Really?"

She nodded. "Imagine if it worked on all boys. How torpid would that be?"

I thought about it for a second. "Or if it worked on your teachers." I shuddered.

"I *hate* my fairy."

"You what?" I stared at her. She was looking straight back at me. "But . . . ," I spluttered.

"I hate it. I've been doing everything I can to get rid of it. I did the not-washing thing. But Mom intervened. I stayed away from boys. Not that that was hard. It was starting to fade . . ."

I hadn't noticed her staying away from Steffi.

"But. It. Will. Not. Go. Away. No matter what I do. I don't even think I like boys."

"But everyone is jealous of your fairy," I said, trying to make sense of her words. "Everyone wants it."

Fiorenze shook her head. "No, they don't. Not if they thought about it."

"And you do *too* like boys. What about Steffi?"

"Who?"

"Stefan." I felt a tiny thrill that he had told me his nickname, but not her.

"Stefan," she repeated. "He's unavoidable. All the other boys obey the rule that protects me, but not Stefan, and he never gets a single demerit."

"But you're always holding hands, passing notes to each other, giggling."

"I don't giggle."

I shrugged even though it was true. Fiorenze was not a giggler.

"And it was Stefan passing notes to *me*. As for the holding hands—I told him I didn't like it. Or him. But it didn't make any difference," Fiorenze said. "The teachers weren't going to protect me because of Steffi's fairy. What could I do?"

"But you were together by first recess of the day you met!"

"I reported him. Three times. But, of course, the teachers didn't do anything." Fiorenze's eyes filled with tears. She blinked rapidly to make them go away. She was safe from a demerit—there were no teachers in sight. "My fairy is the worst fairy in the world," she said. "But at least Steffi isn't as bad as the other boys. I don't think the fairy affects him as much; he's only tried to kiss me twice."

"What does your mother say?" I asked, reeling from what she was saying.

"She hasn't."

"Why not?" I asked.

"You met her. She's not very forthcoming, is she?"

That was an understatement. She was all cryptic sayings.

"You really don't like Steffi?" I asked.

"No, I really don't."

I shook my head. How was it possible not to like Steffi? "Why haven't you asked your father to help you, then?"

"I can't. My parents are . . . Well, neither of them has a lot of time for me. I'm not what they expected."

I didn't know what to say. I didn't know if me and Nettles were what our parents expected, but there hadn't been any complaints. Well, not about who we were, just about what we sometimes did (or didn't do). What did they expect from me and Nettles? That we try hard and be happy? Something like that. My parents didn't have a lot of time, but they gave us whatever we needed of it.

"That's why I tried to join you yesterday, but Tamsin, well, you saw. She told me to go off with Rochelle."

"*That* was you trying?"

Fiorenze ducked her head.

"You didn't even ask if you could watch. You just went away as soon as she told you to."

Fiorenze was still looking down. "She was firm. There's no point arguing with her when she's being firm."

I didn't know what to say. I hadn't realized Fiorenze was such a torpid-heart.

"Did Tamsin show you the book?" she asked.

I shook my head. "I think I saw it, though. In a big metal box?"

She nodded.

"But it was locked up."

"It always is. If only we could read it," Fiorenze said. "Then we'd get rid of both our fairies."

The bell for the end of first recess rang. "Fairy dung!" I yelled. "Late again!"

139

CHAPTER 21

Ruins

Days walking: 69
Demerits: 5−3=2
Conversations with Steffi: 9
Game suspensions: 1
Public service hours: 19
Hours spent enduring Fiorenze
   Stupid-Name's company: 3
Kidnappings thwarted: 1
Number of Steffi kisses: 2
Days Steffi not talking to me: 1

The next morning Steffi was not waiting on my front steps. Even though I was exhausted from Monday night's public service, I'd gotten up early hoping we'd get to talk. He hadn't said a word to me since our fight on Sunday. It was the longest we'd gone without speaking since I first met him. I hadn't had a chance to talk to Rochelle or Sandra about Fiorenze hating her fairy either.

Should I tell Steffi that Fiorenze didn't like him? How

would it feel to be drawn to someone who couldn't stand you?

I had to get him talking to me again. I missed it. He so often said (and did) unexpected things. He looked at things so differently.

I also liked the kissing. Who'd have thought that mixing your saliva with someone else's saliva wouldn't be malodorous? I hoped we'd get to kiss again.

"Wha—," I said.

Large hairless arms closed around me and lifted me off the ground. A huge hand was firmly over my mouth, holding my jaw shut so that I couldn't bite or scream. The hand stank of chlorine.

I kicked hard, and swung my bag to thwack my assailant, but none of it prevented my being bundled into the front seat of Danders Anders's car. A seat belt snapped into place around me. I pressed the release button, but nothing happened.

"Locked," Danders Anders said, folding himself into the driver's seat. "Door too."

It was more like a tank than a car; even so, Danders dwarfed it. The top of his head pressed up against the roof. His knees were in his chest and the steering wheel looked tiny beneath his ginormous hands.

"Liar," he said. "Fairy not gone."

I hugged my bag to my chest and thought about explaining how it was Fiorenze who was a liar, not me.

"Sorry," said a voice from the backseat. I swiveled to see Bluey Salazar blinking at me. He did not look cheerful.

"Sorry?" I asked him.

"I kind of sort of accidentally let slip something that led Andrew to make certain connections—"

"Danders doesn't *make* connections!" I hissed. "His brain's too small."

"Shh," Bluey whispered. "He's right there."

I didn't care.

"Park city," Danders announced. "Emergency." How was he capable of driving when speaking was such a challenge? He hadn't made any connections. Bluey must've flat out told him my parking fairy wasn't gone.

"No!" I screamed. "No parking! I can't be in a car! I can't find parking spots! Don't you understand? My parking fairy is almost gone! This will make her come back!"

"Parking fairy good."

"No! Parking fairy bad. Parking fairy benighted, malodorous, doxy, vile. There is nothing good about parking fairy. I can't do this! I can't feed the bad fairy! I can't starve the good fairy! I can't!"

My eyes were getting hot. I did not want to start crying, even though the odds of any teacher seeing were small. But I was furious. If Danders Anders had been considerably smaller, and I knew it wouldn't get me expelled, I'd have killed him.

"Give money. Not now. Later. Lots of money."

142

"I don't want your money! Not now or ever!"

"You see, Andrew?" Bluey said. "You've driven her insane. You should let her go."

"Yes! Let me go!"

"She go," Danders said, "you stay. Drive car round and round."

"I have classes! I can't be late! Sorry, Charlie," Bluey said again. "But he just picked me up and marched me off campus. He's really big."

"I'm not angry with you, Bluey," I said, though I was. I was angry with him and with Danders and with the parking fairy and my sister and Fiorenze and Steffi and the entire universe. I was bubbling with rage because I could smell all those vile car reeks that my nostrils had been free of for TWO WHOLE MONTHS. Vinyl and plastic and weird car carpet and gasoline underneath it all. The worst smells in the world.

"But you have to let me go, Andrew," Bluey said. "You promised."

"Have money?" Danders asked.

"No," I said, though he could have been asking Bluey. "And if I did I wouldn't give it to you."

"Need gas money."

"You don't have enough money for gas, but you want me to get you parking spots? How are you going to pay me? Unbelievable!"

"Gas money?" he asked Bluey.

Bluey handed him twenty dollars.

"Pay back," Danders said, pressing a button so that Bluey's seat belt retracted and the back door swung open.

"Traitor," I hissed.

"I'll make it up to you, Charlie," Bluey said, stepping out of the car.

I really wanted to smack him but instead I said, "You'd better."

"No worries," he said, shutting the door behind him. "No worries for him," I thought.

"Park city now," Danders Anders said.

He switched on the ignition, the engine turned over, he released the brake, put his foot on the accelerator, and for the first time in two months I was in a car that was in motion heading toward a perfect parking spot. I could feel my fairy getting healthier and heavier.

I closed my eyes, held my breath, and counted to twenty. Maybe by the time I opened them it would turn out this was a dream and I was still in bed.

"Park city now," Danders Anders said. "Emergency."

"Fine then," I said. "My life is over anyway." I could see the school gates out the car window. Maybe if a teacher saw me, they would come to the rescue. Sadly, the car windows were tinted.

Nineteen, twenty. Streets zoomed by and then we stopped at the first traffic lights before the bridge leading into the city proper. Not a dream.

It took more than twenty minutes to weave through all

the traffic to a nondescript terrace house wedged between two skyscrapers. There was a parking spot directly in front of it. Danders Anders squealed with joy. The most malodorous sound in the world.

It was a vastly big parking space. Danders is a terrible parker, but somehow the parking fairy knew that and gave him plenty of space. It still took forever.

He finally got out of the car and slammed the door behind him. I wiggled out of the seat belt and tried the door on his side. Locked. Both doors in back as well. There was no way to squeeze into the trunk from the backseat and anyway it would be locked too. Nothing for it but to squeeze back into the seat belt and wait for Danders Anders to return.

This time I would dob, I decided. The school couldn't mean us not to report something as big as kidnapping. It wasn't right. I wondered if other schools were like that. I'd never asked Nettles if they dobbed or not. It hadn't occurred to me. No curiosity, that's what Steffi said. Was it true? I resolved to ask Nettles a whole bunch of questions the next time we got a chance to chat.

After fifteen of the longest minutes of my life, Danders returned.

"What were you doing in there?"

"Secret. School now."

"Yes!" I said fervently. "If you hurry we might only miss one class."

"Parking fairy good," Danders said. "Get me park after school every day. Need good parks."

"I can't. I have public service! If I don't go I get more demerits."

"Need good parks," Danders said.

I didn't say anything. I was not going to cry in front of Danders Anders.

CHAPTER 22
All Over

Days wasted walking: 69
Demerits: 5
Conversations with Steffi: 9
Game suspensions: 1
Public service hours: 19
Hours spent enduring Fiorenze
    Stupid-Name's company: 3
Kidnappings thwarted: 1
Number of Steffi kisses: 2
Days Steffi not talking to me: 1
Parking spots for Danders Anders: 2
Vows to kill Danders Anders: 7
Kidnappings unthwarted: 1

On account of the perfect parking spot my fairy got Danders Anders right in front of main campus I got to school in time to slide behind my desk in History a fraction of a second before the bell sounded. History: my second class of the day. I'd never missed a whole class before. An automatic three demerits, which brought my total up to five.

Every day after school, Danders had said. If I couldn't escape, then I'd miss public service and then how was I going to get rid of my remaining demerits? Gah!

How was I going to get Danders off my back?

I would dob. There was no other way. Surely kidnapping was serious enough for me to report it?

But Danders Anders was going to be an Our of stellariffic proportions. The school needed him. Government funding was generous, but the school still depended on donations, and the majority of those came from its most successful alumni. Danders promised to be vastly successful. Danders would probably wind up being worth millions, maybe even more, to New Avalon Sports High.

What would they say if I reported him? Maybe I should tell Ms. Wilkinson, my counselor, first and see what she said?

I opened up the reading on the founding of New Avalon. Dry as dust, but at least it was familiar. We'd gone over every inch of New Avalon's early years in middle school and four years before that in elementary. If there was one bit of history I knew, it was the founding of New Avalon. Going over old work might be torpid, but right now that was comforting. I wasn't sure I could have focused on anything new.

I'd been so close to getting rid of my fairy. Two months of hard work, of endless demerits, of aching feet, of my parents, my sister, my teachers all mad at me. All completely undone by a selfish, thick, spoiled, stupid, doxhead water polo player. It made me want to scream.

Sandra sat next to me and slid a note under my tablet.

> Dana Chusan sprained her ankle. Rochelle's the starting center for tonight's game. Wanna come watch?

That was wonderful news for Rochelle and for me—surely there'd be a basketball tryout soon. I should have been over the moon, but all I could think about was my fairy. I forced myself to grin and give Sandra the thumbs-up.

Sandra passed another note.

> And Our Tui broke up with her girlfriend.

I did an exaggerated eye widen even though I didn't care. Sandra nodded and slid me another note.

> What did they expect? Ours should only go out with other Ours. Never works when they don't.

"Reckon," I said just to say something.

"Charlotte Adele Donna Seto Steele," said Mr. Lien, whose fairy had to be an ears-like-a-fox fairy. "I hope you are not conversing with Sandra Leigh Petaculo. I do not wish to start the morning off with a flurry of demerits." He glanced at his tablet. "Even though it seems to be your intention to gather as many as possible. You've already earned three today. Do you really want more?"

"No, sir."

"You may read Chapter Three: The Founding of New Avalon for the class."

"Yes, sir." I read out loud and tried to keep my mind on what I was reading.

The parking fairy was going to ruin my life.

CHAPTER 23

Hope

Demerits: 5
Conversations with Steffi: 9
Game suspensions: 1
Public service hours: 19
Hours spent enduring Fiorenze
   Stupid-Name's company: 3
Number of Steffi kisses: 2
Days Steffi not talking to me: 1
Parking spots for Danders Anders: 2
Vows to kill Danders Anders: 15

Fiorenze came into the library during first recess. Four boys trailed behind her. None of them was Steffi. She didn't look happy. I was starting to understand that her fairy might be somewhat annoying.

Fiorenze saw me looking at her and came and sat opposite me. I wished she hadn't. She seemed to think we were friends now. We weren't.

"I can't talk," I told her. "I have a mountain of homework to catch up on. This has not been a good morning."

"This won't take long," she said. "It's important." A boy I didn't know sat down beside her.

"If you don't go away," Fiorenze hissed at him, "I'll report you."

"I won't say anything," the boy said. "I just want to look at you."

"I'm turning my tablet on," she said. She started writing with her thumbnail. "I'm about to send a message to the head counselor."

The boy stood up. "I love you, Fiorenze," he said and walked away.

"You look tired," she said.

A vastly original observation. Why would I possibly look tired? Could it be my not having had more than two hours' sleep a night in months? Doing public service every night? Walking everywhere? Or could it be because all of that had been completely useless? I'd done everything to get rid of the parking fairy and now Danders Anders had ruined it all. I started to say some of this and stopped. What was the point?

I turned back to my assignment on the first cricket match played in New Avalon. The only sources were two contradictory diary entries and a dispatch back to the old country that had no points in common with either of them.

Sometimes the whole point of history seemed to be that everyone saw things completely differently. Still, for one source to say that the Colonials won, and the other that the Squatters did, and the dispatch to say it was a draw, well, that wasn't seeing things differently, that was lying. But how did you tell who the liars were so many centuries later?

"Look," Fiorenze said.

"Go away. I have to work."

She held out her hand. In the middle of her palm was a tiny key.

"It's a key. I've seen keys before, Fiorenze."

"Yes. It's the key to the box that holds *The Ultimate Fairy Book*."

"Your mother's book?" I asked. "The one in the metal box?"

"Yes."

"Why did she give you the key?"

"It's a copy."

"Why would she give you a copy of the key?"

"She wouldn't."

"Then how did you get it?"

Fiorenze didn't say anything.

"You *stole* it! So you're a liar *and* a thief. No wonder you have to do public service!"

Fiorenze put her finger on her lips. "Do you want to get us—"

"Indeed," said Mr. Caswell, one of the librarians. "I am issuing you both with a demerit. See that your discussion remains quiet. You are discussing homework?"

"Yes, Mr. Caswell. Of course. Sorry, sir." Just what I needed—another fragging demerit!

153

Caswell did a condescending eyebrow raise and walked away. Most of the librarians weren't fond of us students on account of we only ever borrowed books for doing homework, not to, you know, just read. Who had time? The librarians enjoyed giving us demerits. Poxy librarians.

"Where's Stefan when I actually need him?" Fiorenze asked when Caswell was out of earshot.

"You really don't like Steffi?" I asked.

"No. I know there are much worse boys—Irwin Daniels for one. But I just wanted my fairy to go away and then Stefan came along and ruined everything."

"Just like Danders Anders," I said. She nodded. "But maybe we *will* wind up with a fairy like Stefan's," she said. "Or a better one."

"What could be better than Steffi's?"

"Tamsin says there are lots of fairies we don't know about. It could be anything."

"And how're we going to get these super-doos fairies?"

Fiorenze held the key up. "Tonight my mother leaves for a conference on the West Coast. She doesn't get back till Sunday. We've got heaps of time to go through the book and find out how to get rid of our fairies. Why don't you come to my place after public service?"

"Why do you need me?" I asked. I was happy to help her get rid of her fairy, which was as much in my interests as hers, but it was still weird. "You could read the book by yourself. If I had that key I'd have read the whole thing by now." I wished I could steal the key from her, but then

I'd have to break into her house to get to the book. Too complicated. I couldn't even imagine how many demerits I'd get.

Why did Fiorenze think she needed me anyway? We didn't even like each other.

"Tamsin hasn't left yet. I can't get near it until she's gone."

"Yes, but why do you want to share this with me? We're not friends."

"I don't have any friends," Fiorenze said. "Except boys. And Rochelle. But she's friends with everyone."

"So why me?" I said again, to make her answer my question.

"Because you know what it's like to have a fairy you hate. You're serious about getting rid of it. You're the only one I can share this with." She paused. "And because I don't want to do it alone."

"Why not?" I asked. She was so torpid!

"Because. Because what if I get rid of the fairy and then *no one* likes me? Not even the boys . . . You all hate me because of my fairy. But what if you still hate me because of *me*?"

"Voice down. Caswell's looking again," I whispered. I didn't know what to say to her, then I realized that it didn't make any sense. "That still doesn't explain why you need me."

"Okay," Fiorenze said. "I've heard enough to know that some of the fairy-getting-rid-of methods need more than one person or they don't work."

155

"The true reason!"

"You want to get rid of your fairy, don't you?" Fiorenze asked. "Tamsin's book has all the answers. Come to my place tonight and it'll be gone!"

"That would be lovely," I said. "But Danders Anders is kidnapping me after school like he kidnapped me this morning."

"But we told him your fairy was gone!"

"*You* told him. You're the liar, not me. Bluey Salazar told him I hadn't gotten rid of my fairy because I was still walking everywhere and being late for everything."

"The traitor!" Fiorenze hissed.

"Not his fault," I said, turning the page of my book to look more like I was studying. "He didn't know that he was dobbing me in."

"I'm so sorry."

"That's what Bluey said."

"That makes it more urgent that we read the *Fairy Book*."

"If you've never read it," I asked, "how do you know it has all the answers?"

"Because Tamsin knows everything about fairies," Fiorenze said firmly. "She's a fairy genius."

I really hoped so. But what if her book was as unforthcoming and cryptic as she was? "What's her fairy, then?" I asked.

"At the moment?"

"What do you mean 'at the moment'?"

"Well, Tamsin's had at least six different fairies."

"*Six* different fairies!?" When I'd met Tamsin I'd been impressed by the mirrors, but the rest of it had seemed, well, almost torpid. But six fairies? Maybe she wasn't full of fairy dung after all.

"Uh-huh. The current one is a never-being-late fairy. I think it suits her best. She's very, um, OCD. It drives her insane when she's late because of trains or planes or whatever. But now nothing keeps her from being on time."

"And before that?" I asked.

"The first one I know of was a loose-change-finding fairy."

"Hmmm, bog ordinary. I can see why you'd want a different one. But not exactly a nightmare fairy." A loose-change-finding fairy would suit me just fine.

Another of the librarians gave us the evil eye. "The second was a good-hair fairy," Fiorenze said, lowering her voice even further and talking to the book in front of her.

"She got rid of a good-hair fairy?" I squeaked at my homework as quietly as I could. "Why would you get rid of a good-hair fairy?"

"She said she didn't always want to be well-groomed."

"That is the most torpid reason for getting rid of a fairy that I've ever heard of."

"Then there was the—"

"Your mother changes fairies like Ro changes clothes and all she could tell me to do was keep walking?" I whispered, despite wanting to yell.

157

"Tamsin's afraid people will steal her research. She thinks *The Ultimate Fairy Book* is going to change the entire world. But she's scared of anyone else getting the credit. That's why my parents don't speak to each other. Tamsin thought Waverly was stealing from her. She does help people, though. Like she helped you. But not many and she's always vague about it."

"Vague! All she did was stare and take notes. If she's that paranoid what will she do if she finds out that we've looked at her precious book?"

Fiorenze gulped. "We have to make sure she *doesn't* find out."

CHAPTER 24
Metal Box

Demerits: 6
Conversations with Steffi: 9
Game suspensions: 1
Public service hours: 19
Hours spent enduring Fiorenze
   Stupid-Name's company: 3.5
Kidnappings thwarted: 1
Number of Steffi kisses: 2
Days Steffi not talking to me: 2
Parking spots for Danders Anders: 16
Vows to kill Danders Anders: 27

I didn't make it to public service after school and thus my demerit total remained at six. If tomorrow was as bad as today I'd wind up with my second game suspension.

Danders Anders needed to park all over the city. Fourteen parking spots and with each one I felt my fairy getting fatter. The proto-fairy was never going to take over.

If I could have killed Danders I would have. Or broken a few of his bones. Or at least given him some nasty bruises.

He returned to his car for the last time after eleven. I'd almost fallen asleep over my Statistics homework. How was I going to stay awake to concentrate on *The Ultimate Fairy Book*? Poxy Danders Anders.

"You have to drive me someplace," I announced as Danders crammed himself back into the driver's seat. "You owe me." He owed me my life back. He owed me *everything*. I wished him a blighted life and future.

He grunted and turned the engine on. If he were an actual human being with feelings and facial expressions I would have said that he was sad. But he was Danders Anders, so for all I knew he was in ecstasy brought on by a twenty-minute rendezvous with his secret lover. Though given how many stops we'd made, that would be fourteen secret lovers.

Horns sounded.

"You're supposed to look when you drive! Not get us killed!"

Danders said nothing.

"Don't turn right, turn left. You're taking me to Fiorenze Burnham-Stone's house. Cliffside Drive."

"Cliffside Drive," Danders repeated.

✦ ✦ ✦

I followed Fiorenze's directions to get to her bedroom. I put my ear to the door, but heard nothing. I knocked gently, hoping this wasn't all an elaborate payback joke on Fiorenze's part and I was about to wake up her mother, who would punish me by making sure the parking fairy never went away.

Nothing. Just me breathing a little too loud.

I knocked again. What if this really was her mother's room? I counted to twenty and then tried the handle. It turned. I opened the door.

It looked like a library. The walls were lined with floor-to-ceiling bookshelves. Except for where there was a large window. Under it was a desk where Fiorenze was asleep, drooling on her homework. I walked across the huge room and whispered her name, then when she didn't stir, nudged her awake.

Fiorenze blinked at me, pushed her hair back, rubbed at her eyes and mouth, then blinked some more. "You came," she said at last.

I grunted. "Said I would, didn't I?"

She patted her pocket. "Come on, then."

I followed her out of her room and along the corridor and into another, then down some stairs, and up some others, and along yet another corridor.

"It's like a crazy house," I whispered.

"What?" Fiorenze whispered in turn.

"So many doors and corridors and staircases. It's like a fun house. It just needs lots of weird mirrors." It was so quiet. At my house there was always some kind of sound: Nettles's weirdo music, my parents laughing or fighting, the dogs next door.

"Oh," she said. "We have those too. In Tamsin's study."

"I've seen them. Vastly peculiar."

"They work, though."

"I know," I said, remembering the fading white aura of my parking fairy. I feared it would be a lot less faded this time.

"How can your family afford all this?"

"We're rich."

I sucked my teeth. "I *know* that. But this is big even for rich people. Why are you rich? Did your grandfather really have a gold-finding fairy?"

Fiorenze shook her head. "No. It was my grandmother and she had a stealing fairy. No matter what she stole, and no matter how blatantly, she never got caught. All our wealth is stolen. That's why my parents give so much to charity. They're vastly guilty about it. Tamsin doesn't like to talk about her mother."

I didn't know what to say.

"Are you ready to see the mirrors again?" Fiorenze opened the door. And there were me and Fiorenze staring back at ourselves. Automatically I straightened my shoulders and pulled in my core muscles. Fiorenze did the same. I could see the white aura of my parking fairy all right. Brilliant white. It shone. The blue of my proto-fairy was barely there.

"I never get used to that," she said. "Seeing myself from the outside." Her fairy had a red aura. Not quite as brilliant as mine, but plenty bright. It wasn't going to fade away any time soon. "I never look the way I think I will."

"Huh," I said, not entirely sure what she meant. "It's weird seeing fairy auras, isn't it?"

"You get used to them." She walked over to the metal box. I shut the door behind me and crouched down next to her. She pulled the key out of her pocket and looked at it and then at the box.

"It's really big," I said. "Much bigger than you'd need for a book."

"It's a really big book." Fiorenze knelt in front of it and laid her hand on top. The box made her hand seem small; Fiorenze's hands are not small.

"Are you sure your dad's not going to burst in on us?" I asked.

"I'm sure."

"Shouldn't we start looking through it then? It's after midnight."

Fiorenze nodded, but made no move toward opening it.

"What are you waiting for?"

"I'm nervous." She pulled her hand back and put it in her lap.

"But you said your dad won't disturb us. And your mother's on the West Coast, right?" I wondered if she was going to Ravenna. It occurred to me that I had no idea what Steffi's city looked like.

Fiorenze didn't say anything.

"What's up?" The tiles underneath my feet radiated coldness. I pulled a cushion under my butt and crossed my legs.

"I've never seen Tamsin's book before. I don't think

anyone but her has in years. What if it's not so great? Tamsin could have lost perspective."

"Now you say! You do know your mom's a bit nuts, right?"

Fiorenze's eyebrows pulled together and her mouth went down. "Waverly's worse."

"*That's* reassuring. You're really sure he's not coming in here? With, say, an axe?" My voice didn't come out as jokey as it sounded in my head.

"He's not coming in here with anything," Fiorenze said. "He's too superstitious." She still hadn't touched the box.

"Do you want me to open it?" I asked. Fiorenze was squatting, like she was ready to jump up and away as quick as possible. "You don't think it's booby-trapped or anything, do you?"

"Of course not." She put the key in the lock and turned it. The lid popped up immediately. I half expected a hideous siren to go off, or the box to explode, but the only sound it made was a slight creak from the hinges.

We both stared.

CHAPTER 25
The Ultimate Fairy Book

Demerits: 6
Conversations with Steffi: 9
Game suspensions: 1
Public service hours: 19
Hours spent enduring Fiorenze
    Stupid-Name's company: 3.75
Number of Steffi kisses: 2
Days Steffi not talking to me: 2
Parking spots for Danders Anders: 16
Vows to kill Danders Anders: 31

Well," I said at last. "That's a vast amount of paper. How are we going to read it all before your mom comes back?"

The box was almost a meter high. Inside it were four tightly jammed together stacks secured with colored ribbons. The first stack was labeled *Origins,* the second *Earliest Research,* the third *Taxonomies,* and the fourth *Ethics.* It was an insane amount of paper. Reading through it all would take weeks and weeks and weeks. I stared at it in despair. Buried in there might be a way to get rid of the parking fairy that danced white in the mirror. But finding the magical fairy destroyer suddenly looked even harder than it had.

"Wow," Fiorenze said.

"Vastly wow. Where do we start? She must have written down everything ever known about fairies ever."

Fiorenze nodded. "It must be the biggest book in the universe."

"Well, she calls it *The Ultimate Fairy Book*, doesn't she?" The name seemed much less boastful now.

Fiorenze giggled. "No, that's what *I* call it. It's sort of a joke. But maybe it isn't." She grabbed a pillow to sit on and shifted into crossed legs.

"So where do we start?" I asked. "We have to start somewhere."

"With the first one? Origins? Or how about Taxonomies? Do you think there's anything in those about getting rid of fairies?"

"Dunno. What does 'Taxonomies' even mean?"

"Something to do with paying tax?" Fiorenze touched the yellow ribbon around it. Origins and Earliest Research had red ribbons around them and Ethics a green.

"Is the ribbon around the whole stack?"

Fiorenze squeezed her fingers around the edges of Origins and eased it out of the box. It was about four centimeters thick. "Wow, it's heavy!" She put it down between us. "The one underneath it is called Eschatologies."

"What does 'Eschatologies' mean?" I asked. What if we found instructions on getting rid of our fairies but couldn't understand all the fancy words Dr. Burnham-Stone used?

"I don't know."

"Could it be about getting rid of fairies? Should we check?"

"Maybe come back to it?" Fiorenze suggested. "It and Taxonomies. There might be one that's more like what we want."

I nodded.

"We have to make sure the book looks exactly the same when we're finished. Tamsin can't have any idea that we've touched it."

"Of course," I said. "Let's look through all the bundles, maybe we'll find one that says, 'Fairies, Destruction of'?"

Fiorenze smiled. "Sounds like a plan. One stack at a time and we make sure we put each bundle back exactly as is."

I nodded. I wasn't sure what the wrath of Dr. Burnham-Stone would look like, but I was not anxious to find out.

We went through the rest of the stack, but nothing was labeled with anything promising like *Fairies, Extrication of*, though I put aside one called "Proto-Fairies." We put the stack back exactly as it was and turned to the next, but didn't hit pay dirt until the middle of the last stack. "Removal and Swapping," wrapped in a faded blue ribbon that had clearly been tied and retied many times.

"It's very thick," Fiorenze said, handing it to me. "That's at least ten centimeters."

I balanced it on my palm. "More like fifteen. Heavy too," I said, placing it between us. The answers to all my problems could be in this bulging stack of papers.

"Do you want to undo the ribbon or shall I?" Fiorenze asked.

"You," I said.

"You sure?"

I nodded.

"I'm a bit nervous," Fiorenze said, looking down at the bulky bundle.

"You and me both. Make sure you remember how it was tied. We have to retie it exactly the same. And don't wrinkle any of the pages."

"You're right. I'll be careful. But what if—"

"Just open it, Fio." I didn't want to hear what-ifs. It was bad enough thinking them.

She nodded, undid the ribbon, and put the title page aside. The second page was a contents page. There were lots of crossing outs, and scribbles, and words on top of words.

"Thwarting, Stain—"

"Doesn't that say 'starving,' not 'staining'?" I peered closer. It was hard to tell. It was written over words that had been written and crossed out several times.

"What's the difference between thwarting and starving a fairy?"

"What do you reckon bleaching a fairy involves?"

"Or 'Near Dying.' Huh? And I never heard of 'Flensing.'"

"Is that what it really says? And why has she crossed out 'teasing'?"

"And what's 'grunching'?"

"I reckon she's making them up." Each unfamiliar word made me more nervous. Would any of it make sense?

"Shall we look?" Fiorenze asked.

"Well, duh! If we don't get started soon it'll be time for school before we've read anything."

"How about I take Grunching and you take Bleaching?"

"No way. How interesting is Bleaching going to be? I want Grunching. That has to be something wholly doos."

"Fine," Fiorenze said. "I'll take Near Dying, then."

"But that could be doos too."

"Okay, then. How about we split it in half? You take the front section, I'll take the back."

"Done."

Fiorenze handed me the first half. I held the pages firmly, afraid of dropping them. I caught a glimpse of my reflection. The blue aura looked anemic, but the white was dazzling. It was hard to imagine ever getting rid of it.

CHAPTER 26

Bleaching, Starving, and Flensing

Demerits: 6
Conversations with Steffi: 9
Game suspensions: 1
Public service hours: 19
Hours spent enduring Fiorenze
   Stupid-Name's company: 4.75
Number of Steffi kisses: 2
Days Steffi not talking to me: 2
Parking spots for Danders Anders: 16
Vows to kill Danders Anders: 31

I put the heavy pile of papers on the floor in front of me and turned the contents page over, carefully placing it on the floor on top of the title page. "Introductory Notes," it read. I wondered if it would be safe to skip it and glanced at Fiorenze, who was frowning, but seemed to be reading every single word.

The first few pages referred to gazillions of other books on fairies, quoting from them and then (mostly) disagreeing with them. The other weird thing was that she kept referring to other things she'd written and calling herself "Burnham-Stone." Strange. Especially when she started disagreeing with herself.

Like she said that despite Burnham-Stone's argument that "if one's belief system did not encompass the existence of fairies, said fairies would generally be less productive than they were for those whose belief systems were more accommodating," there was plenty of evidence that "fairy productivity had no correlation with the host's belief systems," which I figured meant that she used to think you had to believe in fairies for them to work but now she didn't. That explained Steffi and his fairy.

Then I realized that the first Burnham-Stone had the initial "W" and the second one the initial "T." She wasn't disagreeing with herself. She was disagreeing with her husband.

I also found it creepy that she used the word "host" to refer to the person who had the fairy. Did that mean fairies were like parasites?

One section worried about whether getting rid of your fairy and getting a new one was ethical. There were lots of quotes from various experts on how you were probably meant to have whatever fairy you wound up with and if everyone changed their fairies it could lead to all sorts of terrible consequences. There were no quotes saying what those consequences were. Obviously none of these experts had ever been stuck with a parking fairy.

She also said that there was no evidence to support the

theory that fairies were attracted to "good" people and repelled by "bad" people—"the behaviors of hosts appear to have no effect on their fairies whatsoever." I couldn't wait to tell Rochelle.

The pages were littered with tons of impossible-to-read footnotes. All of it scrawled in her not-the-most-legible-in-the-world handwriting. While there weren't as many crossing outs as on the contents page, there were still many.

I skipped to the first proper section, "Thwarting."

It was exactly what I thought: don't do any of the things that are remotely within your fairy's bailiwick. Thwart the fairy! Only it took Burnham-Stone twenty pages to say so on account of having to list example after example after example and quote everyone who'd ever written about fairies ever. Vastly boring! She concluded by saying that while it was one of the most effective fairy removal methods, it was by far the slowest.

I could vouch for that! It took Burnham-Stone four months to get rid of her loose-change fairy. Though she wrote about one case that took two years. I shuddered at the thought of it.

Starving fairies turned out to be the vegetarian option. Sort of. Only it wasn't all vegetables, just carrots. According to Burnham-Stone, if you stuck to that diet, after two weeks your fairy would be long gone. When she used it to get rid of her good-hair fairy it was gone in twelve days.

She didn't mention how that left her. Twelve days of

nothing but carrots? Wouldn't *you* be gone too? And according to her you could drink only water; anything else delayed the fairy disappearing, or stopped it from working altogether.

In her conclusion Burnham-Stone noted that the diet was dangerous and should not be continued for more than three weeks. On the other hand, the starvation method was as successful as the thwarting method, just quicker.

For me and Fiorenze it was out of the question. Although carrots were one of the few vegetables I liked, all our food was measured and weighed. If we were consuming that few calories a day with so little good fat or minerals or vitamins or protein, we'd be reported to the doctors before the end of the day.

"You got anything yet, Fio?"

She shook her head. "Impossible or too dangerous so far. Though the section I'm reading now is a possibility. Bleaching. You have to lie in a bath of bleach. The trick is to get the bleach to water ratio exactly right. Plus you have to keep it out of all your bits that will sting."

"Hmm." That didn't sound like much fun.

"If you get it right the fairy goes away instantly."

"What happens if you get it wrong?"

"You wind up with third-degree burns, or go blind, or damage your hearing. Or all three. Oh."

"What?" The expression on her face was dire.

"If you really frag it up you die."

"What larks," I said. "I guess if nothing else works we

could try that. But we're not that desperate yet, are we?" I felt desperate.

"Not yet." Fiorenze smiled. "Moving along."

My next one was light deprivation. Two weeks of total darkness? It was about as possible as the nothing-but-carrots method. I could only attempt it during the holidays and even then I couldn't see my parents agreeing. And Burnham-Stone's list of "contraindications," which included depression and suicide, was not encouraging. On the other hand, at the end of it her cat fairy was gone.

The dirt option was the one Bluey had recommended, only he'd said six weeks and Tamsin said four. You weren't allowed to wash your teeth, your hair, your clothes, your anything. We'd be expelled by the end of the second day if we tried it. I wondered how bad you'd smell after four weeks. Vastly bad, I decided.

The next one was completely out of the question. "Near dying" turned out to be exactly that. Burnham-Stone had noticed some people who'd almost died had lost their fairies. At first she'd thought this was the velocity effect. I tried to read the footnote to figure out what the velocity effect was, and failed on account of the teeniness and multiple-crossed-outedness of her writing, but it seemed to be the idea that if you go really, really, really fast your fairy falls off. She discounted it because there were lots of professional skydivers and race car drivers with fairies.

She also said you didn't have to actually nearly die. It

wasn't about seeing the light at the end of the tunnel, but about whether your fairy thought you were in immediate danger of sudden death. So people who'd been held up in an armed robbery had lost their fairies, as had some amateurs skydiving, and people in car accidents who otherwise had been completely unharmed.

If the fairy thought you were about to die imminently, even if you weren't, it jumped ship.

She'd been unable to find a single example of someone with a fatal illness losing their fairy before they died. The fairy didn't jump on diagnosis. People who were deathly ill kept their fairies until they died.

"So, Fio? It says here that if we jump off a building and survive, our fairies will disappear. Apparently they run away if they think you're going to die."

"Um, yay? But wouldn't we actually die?"

"Not if we had a trampoline or something to land on." Even to me it sounded like an injured suggestion.

"I prefer bleaching."

It was almost four in the morning and I hadn't had a proper night's sleep in months and months. I yawned, rubbed my eyes, and tried to focus on the pages in front of me. Why did Burnham-Stone give so many examples? Why did she have to quote so many people, including herself? Why couldn't she get to the point? Her book would have been half the size if she hadn't droned on and on.

Fiorenze yelped.

I startled and scattered pages. "Gah!"

Fiorenze looked up at me, all tiredness gone. "I think I've got it!"

"Really?" My heart beat faster.

"Yes! And it's not *that* dangerous, plus we can do it tonight—"

"This morning."

"We can do it right *now*," Fiorenze said, grinning. "But you might not like it."

"I thought you said it's not dangerous? It's got to be better than bleaching, right? Or dying. It doesn't turn you orange, does it?"

"Orange? No. But it's a bit bloody."

"Tell me." Did we have to cut our little toes off and eat them? Drink blood? Bathe in it? Though where would we get enough blood to have a bath in at this time of night? "How bloody, Fio?"

"We cut our thumbs. Doesn't have to be too deep or anything, but there has to be blood. Also we have to have salt in our mouths when we do it, and it has to be in the dark."

"Well that doesn't sound too bad. If we're careful and don't take out our own eyes we should be fine."

"And . . ."

"And?"

"Well, it won't disappear our fairies exactly."

"How do you mean?"

"We do it together. We swap."

"Swap?" I asked. "What do you mean, swap?"

"Swap our fairies. I'll have your parking fairy and you'll have my boy fairy."

"That's possible? I never heard of that happening. Are you sure?"

Fiorenze nodded. "I don't know if it'll work or not. But Tamsin says that it worked for her. She and Waverly swapped fairies. Do you believe that? I didn't even know. He got her fairy, she got his. That's how she got her current OCD fairy."

"So you'd get my parking fairy," I asked, thinking that sounded very doos indeed. "And I'll have—"

"I'll have all your problems and you'll have mine."

"Why haven't we ever heard of that before?"

"I don't know. But according to Tamsin it not only works, it takes about ten minutes."

Just ten minutes away from having no parking fairy and having Fiorenze's boy fairy instead? The one that made Steffi like her? "Are you sure you want to do that?" I asked. "My problems are vastly malodorous."

"Not as malodorous as mine," Fiorenze said. "Truly, Charlie, my fairy is the worst fairy in existence. You're getting the bad end of this deal. We can keep searching through Tamsin's book if you like."

Was she mad? Nothing could be worse than being Danders Anders's parking slave. *Nothing*.

"You really don't have to swap."

"Yes, I do. I can't stand having a parking fairy for another single day. Let's do it!"

CHAPTER 27

Demerits: 6
Conversations with Steffi: 9
Game suspensions: 1
Public service hours: 19
Hours spent enduring Fiorenze
   Stupid-Name's company: 7.66
Number of Steffi kisses: 2
Days Steffi not talking to me: 2
Parking spots for Danders Anders: 16
Vows to kill Danders Anders: 31

Isn't there a closer bathroom?"

"Sure," Fiorenze said, "but the one we're going to is the darkest."

"It's not near your dad's rooms, though, is it?"

"Oh, no. He has his own bathroom."

"How many bathrooms do you have?"

"I don't know. I've never counted. Maybe twelve, I guess. But this one," she said, opening the door while balancing the bowl of salt and knife, "is the darkest. No windows."

"Okay," I said, following her in.

Fiorenze placed the bowl on the floor and rested the knife on top of it. I put the antiseptic and Band-Aids beside them and shut the door. The knife looked sharp, but I was more worried by the salt. It was *a lot* of salt. We had to put a fistful of it in our mouths while we cut our thumbs.

I like salty things, but not *that* salty. It reminded me of the time me and Nettles had made a cake together—we were both little. We'd gotten the salt mixed up with the sugar, and put in way more than the recipe said because we both have a sweet tooth. It had been the worst shock of our lives when we tasted the batter! I'd almost choked; Nettles had vomited. She'd been so discombobulated by the whole thing she didn't take any photos. But even after we'd drunk liters and liters and liters of orange juice, all we could taste was salt. Water became ocean in our mouths.

What if I couldn't keep the salt in my mouth for the count of one hundred? The swap would be ruined.

"You ready?"

"Yes. We should cut ourselves *before* we turn off the light, right?"

"Tamsin says it doesn't work unless you do everything in the dark."

"Fine. If that's what she says. But no slipping and taking out one of my eyes."

"I'll do my best." Fiorenze sat down with her back against the bathtub. She patted a spot on her right. "You sit here

179

when the lights are off. Just two steps, then sit." She shifted the bowl so it was between us and picked up the knife.

I nodded. "Got it." I reached my hand to the light switch and then paused. "Are you sure you want to do this, Fio? Every girl in school, not to mention some of the boys, well, they'd kill for your fairy."

"They're insane. Ten seconds with my fairy and they'll change their mind. You will too, Charlie."

I doubted that. I'd have Steffi. "My fairy's much worse. You're going to get sick of everyone bugging you to get in their car. Just wait until Danders finds out."

"It'll beat being chased by every boy my age."

"So you're sure?"

"I'm completely sure."

"Me too. Okay, here goes the light." I turned it off.

"Hmm," Fiorenze said. "Turn it back on."

I did. Fiorenze jumped up, shoved a towel in the gap under the door, and then she grabbed some toilet paper to fill up the keyhole.

"It really has to be that dark?" I asked.

"As dark as possible. According to Tamsin, fairies don't like the dark."

"Scared of the dark, and of dirt, and carrots. Fairies are weird."

"No argument from me." Fiorenze smiled, then sat back down, adjusting the knife and salt next to her. "Lights," she said.

I turned them off again. This time we were in complete

darkness. All I could see were the lines and smudges on the back of my eyelids. "Dark enough for you?"

"More than enough. Let's hope it's enough for our fairies."

"Okay, I'm walking toward you. One step, two step. Coming down."

The tiles underneath me were cold. I could hear Fiorenze breathing and feel the movement of air between us.

Fiorenze breathed in sharply. "I just cut my thumb. I'm passing the knife to you, hilt first."

I took it from her and brought the blade across the tip of my right thumb.

Nothing happened.

"Are you bleeding?" she asked.

"No," I said, annoyed with myself. I tried again and managed to break the skin. I brought my thumb to my mouth but didn't taste blood.

"I Iurry. My cut's drying up."

I pressed the tip of the blade in harder and then drew it across quickly. "Ow!" I felt the air against the broken skin, and then felt the blood dripping down my thumb.

"Okay," Fiorenze said, grabbing for my hand and hitting my shoulder.

"Here," I said, grabbing her hand. Clumsily we pressed the two wounds together. "This is so undoos."

I heard the bowl shifting on the tiles. "Oh. The salt!"

"Yes," she said. "I've got a handful. Now you."

I felt along the tiles for the salt bowl, careful to keep

our thumbs pressed together, and got Fiorenze's shin. "Sorry!"

"Hurry up."

I found the edge of the bowl and then slid my fingers into the salt crystals. They were sharp and dry. I gathered as much as I could between my fingers, but couldn't help remembering what it was going to taste like. My stomach contracted and my throat tightened. "Okay, I've got some."

"On the count of three shove it in your mouth. Don't let your hand slip."

"Sorry." I gripped her hand harder.

"Ready?"

I nodded. Then remembered the dark. "Yes, ready."

"One. Two. Three."

I shoved the salt into my mouth, pressed my lips tight together, and tried not to gag. The saltiness was so intense it felt like I was tasting it in my nose. It burned. My eyes watered. Then I remembered I was supposed to be counting to one hundred. I started at twenty. The urge to spit the salt out was so strong that I squeezed Fiorenze's hand as tight as I could.

What felt like hours later Fiorenze mumbled, "One hundred," through a mouthful of salt.

"We're done?" I managed to squeak out.

"Yes."

I leaped up, knocking the salt bowl over, turned the light on, my eyes watering at the insane brightness of it, then I spat the salt into the sink. Fiorenze spat after me.

"Gah," she said, turning on the tap and pushing me aside to fill her mouth with water, rinsing noisily and spitting again.

I stuck my head under the tap in the tub and did the same. But no amount of rinsing and spitting was getting rid of that taste.

"It's so disgusting," Fiorenze said, rinsing and spitting again.

"Do you think it worked? Do you feel any different?" I maybe felt different, but I couldn't be sure. All I knew was that my mouth was a salt lick.

She rinsed and spat again. "Don't know."

I sucked in more water to swirl around my mouth and turn into ocean. "Maybe if we tried drinking or eating something with actual flavor? You know, rather than water?"

"Genius idea. Hey, shouldn't you clean up your thumb?"

I looked at it. A flap of skin was hanging off the top and the cut was bleeding copiously. Pox. I had fencing again today. It was going to be fun holding a foil without making it bleed all over again. "Oops," I said, thrusting it under the tap. "Pass me the Band-Aids."

Fiorenze rummaged around in the cupboard above the sink. "Here," she said, grabbing my hand, dousing the thumb in antiseptic—

"Ow!" It stung something fierce.

"Hush."

She put a big wodge of cotton over the cut. "Hold that there till it stops bleeding."

I did and noticed the time. "It's almost seven, Fio."

"Pox! We haven't put the book away yet!"

"I'll do it."

"No! You might bleed on it."

"How long does it take you to get to school?"

"Twenty minutes if Waverly gives us a lift and the traffic's okay. I'll go beg him and get ready. You can shower in here. I'll grab your bag and some towels. Won't be a sec."

"No worries," I said.

I put a fresh piece of cotton over my cut and held it in place with a Band-Aid. Then I went into Tamsin's mirror room. Through my tired eyes I could see the halos of my fairies. The white was gone. In its place there was a healthy red halo and the same thin blue one of my proto-fairy.

It had worked. I had Fiorenze's fairy; she had mine. With any luck I would never ever hear anyone squeal for joy over finding a perfect parking spot again! I couldn't wait to see Mom, her sisters, her best friend, Jan, and Nana and Papa crushed with disappointment as they trawled the streets of the city in vain, while I convulsed with laughter in the backseat.

I would never smell of gasoline again!

Tomorrow, or rather *today*, was going to be the best day ever. I spun around on my toes and screamed. I'd done it!

CHAPTER 28

Waverly Burnham-Stone

Demerits: 6
Conversations with Steffi: 9
Game suspensions: 1
Public service hours: 19
Hours spent ~~enduring~~ in Fiorenze ~~Stupid Name's~~
    Burnham-Stone's company: 11.14
Number of Steffi kisses: 2
Days Steffi not talking to me: 2

Fiorenze didn't look any more like her father than she did like her mother, except around the eyes. He had a squashed nose, almost like a pug, which made me wonder if he'd been a boxer. His nose looked like it had been pounded long and often.

He nodded when Fiorenze introduced us.

"Pleasure to meet you, Dr. Burnham-Stone," I said, resisting the urge to ask him about his nose.

"Call me Waverly. And you're Charlie? Fio's told me a great deal about you."

She had? Fiorenze continued to shovel in her cereal without looking up.

"All of it praise," he said, staring at me almost as intently as his wife had. I joined Fiorenze in cereal shoveling, despite the fact that it tasted like salt. "I've been looking forward to meeting you. Are you both ready to go?"

We nodded. Fiorenze grabbed our plates and practically hurled them into the sink. I'd brush my teeth at school. Maybe that would make the salt taste go away.

"This way," he said. I wiped my mouth and slung my bag over my shoulder, and followed as he led the way to the garage. It was every bit as large as I expected. Although it housed six cars, there was room for more.

My nostrils filled with the sharp unpleasant reek of gasoline and my mouth with bile. Even if I didn't have a parking fairy anymore, I still hated cars. I wished we were getting a lift to school in anything else. Why didn't they own a helicopter? They were rich enough.

Fiorenze's father unlocked the smallest car and climbed into the driver's seat. Fiorenze slid in back. I sat next to her and put my seat belt on. She hadn't said a word since introducing us. As the garage door opened and he eased the car out and onto the driveway, I thought about asking her if she'd enjoyed the salty breakfast. And especially if she felt any different.

I kind of did feel different. It was certainly weird being in a car that wasn't going to automatically get a parking spot, or rather it was, but it wasn't going to be *my* parking spot! That made being in a car not quite so malodorous.

"How is your campaign to get into the basketball stream going?" Waverly asked as we pulled onto Cliffside Drive. "I hear they're likely to hold a new tryout any day now."

"What's that?" I spluttered. I couldn't believe what I'd just heard. How had Fiorenze known about that? The only people who knew were Rochelle and Sandra and Steffi. And why had she told her father? I glared at the side of Fiorenze's head.

"It would be quite the coup if you made it, wouldn't it?" he asked. "I don't believe anyone's been selected in the middle of the year in a long time."

"Six years ago," I said. "Tyzhe Xian was accepted into baseball." It felt strange and wrong to be discussing my basketball aspirations with anyone other than Rochelle, Sandra, or Steffi. What had Fiorenze been thinking? And what had Rochelle or Sandra been thinking to tell her in the first place?

I wished Fiorenze lived closer to school and we could've walked. At least there wasn't that much traffic getting to the city. It shouldn't be long before we arrived in the brand-new world of Steffi liking me again.

"And she went on to represent the city, didn't she? A lovely precedent. Didn't she have a never-drop-a-catch fairy?"

"That's right. You're a fairy expert too, aren't you, sir?" I asked, hoping he would start talking about himself, rather than me.

"Not 'sir,' Waverly," he said. "I hear you have a parking fairy."

"Um," I said, glancing at Fiorenze for guidance, but her eyes were on her lap. Did she want me to tell her father that we'd just fairy swapped? I didn't think so. She hadn't exactly asked his permission or told him anything about it. On the other hand, she'd told him one of my big secrets. "What's your fairy?" I asked.

"Jukebox."

"What's a jukebox fairy?" I asked, wondering what a jukebox was.

"Wherever I go the music playing is always something I like. I never hear music I hate."

"If you never hear it, how do you know what music you don't like?" I asked, not sure if I'd made any sense. It was spinny trying to figure it out. Didn't you know what you liked in contrast to what you didn't? But if he only heard music he liked, he'd never have any contrast. Did that mean he liked everything?

Waverly laughed. "You're funny, Charlie. I can see why Fio likes you. Your parking fairy doesn't affect traffic, does it? I don't think I've ever gotten through the city this fast before."

"Not that I know of," I said, peering out the window. Seemed like a lot of traffic to me. Just that it wasn't backed up. The footpath was chockers too. Mostly Sports students beautifully turned out in their brown uniforms, ties straight, hats on, heading to school.

One of them was Steffi. Time to test the new fairy.

"Oh!" I exclaimed. "Can you stop here, sir? I mean, Waverly? We could walk from here."

"Of course," he said. "I'll just need to find a—speak of the devil."

A car pulled out just in front of us and Waverly slid his car into its place. "You do have a parking fairy, don't you?"

I made a noise that could have been either a yes or a no. "Thank you for the lift, sir, um, Waverly."

"You're welcome."

Fiorenze was already out on the footpath, students flowing past her. She was grinning.

"Good-bye," I said, shutting the door and turning to Fiorenze.

She hugged me. "It works! Not one boy has spoken to me. Not a single one! Thank you so much!"

I did not return the hug. "You told your father about me wanting to switch to basketball! How did you even—"

"Charlie!" Steffi called from behind us. He was talking to me again. Yes!

Steffi planted a kiss on my cheek. My entire face got hot. The all-the-boys-will-like-you fairy was up and running. I hoped his fairy would protect me from kissing demerits like it had for Fiorenze.

"You look great," he said, grinning. He'd never said

anything about my looks before. "What were you doing in a car? What about your parking fairy?"

"It's a long story," I said. My cheek still tingled. "What are you doing walking to school from this direction?"

"I was rowing on the river with my dad."

"Huh. Didn't know you rowed."

Steffi did his hand-flicking thing. "I do lots of things there's no space for at school. You're really looking lovely today, Charlie." He slipped his hand into mine and my face got hotter, even under my eyebrows. I wondered if you could give yourself sunburn from the inside.

"I didn't think you *could* get lovelier. Hi, Fio," Steffi said as if he were noticing her for the first time. "How's it going?"

"Doos," Fiorenze said, grinning widely as we turned in at the school gates. "*Vastly* doos."

"Excellent," Steffi said, but he wasn't looking at Fiorenze. "You know what I've been wondering, Charlie?" he asked. "I've been wondering where the word 'doos' comes from. I never heard anyone use that word before I moved here."

I had no idea.

"Hey, Charlie," Bluey Salazar said. "I'm so sorry about what happened with Danders Anders. Let me know if there's anything I can do to help. I mean it," he said, staring into my eyes intently. "Anything at all."

"No worries, Bluey," I said. "All is well."

"I'll say it is, Charlie," Freedom Hazal said. "Have you

190

done something new with your hair? You are so pulchy this morning, you've almost broken pulchiness."

"Thanks, Freedom."

It was going to be the best day ever.

CHAPTER 29

A Different Fairy

Demerits: 6
Conversations with Steffi: 10
Game suspensions: 1
Public service hours: 19
Number of Steffi kisses: 2
Boys who like me: Steffi, Bluey Salazar,
    and Freedom Hazal

Bluey, Freedom, Mazza (clean-clothes fairy), and Chook (surfer fairy) almost came to blows over who was going to sit next to me in PR. Ms. Johnson resolved the fight by issuing them each with a demerit and ordering Sienna Bray (never-being-cold fairy) into the seat.

"What's going on, Charlie?" Sienna whispered. Sienna was probably the only student ever to come to NA Sports from an Arts middle school. She was a very promising snowboarder, trampoliner, and freestyle skier. No one knew how she'd managed to discover that she was an athlete while studying finger painting, poems, and finding-the-inner-you. There was a book being run on how long before she'd drop out, but so far she'd surprised everyone.

"New fairy," I said.

Sienna's eyes widened and three notes landed on my desk. "What kind of—"

"Silence!" Ms. Johnson boomed at us. "The next person to say a word without being called on by me, or to throw a note at Charlotte Adele Donna Seto Steele will receive a demerit *and* be sent to the principal's office. Am I clear?"

"Yes, Ms. Johnson," we all chorused.

"Proper protocol on being introduced to a head of state. Freedom?"

"Ah, um, doesn't it depend on which head of state, Ms. Johnson?"

"So you are awake." She started scribbling on her tablet. "I've just transmitted a list of forty countries. Sienna? Correct protocol for the first two." Around the room people started scratching with their styluses.

"Your screens are frozen," Ms. Johnson said. Several people groaned. No way to search for the answers . . .

Sienna reeled them off. She had a vastly sharp memory for someone who'd never had to memorize anything before getting to high school.

I wished I had even half her memory. Miraculously Johnson called on me for thirty-nine and forty, which were the only countries I knew. "Bow deeply and don't speak until they speak to you."

"And the last one, Charlotte?"

"Slight nod of head and shake their hand when offered."

"Excellent. I've just transmitted your assignments. They are due Monday." Johnson ignored the groans. "And the word limit is a hard one. I will not mark any that go over or under it. Understood?"

"Yes, Ms. Johnson."

"Dismissed," she said as the bell for end of class sounded.

Bluey, Mazza, Chook, and Freedom followed me out into the hallway, where Stuart, Richo, and Luca joined us. I couldn't help grinning. Why had Fiorenze hated her fairy? What was there to hate?

"Carry your bag for you?" Chook asked.

"Sure," I said, quickening my pace. I was not going to be late for tennis. I was not going to get another demerit. Then I realized it didn't matter. Not like it had. Tonight I'd get to public service on time because I was useless to Danders Anders. I would work off my six demerits in no time. I'd never have to do another game suspension!

The boys trailed after me, more joining as we passed by. Things were definitely looking up. I spun my lucky cricket ball high, squeezing it between my thumb and fingers in the hope of getting some flipper action going. Some of the girls shot me looks that were less than friendly. Tee hee.

"Are you free for first recess?" Richo asked. "I know this great spot that—"

"Oh, no," Bluey said. "She's recessing with me. We're old friends, aren't we, Charlie?"

"Please!" Freedom broke in. "Charlie and me were in the same preschool together."

"Well, I've only known Charlie for a little while and I *know* she likes me best," Steffi said, planting a kiss on my mouth. It felt so tingly doos that I knew everything was going to be fine.

Bluey, Freedom, and the other boys all gasped.

Steffi smelled delicious.

"She'll be recessing with me. Won't you, Charlie?"

I nodded. "I have to go," I said. "Tennis."

Steffi gave me one more tingling kiss—smack on the lips—and while the boys all gasped and tut-tutted, I slipped into the change rooms.

CHAPTER 30
Best Fairy Ever

Demerits: 6
Conversations with Steffi: 11
Game suspensions: 1
Public service hours: 19
Number of Steffi kisses: 4
Boys who like me: Steffi, Bluey, Freedom, Mazza,
    Chook, Stuart, Richo, and Luca

You look bouncy," Sandra observed. She was tying on her tennis shoes. "Hurry up."

"I do? I guess that must be because I *feel* bouncy." I grinned. I didn't think I'd stopped grinning since I first ran into Steffi. I had the best fairy ever! "So far it's been the most astral morning of all time."

"Yay for you," Heather Sandol said, walking past me with her tennis bag over her shoulder. She did not sound like she meant it. "I'd prefer if you didn't share your wonderful morning with Freedom. You know Freedom? My boyfriend?"

"I have a boyfriend," I said. "Stef—"

"Save it for someone who has some interest in your doings," Heather said, slamming her locker shut and walking away.

"What's with her?" Sandra asked.

"Where's Ro? I want to tell you both at once." I pulled my tennis gear out of my locker and started throwing it on. It was blessedly clean thanks to the ministrations of my concerned father.

"She's out on the court warming up. Tell us what? Hurry up and get your gear on. You don't want another demerit."

I hurried and made it out onto the court just in time to join Rochelle and the rest of B-stream tennis stretching. Rochelle looked up and waved.

Sandra sat next to me, stretched her left leg out in front of her, and leaned over it to work on her hammies. "Since when does Heather Sandol hate you?" Sandra whispered.

Giddo Halliwell blew me a kiss. I blinked. Giddo had barely spoken to me before. Also he was not the kind of person who blew kisses. His other electives were boxing and rugby. He was the proud possessor of a beer fairy. Not to mention he had a boyfriend, Sholto Sung, one of the seniors most likely to become an Our. My new fairy was amazing!

"You are advising each other on hamstring stretch technique?" Coach Ntini inquired. He did not wait for us to reply. "I do not think so. Sandra, stretch over here. Gideon, there."

He raised his voice so everyone could hear. "Stretching

is not a special time for gossiping before training. It is part of your training. And is only truly effective when done in silence. Today our entire session will be conducted in silence."

◆ ◆ ◆

"So spill," Rochelle said. The change rooms were empty except for the three of us, everyone else having dashed off to first recess.

"Fiorenze and me swapped fairies."

"You what now?!" Sandra exclaimed.

Rochelle's mouth dropped open. "But that's impossible! You can't swap fairies."

"You can," I said. "We did."

"So that's what Heather was talking about!" Sandra said. "She's transferred her Fiorenze hatred onto you! 'Cause her Freedom's chasing after you now. And that's why Giddo was winking at you and blowing kisses!" She shook her head. "Because that was odd."

Rochelle's eyes widened. "You really swapped fairies? How?"

"Hey," Sandra said. "Not to mention—"

I did Steffi's hand-flicking thing. "Yes, it's true and real; I have Fio's fairy and she has mine. Isn't it doos beyond doosness? Steffi likes me again. We're linked now!"

Sandra and Rochelle looked at each other and then at me. Their expressions were not from the family of happy faces.

"That's great," Rochelle said at last.

"Once more with enthusiasm," I said. Why weren't they pleased?

"No, really," Rochelle said. "That's wonderful. I'm happy for you."

"Why did Fiorenze agree?" Sandra asked. "Why did she give up her fairy?"

"She hates her fairy as much as I hate mine. She told me. That's why we swapped."

Rochelle nodded. "I can imagine. Must've been tough with no friends."

"A parking fairy would definitely appeal to her. It's more useful. When I get my license—," Sandra started.

"She's crazy! You both are too. This fairy is *so much better* than the parking fairy. You should have seen how Steffi was looking at me. He—"

"Or looking at your *fairy*," Sandra said. "It's all about your fairy now, not about you."

"Oh, no!" I protested. "He was definitely looking yummy eyes at *me*. Remember? He liked me *before* the new fairy."

"But he wasn't talking to you, Charlie. He hasn't sat with us in days."

"We had a little stoush—"

"And your new fairy made the stoush go away?" Sandra asked in a baby voice.

"It's not like that! This is the greatest fairy ever!"

"No, it's not," Sandra said. "Only a fraghead would

199

think that having a fairy that forced boys to like you was doos."

"I'm not a fraghead!"

"You're my friend. I don't want to think that of you."

I stared at her. "It's the best fairy ever! And even if it wasn't, I'm free of the parking fairy. Danders will never bug me again. But it *is* the best fairy ever."

Rochelle patted my arm. "I'm sure it is, Charlie. But we should get to the cafeteria and get our protein quota before next class. None of us has a not-getting-demerits fairy."

We gathered up our stuff in silence. I couldn't believe they weren't happy for me.

As we headed down the hallway many of the boys we passed trailed behind. We accumulated almost all of the B-stream rugby boys. They called out to me, saying Charlie this and Charlie that, and asking a million questions.

"Doos," I said, grinning. "Pretty powerful fairy, eh?"

Sandra cut her eyes at me. Rochelle nodded but didn't say anything.

I didn't let their attitude get to me; I knew I had the best fairy ever.

CHAPTER 31

Impossibilities

Demerits: 6
Conversations with Steffi: 11
Game suspensions: 1
Public service hours: 19
Number of Steffi kisses: 4
Boys who like me: all of them
Girls who hate me: Heather Sandol

The ruggers followed me all the way to the cafeteria. I felt like the Pied Piper, except that the rats probably weren't offering to share protein-rich snacks with him. All of them trying to sit at the same table made me feel like an Our, especially when one of the ruggers handed me a box of chocolates.

"You didn't have to do that," I said, taking them and smiling at the boy. Why had Fiorenze found this so irksome? I loved all the attention.

"No," Steffi said, "you really didn't. That's my seat, I believe," he told the chocolate-giver, muscling him out of the way and sitting next to me. "You all need to quit bothering her. She's my girlfriend, not yours!"

His *girlfriend*! Steffi'd never called me that before! If my new fairy weren't invisible I would have kissed it.

"They're not bothering me," I said, basking in the adulation. Boys other than the ruggers were crowding around me as well. Steffi had never called Fiorenze his girlfriend. I couldn't stop smiling.

"You're all bothering *me*," Sandra said, glaring at them. "I'm trying to eat!"

"What is going on?" Coach Van Dyck demanded.

"Nothing," said one of the rugger boys. They all stepped back together. The boys who were farthest from Coach scuttled away. A thick-necked rugby boy scuttling was quite a sight.

"Charlie has Fiorenze's fairy," Sandra told her. "They swapped."

"That's impossible," Coach said.

"That's what I thought," Rochelle said. "But behold." She gestured to the many boys looking at me longingly.

"I've never heard of such a thing," Van Dyck said.

Coach Panesar, the A-stream skiing coach, joined her. "What is going on here?"

"Fairy swappage: Charlie, Fiorenze. The boys like Charlie now," Sandra said.

"That's impossible!" Panesar said.

I sighed. "Everyone keeps saying that. No disrespect

intended, Coaches, but look at all those boys and look where they're looking. At me." It was hard to say without sounding smug. "How many boys have gotten demerits for hassling Fiorenze today? And how many boys are following me around?" I couldn't help thinking that I was much better at this fairy than Fiorenze was.

The two coaches exchanged skeptical glances. The bell for the end of first recess sounded. Rochelle, Sandra, and I had not eaten a thing. I could tell they blamed me. Grossly unfair. Could I help it if I was enjoying myself?

"Get to your classes!" Coach Van Dyck yelled. "You know you'll get a demerit for lateness."

◆ ◆ ◆

I made my way to Accounting, walking as fast as I could without actually running, pausing only to shove the chocolates into my locker.

"Charlie," Freedom began, just as we turned into the classroom.

"Not talking to you," I said. "Heather doesn't want me to." I was not going to risk any more of Heather's wrath.

"Oh, Heather," he said. "She's just—"

"Charlie," Bluey said, "I've made sure that Danders—"

"Silence," Mr. Vandenhill (eyes-in-the-back-of-his-head fairy) said. He was chalking strings of numbers on his special blackboard. His class was the first time any of us had ever seen one. The chalk made me sneeze. Vandenhill had been known to give students demerits for sneezing. "Anyone who is not silent or sitting when I turn around will be given a demerit."

I sat. Freedom forced his way past four other contenders to grab the seat next to me. Along with Statistics, Accounting is a Rochelle-and-Sandra-free class, so who sits next to me varies.

"Go away!" I hissed as a shower of notes landed on my desk.

"A demerit for Charlotte Steele," Mr. Vandenhill said, chalking the last string of numbers on the board.

"But, sir—"

"And another one for dissent." He consulted his tablet. "A second game suspension for you. Fencing." He walked to my desk and brushed the notes to the ground. "Care to go for the hat trick?"

I looked down at my desk. "No, sir." Eight demerits. I'd just gotten my second game suspension. I couldn't get to public service soon enough. I'd get through the game suspension. I'd work away all my demerits. Getting rid of the parking fairy meant everything was going to be okay.

"Can you explain to the class what absorption costing is?"

My mind went blank. Well, not blank—it was full of thoughts: about my new fairy, and what it felt like to have all the boys following me around, sort of tingly and cheek warming but also strange and wobbly making, about Steffi, about the horrors of accounting and Vandenhill, but there wasn't a glimmer of an inkling of a notion of what absorption costing was. "Um . . ."

"Um?" Vandenhill raised his eyebrow. "Did you not do your assigned reading, Charlotte Steele?"

I *had* done the reading. Last night in Danders Anders's car. Why couldn't I remember it? "Yes, sir."

"Then what is absorption costing?"

"I don't remember, sir. I did so much reading last night that it's fallen out of my head." I was so tired it was hard to remember my own name.

"Another demerit. And you will transmit your assignment on absorption costing by first bell tomorrow."

I watched the assignment appear on my tablet. It looked long. Less than five minutes into class and I'd earned three demerits, a game suspension, and an epically long extra assignment. Even for me it was impressive. My grand total was now nine. All I had to do was get through the rest of the day.

Freedom put his hand on my knee. I shoved it off. "You're so pulchritudinous, Charlie."

Vandenhill saw the whole thing. "And that would be three demerits and a visit to the principal's office for you, Freedom Hazal."

"Sir?" Freedom asked.

"Now," Vandenhill said. "To return to absorption costing," he continued as Freedom picked up his bag and slunk out the door, casting a longing look back at me. "What are you doing, Bluey Salazar?"

Bluey was halfway out of his seat. "Um. I thought I should sit down next to Charlie."

"One demerit and stay where you are. I would like to remind everyone this is an accounting class, not an ogling-Charlotte-Steele class."

There was a murmur around the room. I could feel everyone looking at me; not all of them were looking with admiration. My cheeks burned.

◆　◆　◆

They were still burning when the bell for end of class sounded. I shoved my tablet into my bag and made my way out of class with Bluey chattering away beside me. Freedom Hazal was waiting for me in the corridor. He looked all dewy. Like he might cry if I didn't talk to him. I nodded briefly.

"Hey, Charlie, whatcha doing after school?" Freedom asked.

"Public service. Weren't you supposed to go to the principal's office? I can't be talking to you. Heather won't like it." I smiled, trying not to be too mean about it, but I didn't need more hassling from Freedom or Heather.

"That's right," Mazza said. His arms were wrapped around the biggest bunch of roses I'd ever seen. "You need to leave Charlie alone." He turned to thrust the roses at me. "These are for you. I bought them for my mom—it's her birthday—but you should have them."

"Thanks, Mazza," I said, almost falling under their

weight. They were bigger than me. "They're gorgeous. But shouldn't you give them to your mom?" I asked, though I couldn't actually see him.

"I'll get something else for her. I want you to have them."

"Okay," I said. I didn't have time to argue. Which locker was I going to stash them in? My main locker was already full and my tennis, fencing, and cricket lockers were too crammed with gear. Then I had a brain wave.

"Could you mind them for me, Mazza? Till after school? I'll get a demerit if I bring them to class."

He slapped his forehead. I had never seen anyone do that before. "I'm so sorry! I can't believe I didn't think of that!"

One of his friends started to talk to me, and then Freedom and Bluey tried to get me to meet them after school since they were now convinced I was meeting Mazza. I had to bite my lip to keep from giggling.

"I gotta get to class. Demerits, don't you know? Remember them? See you all later!" I took off at a run, laughing.

I was a natural for the every-boy-will-like-you fairy: I knew how to deal with Freedom and the rest, and if *that* didn't work I could always outrun them.

CHAPTER 32

Possibilities

Demerits: 9
Conversations with Steffi: 11
Game suspensions: 2
Public service hours: 19
Number of Steffi kisses: 4
Boys who like me: all of them
Girls who hate me: Heather Sandol

Danders Anders was the first one to meet me after school.

"Park," he called, opening the door and gesturing for me to get in. "Emergency."

I leaned in through the door. "The parking fairy's gone," I told him. "I can't help you."

Danders shook his head.

"Truly, Andrew, it's gone this time."

"Lies."

I shrugged. I was relieved I'd gotten through the day without earning a school suspension, plus Danders would believe me soon enough. I climbed in, tossing my bag onto the backseat, and reached out to close the door.

"Wait!" Mazza came running up, yelling and breathless. "Charlie! Your flowers! I thought! We! Could! Hang! Out!"

A billion roses pressed into my face.

"Can't, Mazza," I said, my eyes watering from the rose fumes. "I've got public service. Andrew here is kindly giving me a lift." Danders didn't say anything. "Could you put the flowers in back?"

Danders made the door click open and Mazza laid them reverently on the seat. He closed the door and the car filled with the smell of roses. I coughed. It was like being in a florist. I wound down the window.

Danders didn't say anything as he drove into town. He remained silent as he circled one block four times.

"This where you're hoping for a parking spot?" I asked at last.

"Parking fairy gone?" Danders asked.

"Parking fairy gone," I confirmed.

He sighed. It was probably the saddest sound I'd ever heard.

"Will you drop me off at public service?" I asked. "I'm at Hillside cemetery."

Danders sighed again.

"What's your emergency, Andrew? You really do have an emergency, don't you?"

"Money," he said, and he made the word even sadder than his sighs.

"But you'll have lots of money next year. When you're an Our."

"Next year," Danders said as if that was too far away too imagine.

He let me off at the cemetery.

"Good luck," I told him. "Hope your money worries are over soon."

He said nothing.

✦ ✦ ✦

Fiorenze dashed over to hug me. She was covered in dirt and I hadn't put my vest on yet. "You're making me dirty!" I shouted though I didn't really care. It felt wonderful to be at public service again, making my demerits go away.

"Sorry," she said, sounding not even slightly sorry and steering me toward where she was working. "Guess what? I walked part of the way here! Can you believe that?"

"Um, yes?" I brushed off the dirt she'd gotten all over me, pulled my vest and gloves on, then bent down to pick up a chewing gum wrapper, which I dropped in the non-recyclable sack.

"Waverly dropped me off," Fiorenze said, adding a handful of weeds to the compost sack, "and on my own I walked past a bunch of boys and they didn't even look at me! All they cared about were their boards. I'm so happy! I love your fairy! I mean *my* fairy."

I grinned. "I love your fairy too! My fairy! Our fairies! Poor Danders couldn't find a parking spot! I'm free!"

"That's stellar! We're both free!"

"And the boys at school are being so sweet," I continued, grinning at the thought of Steffi's kisses. "You should see the flowers they gave me!" Then I remembered that the roses were still on the backseat of Danders Anders's car. Oh well, it was the thought that counted, right? "Me and Steffi are boyfriend and girlfriend now. I really like him."

"That's even more stellar, then," Fiorenze said. "Though he liked you before the fairy."

"I *hoped* so, but it was hard to tell. You know, what with you having the fairy and all."

"Which means the fairy's only *strengthening* his feelings about you."

He had said all those lovely things about me. Stuff he'd never said before. "Can life get any better than this?"

"Doubt it," Fiorenze said, picking up a used condom and depositing it in the nonrecyclables. "Ewww. Just as well these gloves are so thick."

"Isn't it? I'm doing eight hours tonight and I'll be quiet as a mouse tomorrow. I am not going to get a school suspension!"

"Eight hours? The cemetery closes at eleven."

"Oh right, five hours, then," I said, dropping a candle stub in the nonrecyclables bag. "I've been meaning to ask, but what did you do to get demerits? You're always so quiet in class. I've never seen you in trouble."

Fiorenze laughed. "I broke a vase over Freedom Hazal's head."

"How come I never heard that?"

Fiorenze shrugged. "Freedom wasn't exactly boasting about it. He told everyone it was a boarding accident."

"Yay you! I think the fairy works extra-strong on Freedom."

"It does," Fiorenze said firmly.

"He's creepy."

"Not as creepy as Irwin Daniels."

"Irwin Daniels is a creep?" I asked.

Fiorenze nodded. "Him, I punched. Every demerit I've earned has been because of the boy fairy."

"But I thought the rule protected you?"

"Mostly. But sometimes the boys get out of line. I'm supposed to tell the teachers and not take matters into my own hands."

"Not break stuff over their heads or punch them?" I asked.

"You got it."

"You know, the boy fairy is a great way to figure out who the creeps are. Most of the boys have been gentlemanly. I haven't had to use violence."

Fiorenze didn't say anything. I wondered if she was embarrassed that I was handling the fairy so much better than she had.

"I'm really glad we swapped," I said.

"Me too."

I managed five hours. Fiorenze left after three, her demerits all scrubbed away.

CHAPTER 33

Less Than Doos

Demerits: 9 — 5 = 4
Conversations with Steffi: 11
Game suspensions: 2
Public service hours: 24
Number of Steffi kisses: 4
Boys who like me: all of them
Girls who hate me: Heather Sandol

The next morning as my dad dropped me off, a mob of boys congregated around the car. They surged forward as I opened the door.

"You haven't done anything to annoy anyone, have you?" Dad asked, reaching across to close the door. "Looks like they have pitchforks hidden behind their backs."

"Dad!" I grinned. "Don't be torpid. They're just pleased to see me." I couldn't see Steffi anywhere amongst them.

"All of them? I didn't know you were friends with that many boys. You're sure?" he asked, looking out the window at Bluey, Mazza, Freedom, and the rest, who, while they didn't actually have their faces pressed up against it, were pretty close.

"A hundred and ten percent sure." Though I had to admit the boys didn't look quite as smiley as they had yesterday. Probably they missed me. I kissed Dad on the cheek and slid out of the car.

The boys started talking to me all at once. It was like the sound a crowd makes when it's the finals and you're out in the middle of the field with the red ball in your hand and your team only needs to bag a few more for the win.

A roar.

You can't distinguish your name from your team's from your city's. The boos from the yays. All you can do is narrow your focus to the batter and the wicket they're guarding. To making those stumps explode.

Or, in this case, to finding a path past the school gates and into Biology. Even though Mr. Kurimoto was probably the only teacher in school who didn't issue demerits. All he cared about were red blood cells and fast-twitch muscles. But his was the only compulsory class I enjoyed.

"Hi," I said, smiling all around me, wondering where Steffi was. I thought about pulling out my lucky ball, but there wasn't exactly much room for spinning it. "Coming through. Hope you're happy. I'm happy. We're all happy. Happiness everywhere. Ow!" This last because my hair was being yanked. I turned. A boy I didn't know had his hand in my hair. "Let go!"

"Can't!" he said. "It's my school ring. In your hair."

Desperately he tried to untangle his ring, while at least a dozen other boys yelled at him.

"Stop it!" I yelled back. "Be quiet! I can't hear my own thoughts."

The boy's hand came free, but there was still something in my hair.

"My ring," he said.

"I'll get it to you later," I told him. "But if we don't get to class soon we'll all get demerits."

This got through to some of them and my way into the science block became clearer. Eyes on the stumps, I told myself. Bluey, Mazza, and Freedom buzzed along beside me as I tried to get the ring out of my hair.

"Sit with me at first recess, yeah?" Freedom was asking. Mazza and Bluey were saying pretty much the same thing, though Mazza was also asking where in my bedroom I'd put the roses and if I'd thought of him as I looked at them. I didn't have the heart to say they were probably still in Danders's car and that the only person I'd been thinking of when I passed out last night was Steffi.

"My stop," I said, pushing past them into Biology. All the male faces in the room turned to me as if they were flowers and I the sun. I smiled and slid into my regular seat next to Rochelle. She smiled too, but I could tell she was still unhappy with me.

"What are you doing?" she asked.

"There's a ring in my hair."

"Let me. No, don't pull away from me. Here," Rochelle said as it came free.

I took the ring from her. The side of the crest was dented. I pushed at it to no effect and then gave up and put it into my pocket. "Fiorenze likes my parking fairy."

"I'm sure she does."

"This swap is working out." A note landed on my desk. And then another. Then three more.

"Mmm."

"What?" I asked.

"There are rumors flying around, Charlie. They're not kind."

"About me?"

"About you."

"The immune system," Mr. Kurimoto said, stalking into class, late as usual. "What can you tell me about the effects of extreme fitness on the immune system, Rochelle?"

Someone put their hand on my shoulder. I startled and turned around. Irwin Daniels was licking his lips.

"Desist!" I hissed.

"Why?" he whispered. "You want me to touch you, don't you?"

"No!" Fiorenze was so right about Irwin.

"You're the one with the fairy that makes me feel this way," he whispered, leaning forward and stroking my hair and then my back. I shook him off again. "Quit it!"

"Shouldn't have stolen Fiorenze's fairy, then, should you?"

"Did not," I said, leaning as far forward in my seat as I could. Why would he say such a torpid thing? It was just as well most boys weren't like Irwin or Freedom.

"Rumors like *that*," Rochelle said under her breath.

"Irwin," Mr. Kurimoto said. "Keep your hands to yourself. Do you agree with Rochelle's and Meike's answers? Why?"

◆ ◆ ◆

Fencing was next. I sprinted the whole way, ducking and weaving, with Rochelle running interference and setting awesome picks. It was fun but exhausting, and I couldn't help missing when we played ball together all the time. She said good-bye, heading off to basketball (just to make my pang of envy bigger), and I collapsed onto the nearest bench. If I made it into the basketball stream then *everything* would be perfect.

"How much did you pay Fiorenze to get her fairy?"

I looked up. Heather Sandol and her best friends, Alicia and Tracy, were staring at me with their hands on their hips. I'd heard the expression "lips curled with contempt," but now I was seeing actual lips actually curling.

"I didn't. We swapped."

The withering-glare triplets said nothing.

"I just wanted to get rid of my parking fairy."

"Yes," Tracy said. "Because they're such a trial."

"No boyfriend of your own," Heather said. "So you had to steal Fiorenze's fairy."

"I didn't steal it!"

"That's injured," Alicia said. "You're injured." She spat. The globule landed just in front of my feet. "None of the boys like you, Charlie. You're forcing them to. Against their wills. You're turning the boys into zombies."

"What?" I began. "It's not like that."

"It's malodorous," Heather said. "I used to like you. I thought you were funny. I had no idea what you were really like. It's not just Freedom. It's all the boys. At least Fiorenze didn't *enjoy* her fairy."

"I don't enjoy it," I protested even though I did. "I just wanted to get rid of my parking fairy. Swapping was the only way."

"She seems to be under the misapprehension that we're talking to her," Heather said, turning her back on me. Tracy and Alicia did the same. "Where could she have gotten that idea from? She wanted the boys, didn't she? Well, now they're *all* she's got, 'cause no one else is going to talk to her."

"Absolutely no one."

218

CHAPTER 34
Love and Hatred

Demerits: 0
Conversations with Steffi: billions
Game suspensions: 2
Public service hours: 28
Boys who like me: all of them
Girls who hate me: Heather, Alicia, Tracy,
    and all their friends

Life with a boy-attracting fairy was a vast improvement. After two days my demerits were down to zero and the game suspension (fencing) I served on Saturday meant that I'd caught up on all my homework. By Sunday night I'd even managed to study ahead of time and review a week's worth of tennis and cricket training videos as well as two days of fencing.

I hadn't seen much of Steffi, though. He was great at school—all kisses and compliments—but I didn't see him outside it. Not that there was much time for that, what with all my demerit erasing, not to mention catching up with homework. He was probably as busy as me.

It was true that—except for Rochelle, Sandra, and Fiorenze—the rest of the girls were barely talking to me, but I figured they'd get over it eventually. Fiorenze had gone out of her way to stop the rumor that I'd stolen her fairy. Plus we were hanging out together, which seemed to be proof enough for some people, though not Heather or any of her minions.

There was still no rule protecting me like the one Fiorenze had had but maybe on Monday. Mr. Kurimoto and Coach Van Dyck were pleading my case. Kurimoto had believed me right away (how could he not with both Irwin Daniels and Freedom Hazal in his class?) and Van Dyck had finally come around. Still, even if the rule didn't come in, I was better at managing the boys than Fiorenze had been. As long as I avoided Daniels and Hazal, I'd be fine.

Monday—my first demerit-free day—was going to rule. The whole week would be fabulous. I could feel it.

✦   ✦   ✦

It wasn't. By lunch I'd earned a demerit for fending off Irwin Daniels and another one for yelling at Freedom Hazal. I'd hung out with Steffi on my breaks, but it was hard with all those other boys around, and, well, I had to admit that he wasn't quite the Steffi he'd been before. Like, the first thing he told me when we all sat down at lunch was how beautiful and soft my skin was, how gorgeous the color.

Sandra coughed. A mocking cough. She'd been doing that a lot since the swap.

"Have you done something new with your hair? It's so shiny," Steffi said. My hair was not shiny. He'd never said anything like that to me before the fairy. Now it was pretty much all he said.

"Go away!" Fiorenze hissed at the rugger boy who tried to sit down between her and me. The five of us—me, Steffi, Fiorenze, Rochelle, and Sandra—were squeezed around a two-person round table. Easier to keep anyone from joining us.

"You need to lose the fairy," Sandra said, glaring at me. "You may love it, but we hate it."

No one said anything. Not even Steffi. Them not being happy for me made my own new-fairy happiness smaller. They almost made me wish I'd gotten some other kind of fairy. One they'd approve of.

✦ ✦ ✦

By Wednesday things were much worse. Even though I was getting rid of most of the demerits I earned during the day at public service, it kept cutting into homework time.

Then Irwin Daniels tried to drag me into a broom closet. Two rugger boys rescued me, ripping the sleeve of my jacket in the process. Then they got into a fight over who was going to escort me to my class, while Heather Sandol and her minions hissed abuse. Apparently hissing didn't count as talking to me.

221

I ran. The entire D-, C-, and most of B-stream rugby ran after me.

✦ ✦ ✦

Rochelle found me cowering in one of the stalls of the tennis changing rooms. She banged on the door. "Charlie? Charlie? I know you're in there!"

"Yes," I said. "I am in here." I'd put the lid down and was sitting on it, hugging my bag tight, and wishing for the first time that I had listened to Fiorenze.

"What are you doing?" Rochelle asked. "Why weren't you in Bio? Where were you at first recess?"

"I couldn't."

"Couldn't what, Charlie? Come out of there." She banged on the door again. "Stop being ridiculous!"

Maybe I was being ridiculous, but I couldn't go out there again.

"Charlie?"

"They tore my jacket off! My shirt is torn too!"

"Class just started. There's no one out there."

But it was a lot better in here—despite the small space, the chewing gum stuck to the walls making the graffiti hard to read, and the smell—than it was out there.

"And there's no one in here but me, Charlie. No Heather or any of her Heather-ettes for you to hide from."

"I'm not scared of Heather Sandol!" I wasn't *scared* of her, it was just less than doos being around her and

222

her Heather-ettes, which seemed to be every girl in school.

"Of course not. You've just set up camp in there for your health."

"I'm sick."

"Are not."

"How do you know I'm not?" I asked.

I heard her sigh. A vastly impatient sigh. "You'll have to come out sometime, Charlie. Why not now?"

I shifted my legs only to discover that my left had gone to sleep. I grunted. "Okay, I'm coming out." I stood up, slipped my bag over my shoulder, and opened the door. "But you're not allowed to say *I told you so*."

Rochelle patted my shoulder. "So you've realized that having a boy fairy is not the most fabulous thing in the whole world?"

I nodded. "It was a malodorous mistake. Why didn't I believe Fiorenze?! She *told* me. I just didn't think every boy being in love with me would be a problem. And it wasn't at first." I'd thought I could handle it, that Fiorenze's problem wasn't the fairy but her not being able to cope with it. Yet I wasn't any better at it than she was.

"Well, not every boy. You're safe from seniors."

"There's that."

"I don't think any of us realized how bad it was for her," Rochelle said. "She's had rules protecting her. Which you will have too any minute now."

"At least Kurimoto and Van Dyck believe me."

"Them plus overwhelming evidence," Rochelle said. "I'm sure the rule will cover you by the end of the week. Why don't we both get to class now?"

"You'll run interference?"

"Of course. It's not all bad, Charlie. Now you know Stefan likes you better than Fiorenze—he's barely talked to her since you two swapped."

"Well, yes, but that also means he's only with *me* because of the boy fairy. Don't get me wrong. I like being with him, but, well . . ." I didn't want to admit out loud that I'd turned Steffi into a love-zombie just like Heather Sandol said. I didn't want him liking me because of a fairy. I wanted him to like me because of *me*.

"He's not been the same, has he?" Rochelle said.

"No, he hasn't." I wondered if it meant Steffi didn't like me after all. Or maybe he had, but the fairy *making* him like me had killed off any real liking for me.

Fiorenze came running into the bathroom. "Charlie! There you are!"

We both turned to her. "What's wrong with you?" I asked.

"Danders Anders."

I would have been tempted to say *I told you so*, except that her *I told you so* was vastly bigger than mine. "Oh," I said instead.

"He grabbed me in the corridor and told me like a hundred times he could give me lots of money if I'd be his parking fairy girl."

224

"But he told me he doesn't have any money."

"When I said no, he picked me up as if I were a cat! He would have taken me out to his car then and there, but Coach Mbeki intervened. She gave him a demerit. I know he's going to come searching for me again as soon as he can. Wherever Danders wants to go, he wants to go there right this minute; he won't take no for an answer."

"No, he won't," I said. "He never does."

"Hasn't he heard of taxis?" Rochelle asked. "You don't need a parking spot if you go in a cab."

"Danders loves his car," I said. "*Loves* it."

"What are we going to do?" Fiorenze asked. "I can't spend all day hiding from him!"

"How did he even know you have the parking fairy now?" Rochelle asked.

"Bluey told him."

"Bluey talks too much," I said. First he'd betrayed me and now Fio.

"He thought he was helping you," Fiorenze said. "Getting Danders off your back."

"Hmmph," I said.

"So what are we going to do?"

"Can't you swap your fairies back?" Rochelle asked.

"No!" we both yelled. The thought of my parking fairy returning made me want to scream, tear my hair out, and give up sports for macramé, interpretive dance, and making up injured stories in the front row of some torpid Arts school. Over my dead body.

"Okay, okay," Rochelle said, holding up her hands. "It was just an idea."

"Bleaching?" Fiorenze asked.

"Where are we going to get bleach at school?" I asked, though I was desperate enough to try it. "Not to mention no bath tubs. Do you even remember what the proportions are meant to be?"

"Nine to one? Ten to one?" Fiorenze shook her head. "I can't be sure."

"Nearly dying, then," I said. "It's gotta be the near-death thing."

"I am not jumping off the roof of this building!" Fiorenze exclaimed.

"We could pull out the mats from gymnastics. Land on them."

"Don't you think the gymnastics squads will notice?" Fiorenze pointed out. "Plus they're not rated for people jumping off the roof. It's a long fall."

"What about jumping from the high board?" I asked.

"Would a fairy believe that would kill us?"

How was I supposed to know what a fairy would think? "We could call your mother and ask."

Fiorenze looked at me with a most unkind expression.

"Fio, we have to think of *something*. I'm not going through another second with this poxy fairy. I'm so over injured fairies I can't even tell you."

"What are you two talking about?" Rochelle asked.

"Nearly dying," Fiorenze explained. "It gets rid of fairies."

"Isn't that a bit drastic? I imagine that in the attempt to *nearly* die some people *actually* die."

"It's not that kind of nearly dying," I said. "You just have to do something the fairy thinks will kill you. Like jumping off a building."

"Last I heard," Rochelle said, "that really can kill you."

"Not if you land on big padded mats."

"Hey," Rochelle said. "What about luge?"

"Luge?" I said. "That's the sled sport, right?" There was a luge stream, like there was a skiing stream, an ice hockey stream, etc., but us summer sports streamers didn't have much to do with the winter sports types.

It doesn't snow in New Avalon, or anywhere on the East Coast, but we're New Avaloners, so we have to be the best at everything. Which is why New Avalon Sports High has a vastly big Luge Hall, as well as a Skiing Hall and an ice rink. That doesn't stop winter sports being weird and the people who do them weirder. Why would you be into snowboarding when you've never seen real snow?

"Don't you remember?" Rochelle asked. "Last year Teddy Rourke snuck into our school on a dare and broke like a billion bones when he got onto a luge track. He'd never done it before, and he went zooming down faster than light, then flew off the track at the very first turn and—"

"See, Ro, that sounds *actually* dangerous."

"But not fatal. Anyway, when he got out of the hospital he didn't have his fairy anymore."

"That's right," I said. Teddy Rourke was at Nettles's

school. She said he was crazy. He'd also been given a quokka as a get-well present. Nettles went on about how he'd gotten one when he was much less responsible than she was. "It was a sleep fairy. No matter how much sleep he got, he felt great, even no sleep didn't affect him, but ever since the accident he has to get the same amount of sleep as everyone else."

Rochelle nodded. "If you two get onto the luge track and go zooming down it, your fairies are guaranteed to think you're going to die. Neither of you has ever done luge before, have you, Fio?"

She shook her head. "But how come the people in the luge streams have fairies?"

"Their fairies mustn't think they're going to die because it's something they do all the time," I answered. "Same as for skydivers and racing car drivers. Plus your mom says that people with dangerous jobs *do* have fewer fairies than regular people. I think the luge thing might work."

"But I don't want to break billions of bones!"

"We might not break any."

"You're both vastly more coordinated than Teddy Rourke," Rochelle said. "He's at an Arts school! You probably won't break more than a couple of bones. But you'll both most likely be busted if you do it. That would be a whole lot of demerits!"

"That's why you're going to go get Steffi for us," I said.

"Brilliant idea!" Fiorenze said.

"Not bad," Rochelle said. "Stefan will shield you from demerits."

"You know about his fairy too?"

"Please! Who doesn't?"

"So you'll do it for us?" I asked, showing her my pleadingest face.

Rochelle looked at me and then at Fiorenze.

"Please, Ro? I can't go out there 'cause of you know why, and Fiorenze can't 'cause of Danders. We have to get rid of our fairies."

"Okay."

"You'd better hurry," Fiorenze said. "If we do it now before lunch starts, no one will see us."

"If there's no training going on in the Luge Hall now or at lunchtime."

Fiorenze's face fell. "I didn't think of that."

"It's okay, Fio, I said I'd do it. But remember you both owe me for the demerits I'll rack up."

I kissed Rochelle on the cheek. "Vastly. We'll be your slaves."

Fiorenze nodded. "If we aren't dead, that is."

CHAPTER 35
Crossing the Field

Demerits: 4
Conversations with Steffi: billions
Game suspensions: 2
Public service hours: 35
Boys who like me: all of them
Girls who hate me: almost all of them

I peeked out of the changing room doorway and, seeing no coaches or teachers, I slipped out into the corridor. Fiorenze followed. We headed left down the corridor. The teachers' lounge room was down at the other end, which made it way too risky, even though that would lead us to the Luge Hall quicker. We scurried along as fast as we could.

"So, Fio?" I whispered to her. "Thanks for not saying *I told you so*."

"Thank you for not saying the same."

"Your *I told you so* is much more justified than mine," I whispered, turning the corner. The unmistakable silhouette of Danders Anders loomed, coming toward us. "Pox!" I grabbed Fiorenze and pulled her back.

"What?"

"Danders, heading this way."

"Let's just make a run for it, then," Fiorenze said, gesturing to the steps and beyond the field, the Luge Hall. "Go direct."

"Go visible, you mean. The Rugby A's are out there. We'll be busted for sure."

Fiorenze pulled me down the steps and out the door. "Not if we walk with a purpose, like we're *meant* to be going there."

"Have you tried that?"

Fiorenze nodded.

"Does it work?"

"Sometimes."

"Whatever," I said.

Fiorenze straightened and walked down the steps onto the paddock. I did the same, keeping my eyes locked on the Luge Hall in the distance.

We walked past the thick-necked rugby majors attacking large padded tackle dummies. Their head coach blew her whistle a lot, leaving the actual yelling to her two assistants.

"Stupid game," Fiorenze said under her breath.

"I cannot argue."

Only a few of the boys turned to look at me longingly. "Just as well your ex-fairy only works on boys your age."

"Isn't it?"

"Quite the relief."

Up ahead I could see that the main doors to the Luge Hall were closed. "Is that a bad sign?" I asked Fio.

"I think they're always closed. They have to keep the cold in so the ice doesn't melt."

We walked past the main doors. It was a relief to be out of everyone's sight.

"I'm not sure I've seen a luge before," Fiorenze said. "Do you say that you go 'on a luge' or 'in a luge'?"

"Um," I said. "Don't ask me. I don't know anything about snow." I nudged her. "Our fairies will definitely be convinced we're going to die."

"They might be right," Fiorenze muttered.

"Don't jinx us, Fio!"

"Sorry."

"Whatever happens—if the fairies are gone it'll be worth it, right?"

"Absolutely. Worth several broken bones—"

"Shush!"

We walked past Luge Hall's growling array of air conditioners, spitting hot air at us. The solar panels on the roof would be completely bathed in sunshine. It hadn't rained in days.

The bell for the end of class sounded. I risked a glance back and saw Danders Anders heading toward us.

"Pox! Not Danders again!"

Fiorenze sprinted toward the fire exit, with me right behind her.

CHAPTER 36
Luge Hall

Demerits: 4
Game suspensions: 2
Public service hours: 35
Boys who like me: all of them
Girls who hate me: almost all of them

Fiorenze slipped in the back entrance. I followed, closing the door behind us. It was like walking into a giant brightly lit freezer. The cold cut straight through my uniform. We might as well have been naked and barefoot.

"Brrr," Fiorenze said. "Where do we hide?"

The hall was vast. I half expected icicles to be dangling from the ceiling, which was at least thirty meters up. Three winding icy tracks took up almost all of the space. The largest one started at the ceiling line. It wound around and around the hall; two smaller tracks were nestled inside it. The outsides were made of concrete, the insides were gleaming white ice. Along the wall to our right was what looked like a storage room.

"Behind the tracks." I pulled her toward the bottom of it. "Danders won't see us if we duck behind here."

"He will if he comes in the front way."

And because Fiorenze was set on jinxing us, the front door immediately began to open. We had just enough time to scramble up and dive behind the other way as the bell for lunch sounded.

I hoped it was louder than the sound of us landing hard on the floor. Fio's face changed color. I imagined mine was doing the same. My shins were going to be covered in bruises.

"Fiorenze!" Danders called out.

We scrunched closer together. I couldn't see him. I hoped that meant he couldn't see us.

"Fiorenze!"

It was even colder crouched on the ground. I wondered if that was because heat rises. Did that mean cold congregates on the ground?

"Fiorenze," Danders called out again in his booming voice. I wondered if he'd ever thought about training as an opera singer. My nose tingled. A sneeze-is-on-the-way tingle, not a touched-by-Steffi tingle. I pressed my finger under it, praying the sneeze would go away. My nose was even colder than my hands.

"Fiorenze!" he called louder this time, making us both startle.

"Your fairy is so much worse than I thought it would be,"

Fiorenze whispered right in my ear. "Danders is a nightmare."

I put my fingers over my lips and Fiorenze nodded. But I couldn't help being pleased that someone finally understood about the parking fairy.

I heard the front door opening or closing.

Fiorenze and I looked at each other.

"Want Fiorenze," Danders said in a more conversational voice.

"She's not here," I heard Rochelle say. "She doesn't do winter sports."

"Saw her."

"You saw her in here? That's odd," I heard Steffi say. "She's allergic to snow."

I wondered if it was possible to be allergic to snow.

"Outside," Danders said.

"You saw her outside?" Rochelle asked. "Or you want us to go outside?"

"Saw. You her friend?"

"Oh no!" Rochelle said. "I can't stand Fiorenze."

"Me neither," Steffi said. "She's most undoos."

It was probably the first time I'd ever heard him say "doos." Fiorenze nudged me and made a face. I told her with my mind that they didn't mean it, that we all liked her now. As I thought it, I realized it was true. I hadn't resented being with Fiorenze for ages now.

"Why you here?" Danders demanded.

"We do winter sports," Rochelle said.

"Luge and skiing," Steffi corroborated.

"We are very fine skiers," she added, which I thought was a bit much.

"Where Charlie?"

"Don't know," Rochelle said. "She doesn't do winter sports either."

The front door opened. We peeked out cautiously. Rochelle was at the door, making sure Danders was truly gone.

We slipped out from behind the track just as Steffi called my name.

"Hey!" he said, grinning. He slid his arm around my waist and kissed me. My heart soared, but the thought that it was just the boy-attracting fairy in action made it sink at the same time, which made me burp.

"Hello to you too." Steffi laughed. "Even with a red nose you look great."

"He's gone," Rochelle announced, closing the door. "Hey, Charlie, Fio. Glad you made it. Guess what?" she said, turning to me, opening her eyes so wide I worried they might fall out. "They just announced basketball tryouts! For next week."

"No!"

"Yes!"

I screamed and we hugged each other.

Steffi gave me another kiss. "That's so great. You are on that team!"

"Yay!" Fiorenze said. "But shouldn't we get started? Time and all that."

"How?" Rochelle asked. "It's not like either of you knows how to ride a luge. Pox, it's cold in here!" She shivered and hugged herself.

We admitted our ignorance and acknowledged that, yes, it was cold. Fiorenze's nose was red and running. I imagined mine was too. How long before they turned blue and fell off? I wished I had Sienna Bray's never-getting-cold fairy.

"How hard can it be?" Steffi asked. "You jump in a boat thing and someone else pushes it. I bet you'll be really good at it, Charlie."

"Don't we have to wear those tight suits?" I asked.

"That's only for going super-fast," Rochelle said. "You just have to almost die."

We looked up at the top of the longest track. It gleamed white. So bright it made my eyes water. It started high and went on for ages. I followed the track all the way from the top to the bottom, saw the white disappear on the turns, replaced by the concrete gray outsides.

"Well," Rochelle said, "falling all the way down—that could almost kill you for sure."

Fiorenze and I looked at each other.

"Let's get started," I said, walking over to the room I hoped was full of luges. "There's only twenty minutes left of lunch." I tried the door handle. "Pox," I said. The door was locked. "Anyone know how to pick a lock?"

"Yup," Steffi said.

We all looked at him.

"I'd love to pick a lock for you," he said, kissing my cheek. He fished a smallish leather pouch out of his bag and opened it up to reveal several long, thin metal things. He looked at the lock and then at the metal needle things and pulled out the largest one. I moved aside and he started poking at the lock with it.

"You just happen to have that thing in your bag?" I asked.

"Lock pick. Yup," Steffi said, not looking up. "Never know when you're going to need one."

None of us said anything but I could almost hear Rochelle and Fiorenze thinking. It did not seem the doosest thing in the world for someone with a never-getting-in-trouble fairy to have such a skill. Not that I wasn't grateful on this occasion.

"Bingo," Steffi announced, standing up and giving me a hug. He opened the door to reveal a vast treasure trove of lugey-type apparatuses. Three of the walls were covered floor to ceiling with different kinds of sleds. Some looked like long, skinny racing cars with blades instead of wheels. Most of them weren't nearly so fancy, they were just a small base, with teeny rails on the side. I tried to imagine sitting on something that precarious while sliding down that huge long track. My fairy would leave me in seconds.

"Hey, aren't these the suits?" Rochelle said, pointing to racks of what looked like human skins on hangers. That is if human skins were bright golds, pinks, blues, oranges, greens, and reds, and were kind of shiny with lightning flashes and butterfly designs on them. Rochelle went through until she found two to fit me and Fiorenze. The one for me was half the size of the one for Fiorenze.

"Hey! I'm not *that* little."

No one said anything, which was vastly annoying.

"And here are gloves and booties."

I took them from her. The gloves were vicious-looking, with little spikes all over the fingertips.

"So which one of these should we use?" Fiorenze asked, surveying the racks of sleds hanging from the walls. "I think I'd be happier in one of the ones that looks like a car," Fiorenze said.

"I agree," I said. "Wow, those blades look sharp."

Fiorenze nodded. "I'm having visions of us losing fingers rather than fairies."

"Once more with the jinxing, Fio!"

"Sorry," she said.

It hadn't occurred to me that luges would run on blades. I'd thought they'd be smooth on the bottom like a canoe. But sharp worked. This was *supposed* to be dangerous. But I didn't want it to be losing-fingers dangerous, just losing fairies. "Our ignorance is helpful, right? Better chance of dying."

They all stared at me.

"What?" I asked.

"You said 'dying,' Charlie."

"Sorry, I meant *nearly* dying."

"Now who's jinxing?" Fiorenze asked.

CHAPTER 37
Cold and Ice

Demerits: 4
Game suspensions: 2
Public service hours: 35
Boys who like me: all of them
Girls who hate me: almost all of them

The suit felt weird and uncomfortable and itchy. It was the tightest thing I'd ever worn. "This is malodorous," I declared.

"At least it's warm," Fiorenze said.

She was right. It was a lot warmer than our school uniforms. Once I put the gloves on, the feeling started returning to my fingers and toes.

"Warm?" Rochelle said, looking at Steffi.

They grabbed themselves suits and started wriggling into them.

The luge we chose was much lighter than we expected. Getting it to the bottom of the track was easy, getting it any farther, not so much.

"How do we get it up there?" I said.

"There's a ladder over here," Steffi called. The three of us walked over and stared up the narrow insubstantial ladder ascending meters and meters above our heads.

"It has *blades*," Fiorenze objected. "We can't carry it up a ladder."

"Especially not the world's tallest ladder."

"It's making me dizzy," I said.

We walked back around to the front of the track. It looked like a frozen water slide. The ice coated the whole thing so that you could slide along the sides as well as the bottom.

"Push it up?" Fiorenze asked.

None of us could see what else to do.

Rochelle and Fiorenze being the biggest and strongest got onto the track first. Rochelle immediately fell over and slid off, landing on her knees with a thump. "Slippery," she said, as if an explanation were necessary.

"The toes of your booties have grippy things," Fiorenze said, demonstrating by walking farther up the track on tiptoe. "If you walk on the front of your foot you won't slip."

Rochelle looked at her dubiously and climbed back onto the ice, tentatively testing it. "She's right."

They climbed a bit farther up, leaning forward, and grabbing the sides of the track when slipping seemed imminent.

When they were ready, Steffi and I pushed the sled up the track. It occurred to me that being behind the sled increased the chances of being run over by it and losing fingers.

I looked ahead to where the track began. It was a long, long, long way away with many twists and turns. I pushed harder, teetering on my tiptoes.

Then Fiorenze and Rochelle grabbed hold of the sled and it lightened.

Steffi and I pushed, making sure to be on the front of our feet. Before we'd made it around the third turn, the arches of my feet were screaming and sweat ran down my face.

"Do your feet hurt?" I asked Steffi.

"Yes."

"Are you sweating into your eyes?"

"Yes. But I comfort myself with the fact that my nose is no longer so cold it's about to drop off and that I'm here with you."

None of us spoke after that. It was too much effort. We pushed and pulled the sled centimeter by centimeter up the track. Each step my feet hurt more, my fingers became crampier, and my sweat turned into a tidal wave.

And then at long last we had the sled in position on the dead flat straight at the very top of the track. It was wider here and the sides were less curved.

"Gah," Fiorenze said, collapsing onto the wooden platform that marked the start."

"Double gah," Rochelle said, falling beside her. "My feet!"

"Triple," said Steffi.

"Times a billion," I added, flopping down beside them, rubbing my burning arches with my cramped fingers. The others were doing the same thing. None of us had ever walked up a hill on our toes while shifting a sled. "That has to be the most injured sport ever."

"Agreed."

"And we haven't even gotten to the sporty bit."

"Um," Steffi said. "What's that?"

I looked up from my feet. He was pointing at what looked like an elevator. He stood up and hobbled over to press the button.

"No way," Rochelle said. "If it's big enough to fit a luge I'm going to scream."

The doors opened. The elevator was big enough for any number of luges.

Rochelle screamed.

Steffi laughed. Fiorenze and I looked at each other and then at our hands and feet. All that effort and pain and time . . . How had we not noticed an elevator?

"You'd better hurry," Rochelle said. "Lunch was over ages ago. I don't want to think about how many demerits I have now."

"Are you ready to do this?" Fiorenze asked me.

I wasn't sure I was. I was overheated and tired and my arches burned. But I wouldn't be standing on them screaming downhill on a sled. "Sure," I said. "Let's ditch our fairies."

We both stood up. It hurt.

"Sounds like a plan," Steffi said. He wrapped me in a huge hug and kissed me on the lips. Rochelle and Fiorenze looked the other way. "Okay, hop in."

We hopped. Fiorenze clambered to the front of the sled. I arranged myself behind her. "Not exactly comfy, is it?"

"I don't think nearly dying is meant to be comfortable," she said, twisting around so I could hear her.

I looked in front at the edges of the track curving around us, brilliant and white. It was a pity we hadn't worn sunglasses. Sitting down, I couldn't see over the sides, I couldn't see how far we would fall should it all go horrendously wrong. I didn't need to see it. We would fall far. Breaking legs and arms wasn't too bad—we'd all done those—but broken necks? Not so doos. We were only supposed to *nearly* die.

I focused on the white shining track, on the boy-attracting fairy being so scared it would run away.

The sled shifted a little. I turned to see Steffi and Rochelle bent with their hands on it.

"Ready," Steffi called. I wondered if we were supposed to be wearing goggles. Wouldn't the air rushing by make our eyes water even worse than the cold?

"Ready," Fiorenze said.

"Ready," I repeated.

They pushed.

We moved.

A little bit.

They pushed again.

We moved a little bit farther. My nose was starting to feel cold again and my eyes too.

244

I turned around. "Maybe you need to start pushing from a run up," I suggested.

"No way," Rochelle said. "What if I slip and go hurtling down to the bottom? No way am I losing my shopping fairy! It was bad enough pushing the poxy thing up here. I was terrified I was going to slip."

Steffi shrugged. "No run up."

I turned back. We were less than two meters from where it started to slope. They pushed again, and then again, and at last we were heading downward, moving not very fast at all.

We came to a halt at the first turn.

"Oh, come on!" I said. "The ice is slippery! This thing has blades. Why aren't we zooming along?"

Fio twisted to face me and the sled shifted forward, but then stopped again. "Pox," she said. "I think we'll have to get out and push."

"This is malodorous," I said. "Plus I am so cold I think death is imminent."

"I don't think death by freezing is sudden enough to get rid of fairies."

"Very droll," I said. "Why are we not going fast? There is ice. There are blades."

"Should we try pushing with our hands?" Fiorenze suggested.

I couldn't see what else we could use.

The sled had come to a rest against a right-hand turn,

so we reached out with our left hands, which meant once again I whacked my stupid healed fairy-swapping injury. Poxy thumb! It was mostly healed, but the cold was making it hurt again. We pushed, I winced, the sled moved.

And then stopped again.

"Should have jumped off Merckx. I'm pretty sure it's the tallest building at school."

"Isn't Martin a little taller?" Fiorenze asked.

We pushed the luge the rest of the way around the turn until it started to slide down the straight before coming to a halt at the next turn.

"I think it's because we're not leaning with our bodies," Fiorenze said.

"How do you mean?"

"We've got to lean the way we want it to turn. See the next turn after this one? It's going right, so as we approach we've got to lean right. All the way right. You know, like when you're riding a bicycle."

Obvious! If she'd explained it better in the first place I would have known what she meant. It was just like boarding. "I got it."

We used our hands again to push the sled forward, until the blades started shushing across the ice and we were around the corner. We leaned to the right, and took the corner without stopping; we were even picking up speed. Actual air brushed past our faces until we came to a juddering halt at the next turn.

The turn came sooner than expected, we hadn't shifted in time.

"Pox!"

Fiorenze said something.

"What?"

She turned. "We didn't shift direction. How stupid are we?"

I sucked my teeth. I didn't think *I* was stupid at all. The sport of luge, on the other hand . . . "We'll get it right next time."

Fiorenze made a noise between a grunt and groan.

"Are you scared?" I asked.

"I'm a smidge afraid that my nose and ears are going to drop off from the cold."

I teeth-sucked.

"No," Fio said, "I'm not even a little bit scared."

"Me neither. I can't imagine our fairies are either."

There was nothing remotely scary about our stop-and-start slow descent. The only things Fiorenze and I were likely to die of were cold or boredom.

We made it around the next turn. But not the turn after that. They kept coming up on us before we had time to shift. We slowed down or stopped and had to push, and repeat, until we got to the end of the track. I doubted we'd ever gone more than five kilometers an hour. I could walk faster.

Much.

CHAPTER 38

Trying to Nearly Die

Demerits: 4
Game suspensions: 2
Public service hours: 35
Boys who like me: all of them
Girls who hate me: almost all of them
Luges dragged up the ice: 1
Luges ridden down the ice: 1
Near deaths: 0

Steffi helped me out. He was grinning. "You two sure took your time—"

"You can't be in here!" said a boy I didn't recognize. "You're not on the team!"

"No, we're not," I said.

The boy turned to me. His face softened.

Fiorenze nudged me. "Your fairy survived the searing speed," she said.

"Why are you in here?" the boy asked. "I'm Nick."

"He's a luger," Rochelle said. "Who likes you."

"Such a surprise," Fiorenze said.

Nick wasn't listening to either of them. "You're gorgeous," he told me.

"No, I'm Charlie."

"Sorry," Nick said. He was so light skinned that his blush showed purply red on his face and neck.

I pointed to the top of the track. "Me and Fio want to ride this luge all the way down that. We want to do it fast and scary."

"Oh, no," Nick said, shaking his head. "That's too dangerous to start on. Though you two made it seem safe as houses. Do you know I've never seen anyone go down it that slowly? Amazing. You were doing everything wrong. You didn't even steer."

"Steer?" Fiorenze asked.

Nick pointed at a piece of rope. "The driver steers with that and the braker brakes."

"Oh," I said. I hadn't even noticed the rope.

"And you were both sitting up. That slows you massively. You should have been lying down."

"Right, so we steer the luge and lie down in it. What else?"

"Bobsled, not luge. Also it's a three-person, not a two. That slowed you down as well. You also need to lean with the turns. You two seemed to be doing the opposite. It was uncanny.

"Then you have to know the course. We memorize them. Each turn has a number." He started to recite them.

I tuned out, but Fiorenze was nodding.

"Nick," I interrupted. "We have to do this now. I have no idea when your fellow lugers will show up."

"Sliders. We're called sliders. But they won't be here today. They're away at a meet on the West Coast."

That was an excellent piece of luck. I wondered if it was Steffi's fairy's doing—keeping us out of trouble.

"Why aren't *you* there?" Rochelle asked.

Nick looked down. "Didn't pass the physical. Broken arm. It's pretty much healed. But not enough for Doctor Tahn. You know how they are."

The four of us nodded. Over the years we'd all had doctors tell us we couldn't play when we knew we could.

Nick picked out a bobsled he thought was appropriate for us novices and led us to the elevator past the ladder and behind the tracks.

"What are those," I asked, pointing at two helmetlike objects in the sled. Rochelle pressed the button.

"Helmets."

"No helmets," I said.

"What?" Nick looked horrified. "You have to wear a helmet!"

"Nope."

"Maybe we should," Fiorenze said.

"You really should," Nick said. His face was going red.

"How scared is a fairy going to be if we're wearing helmets? C'mon, Fio, do you want to get rid of your fairy or not?" I glared at her.

Fiorenze put her hands up. "Fine. But I want it noted that if we die because of no helmets, then it's your fault."

The elevator doors opened.

"It's noted. Get in the poxy elevator."

Fiorenze, Steffi, Nick, and me stepped in. Rochelle didn't. "I'll see you both at the bottom," she said. "Good luck."

"Don't want to risk your beloved shopping fairy?" I asked.

"Too right," she said. "I'll be the first to congratulate you on being fairy-less. Break a leg!"

"Ro!" Fiorenze and I exclaimed. "Way to jinx us!"

"Sorry! Lose a fairy, I mean."

❖   ❖   ❖

This time we made it to the top in what felt like seconds but was long enough for Nick to start drilling us on the course details. All I could take in was left, right, left, turn twelve, up, down, turn fourteen, blah blah blah, but Fiorenze seemed to be listening.

"Are you sure you want to do this?" Nick asked me again. Since he first saw me he hadn't addressed his comments to anyone else. Most disconcerting. "It's dangerous," he continued. "I didn't do a run this advanced until more than a year after I'd started, and I was jumping the gun."

"We're sure."

Nick sighed. "Recite the course."

Fiorenze did and I mumbled along with her.

Nick got into the bobsled to demonstrate how we were supposed to sit, or, rather lie down. He looked like a corpse. "See?" he said. "This way's more streamlined than sitting up and leaning forward. I'm offering much less resistance." He climbed out and smiled at me. "Got it?"

We nodded.

"Show me, then, Charlie."

Fiorenze climbed in first. Nick seemed a bit put out at having to look at someone other than me.

"You'll be steering. Take this." He put the rope in her hands. "Pull this way for right, that for left."

Fiorenze nodded.

"Now you, Charlie."

I got in and arranged myself as directed. I didn't like not being able to see in front of me. Wasn't that dangerous? Though dangerous was the point.

"Your chin should be tucked in more." Nick adjusted my chin, unnecessarily running a finger down my cheek.

I sat bolt upright. "No touching!"

Nick's face went purple. "It was an accident," he mumbled.

"Was not."

Fiorenze coughed. "Shouldn't we be getting on with it?"

"Right," Nick said, turning his gaze back to me. "The start is tricky because you're running on ice while pushing the sled along, then jumping in. Professionals don't always get it right. And if you muck up the start, well, how do you think I broke my arm?"

We nodded again.

After one lingering glance back at me, he took off running alongside the sled, making it look almost graceful, then swung himself into place, lying completely straight and flat with his hands pinned to his sides. He came to a halt a few meters before the descent, climbed out, and started hauling it back. Steffi ran out to help him.

"Do you think you can do that?"

Fio and I both nodded even though we had no chance at all. But getting it right wasn't as important as getting it scary.

"Promise you'll be careful," Nick said.

"I'll be careful!"

"Ready?" Fiorenze asked.

"Ready," I said. Steffi gave me a kiss for luck and Nick glared at him.

We got in position beside the bobsled.

"We'll definitely go faster this time," I said.

Fiorenze nodded.

"It will be vastly scary. Nick's assessment of our competence will be shared by our fairies. They'll be gone within seconds."

Fiorenze laughed.

"On three. One. Two. Three."

We took off running on the tips of our toes.

Mine cramped up instantly.

The pain was too much. I screamed. I tried to switch to running normally. My feet slipped out from under me. I lost my grip on the sled and went flying down the track on my stomach.

Fiorenze skidded beside me, screaming. I could hear the shush of the sled's blade just behind us. We were going to lose fingers *and* break bones. Why had I rejected the helmets?

"Bloody benighted fragging poxy doxhead fairies of dung!" I screamed. Or at least that's how it was in my head. I think it came out as a strangled *aargh*.

I was going so fast water streamed out of my eyes and down my face. My body shifted right, then left, then right, going with the turns without my doing anything on purpose. I was just falling. I could imagine the fright a fairy would be experiencing, because I was experiencing it.

The track zoomed by so fast now that everything was spinning in white. It and Fiorenze's terrified face were all I could see.

I didn't want to die.

I didn't even want to *nearly* die.

If I were a fairy I would have jumped off by now.

Then I did jump off. Fiorenze too.

There was no ice underneath me, just air. And a sled flying over my head.

◆ ◆ ◆

The jolt went through my entire body. Even my toenails rattled.

Beside me someone groaned.

254

I turned my head.

It was Fiorenze. She was sitting up. She smiled at me. It lacked wattage.

Neither of us said anything for a dazed second. Or minute. Or hour. It was hard to tell.

"Are you all right?" Steffi asked. At least I thought it was Steffi. The sounds were far away.

"I think so," I said, sitting up.

Bad idea. My head throbbed.

Fiorenze tried to stand up. She wobbled.

"Steady," Steffi said, grabbing her shoulder. He guided her as she sank back down. I bet I would wobble too. In fact, it felt like I already was.

"I can't believe I just helped you do that," Nick said. I made myself focus on his face. His face was more purple than before. Veins stood up on his forehead. I wondered if they were love veins. "The sled is cracked all the way through. We're going to be so demerited we wind up expelled."

"Relax," I said. "Stefan's here. He's got a don't-worry-it'll-be-fine fairy. Hey! You don't like me, do you, Nick?"

"You destroyed a sled!"

"Do you want to go out sometime, Nick? We could see a movie or go to the beach."

Nick looked at me as if I had gone insane.

"Fio! Fairy's gone!" I yelled, even though it hurt. "My fairy's gone!"

"Yes," Fiorenze said. She made another stab at standing.

255

"Careful," Steffi said, offering her a hand. "You don't look so great."

"I've felt better," she said in a voice as wobbly as she looked.

Steffi offered me his left hand, while keeping Fio steady with his right. I took it. "You don't look okay either," he said.

"Okay," I said. "Yes, that is me." The hall looked bigger than it had. The ceiling was now farther away than the sky. Also it had been redecorated with lots of wiggling dots.

"I don't think so, Charlie," I heard Steffi say. "Your eyes are all white."

CHAPTER 39

Fairy Free

Demerits: 4

Game suspensions: 2

Public service hours: 35

Boys who like me: none of them?

Girls who hate me: almost all of them

~~Luges~~ bobsleds dragged up the ice: 1

~~Luges~~ bobsleds ridden down the ice: 2

Near deaths: 1

I didn't pass out, but I was pretty shaky being led to the doctors' offices. They prodded and measured and scanned us and then dropped us in the waiting room with a diagnosis of mild concussion.

Fiorenze sat beside me, with her chin resting in her hands. She did not look happy. But then, we had almost died.

"My fairy's gone," I said.

She looked up. "Yes, I expect mine is too."

"I'm so happy," I said, though my head throbbed. "Did you see the way Nick looked at me? Pure hatred. It was beautiful! I wonder what my proto-fairy's going to be? Do you think it will come out of hiding now?"

"I don't know. It might be gone too, you know."

"Don't be silly. It's a proto-fairy, not a real fairy. Aren't you excited? Maybe you'll have a brand-new fairy too! Is it too much to hope for a shopping fairy?"

Fiorenze shuddered. "I hope not. I never want another fairy."

I stared at her. "You don't want a fairy? That's all I've ever wanted."

"I hate fairies," Fiorenze said. "I just want to be me on my own without their help. Their help is malodorous. I hope the parking fairy is truly gone."

"You don't know if it's gone?" I asked. "Don't you feel lighter? I feel lighter." Though that could have been the dizziness.

"It's not like there's been a chance to get in a car and test it. I assume it's gone. *I* definitely thought we were going to die."

"Me too! When we went flying off the track! Whoa! How far do you think we fell?"

"Stefan said it was only about a meter. How do you feel?" Fio asked. "I mean other than all jibbery about the fairy's absence."

"My head hurts."

"Me too. Our heads are rattled," Fiorenze said. "Thanks for vetoing the helmets."

"We'd still have our fairies if we'd worn helmets. Besides,

neither of us passed out. We only have mild concussion. That's nothing! Our near-death experience went perfectly."

Fiorenze forced a smile.

"Why so glum?" I asked her.

"We're in trouble," Fiorenze told me. "The bobsled was a write-off. And we racked up serious demerits for all the classes we skipped. The principal wants to see me."

"How do you know?"

"Doctor told me."

"Well, um, that might not be as bad as you think." I wondered why the principal hadn't asked to see me.

"It's the *principal*, Charlie. No one sees her unless things are bad. What if we get kicked out?"

"We won't be," I said, even though I was worried. "We're both good students. I mean, except for Accounting and Statistics and PR. But you're brilliant at those. And all your other compulsories. We're both at least top ten percent for our electives. You're captain of Basketball B! Plus we've got extenuating circumstances: our fairies. Not to mention Danders Anders's kidnappings. Surely they'll give us a break because of all of that?"

"I'll find out, won't I?" Fiorenze sounded mournful. "I love this school. I can't imagine having to go somewhere else. Ever since I was little this is where I wanted to go."

"Me too."

Dr. Tahn called me into her office again. She asked me again if I knew who the mayor was, and Our Zora-Anne, and what year it was, and what my name was. She didn't make any jokes. It was unnerving. This was Dr. Ha Ha! She always made the most injured jokes imaginable.

My heart squeezed tight in a way that made breathing awkward. Maybe we really were in danger of being expelled.

The feeling expanded when Dr. Tahn told me to report to the principal's office.

CHAPTER 40

Gambling

Demerits: 4
Game suspensions: 2
Public service hours: 35
~~Luges~~ bobsleds dragged up the ice: 1
~~Luges~~ bobsleds ridden down the ice: 2
Near deaths: 1

It was my first time.

Although I'd been in a lot of trouble, I'd never had to report to the principal. Only the most disruptive, disorderly, and difficult students went to the principal's office. Sometimes they didn't come back.

Fiorenze was already there. I smiled and waved, hoping a cheery front would quell the butterflies in my stomach. She nodded slightly.

"Charlotte Adele Donna Seto Steele?" called the stern-looking man seated behind the desk.

"That's me."

He scribbled something on his tablet. "Sit over there,"

he commanded, pointing to the seat farthest away from Fiorenze. "Not a word until you're called."

"Yes, sir."

I wiggled my fingers at Fiorenze. She smiled.

"No hand signals either, Ms. Steele. You are in trouble. You should adopt the demeanor of someone so situated."

I put my hands in my pockets, wondering how much worse I'd made my situation by annoying the principal's assistant.

He turned to Fiorenze. "You may go in now."

She stood up.

"Good luck," I said.

"Thanks," she said, walking past the assistant to the door behind him.

Now I just had to wait until it was my turn. The butterflies in my stomach were not as steady as they had been when I first came in. The thought of expulsion terrified them. Me too.

Whatever the principal asked me, I was going to tell the truth. And not just because being busted lying was a bad thing. The truth was on my side. I really hadn't been such a bad student. I would explain that. Explain how hard I'd worked and that I'd work even harder now that my malodorous fairies were gone. I'd promise whatever was asked. I'd go to public service every day, including Sundays. Whatever it took.

The assistant made half a dozen phone calls, most of which seemed to be about raising money, though after a while I noticed that Danders Anders's name kept coming up. I wondered if the powerful Water Polo Association was using its muscle to make sure that he graduated early so he could represent New Avalon in the world championships. Figured.

How many demerits did you get for breaking a luge? Or bobsled or whatever it was? Had Steffi being there saved us from that?

I looked at my watch and caught sight of the day, which rang a bell. Wednesday. What was special about this Wednesday?

Nettles. Her concert. Monkey Knife Fight. I'd promised I'd try and make it. Well, if I was expelled I certainly would. And if I wasn't expelled, then I'd find a way. I owed her. I'd been a slack sister this year.

The principal's door opened and Fiorenze came out. I couldn't read her face, but then, she'd never had a very readable face. She didn't look sad, but she didn't look happy either.

The butterflies were now having knife fights in my belly. Butterfly Knife Fight. I wondered how they'd do against Monkey Knife Fight. Butterflies were fragile and little and monkeys were big and hairy. But butterflies could fly. Maybe they'd flutter over the monkeys and drop their knives on them.

"Charlotte Adele Donna Seto Steele?" the principal's assistant said, pulling me away from the butterflies and monkeys.

"Yes, sir."

"The principal will see you now."

"Thank you, sir," I said and walked toward the door. I took a deep breath and walked through. It closed behind me. Must have been the assistant, but it felt like it closed on its own.

The principal was a tall white-haired woman with the lightest skin and eyes I'd ever seen. I hadn't realized it was possible to be that pale. I wondered if she had some rare skin disease and that's why she so rarely appeared before the students. Or maybe she was a vampire.

She held out her hand and we shook. Her grip was firm and her hand warm. Too warm for a vampire.

"Take a seat," she said, sitting herself on the sofa. I sat in the lounge chair.

"So how are you doing, Charlie? You've been racking up quite a few demerits, haven't you? You already had four and today you amassed eighteen. That's twenty-two altogether."

"Yes, Principal." Eighteen?! How many classes had I missed? I guess luge—bobsled—destruction warranted quite a few. Plus I hadn't gone to either recess or lunch, so I hadn't clocked in my calories. Maybe I was lucky it was *only* eighteen. If you could call waiting for your principal to tell you that you're expelled "lucky."

"Fiorenze tells me it's because of your fairy?" She sounded almost concerned. Velvet glove, iron fist, I reminded myself. She was going to be all sweet and kind and then throw me out on my ear.

I nodded. "I just wanted to get rid of it. I didn't want to get into trouble."

She nodded back at me sympathetically. "Too many people wanting to use you to park their cars?"

"Yes," I said. "And I don't even like cars."

"Me neither," she said. "Dreadful contraptions. I'd much rather walk. Or ride my bike."

"I love bikes. They make me happy. I miss them," I blurted.

She smiled. "I rode in five different Tours. I still ride whenever possible."

"That must have been great," I said. When was she going to interrogate me? Or was this her subtle way of doing it? Was this the velvet glove? "More fun than cars," I added.

"Andrew Khassian Rogers has been borrowing you to ride in his car quite a lot, hasn't he?" she asked. If anything she was looking even more sympathetic. It was disconcerting. "Tell me about it."

"Well," I said. Why was she asking me about Danders Anders?

The principal nodded, encouraging me to continue.

I told her all in a rush that even to my ears didn't quite make sense. "And this week," I finished, "he kidnapped me so my fairy came back even though it had been just about to disappear from all the walking. That's why me and Fiorenze swapped. I know everyone says it's impossible. But it really isn't. But then it turned out that her fairy was even worse, and that's why we broke the luge. I mean, bobsled. We're vastly sorry but I'm glad our fairies are gone. They were the worst fairies ever."

"I'm sure," she said. She sounded like she was humoring me.

"What's your fairy?" I blurted out. I couldn't help it.

"My fairy? I don't have one."

Did that mean she didn't believe in them? Steffi was the only person I knew with a fairy who didn't believe in them. If she didn't believe in fairies, then she'd never accept our explanations for how the luge or bobsled or whatever it was had been destroyed.

I was going to be kicked out of New Avalon Sports High. My life was over.

"And where did Andrew take you, Charlie?"

"Andrew?" I asked. "In his car, you mean?"

"Yes, where did he want to park?"

"All over."

"Can you be more exact?"

I wasn't sure. I hadn't been paying much attention. "Well, he took me to lots of places in town. There was this old terrace. And different shops and restaurants. Dana's Crabhouse, Tweezies, and Burt's something or other. And one skyscraper. The Connors building. It wasn't very big. For a skyscraper, I mean. And he'd go in for anywhere between ten minutes and an hour."

"Do you think if we drove around town you could spot the places again?"

I stared at her. This wasn't about me and my demerits. This was about Danders Anders.

"Yes," I said. "Most of them. At least two were on Chappel Street. Is Danders—I mean, is Andrew in trouble?"

"Charlie, you understand that this conversation is confidential? You can't discuss it with anyone else."

I nodded.

"Did Andrew ever give you money for helping him with his parking?"

"He used to. But he says he's got no money anymore. He said he'd pay me later."

"Did he say how he was going to get more?"

"No." I paused. "I don't think Dand—Andrew means to be bad. He's just . . . He thinks differently."

"Did Andrew tell you what he was doing at any of the places he made you stop?"

"No."

"Did he ever mention gambling to you?"

"What?!" That's what Danders had been doing? That's why he was broke now? "Is he going to be expelled?"

"I can't discuss that with you, Charlie. But I can tell you the charges against him are serious. Would you be prepared to tell a court what you have told me?"

I didn't know what to say. What would happen if I dobbed on Danders Anders? It's not like he'd kill me. He wasn't malicious. Would it jeopardize my career at school? Did the principal want me to testify or not?

Then I realized who the real danger was: the Water

267

Polo Association. They were notorious. They would definitely go after me for blackening the name of next year's star recruit!

"Charlie?" the principal asked.

"Um," I said.

"New Avalon Sports High will support you in whatever you decide, Charlie. You have my word that if you choose to testify there will be no repercussions. This school has put up with bad behavior from some of its star students over the years, but Andrew Khassian Rogers's behavior sets a new low. We will not tolerate it."

"Kidnapping and gambling are bad."

"Yes. Those are *not* his only infractions."

I wondered what else he'd done. He couldn't have thrown a game. Water Polo A hadn't lost once since he joined the team. "Do you know why he started gambling? Dan—Andrew's not a bad person. Maybe there was a reason he needed money?"

"Perhaps," was all she said before changing the subject. "You and Fiorenze will have to pay for a new bobsled. I have reduced your demerits to ten, which leaves you with one game suspension. Tennis, I believe. I advise you to keep up your public service until they are erased. Fiorenze assures me that you are unlikely to gather any more demerits now that your fairy is gone."

"Yes, Principal. Thank you, Principal." I'd never heard of anyone having that many demerits wiped out before.

"Good luck, Charlie. And let me know what you decide. Do not talk about this with anyone."

"I won't, Principal."

"You may return to class, Charlie, if you'd like. Dr. Tahn says you should be fine, but if you'd prefer to rest or go home, you may."

"Thank you, Principal," I said, going out the now open door.

CHAPTER 41

Friends Again

Demerits: 10
Game suspensions: 3
Public service hours: 35
~~Luges~~ bobsleds dragged up the ice: 1
~~Luges~~ bobsleds ridden down the ice: 2
Near deaths: 1
Visits to the principal: 1

The first thing I heard in Fencing was that Water Polo A had lost its first game in three years that morning.

Fiorenze and I stared at each other. Danders Anders had offered her *lots* of money when he'd grabbed her. But on Wednesday he hadn't had any. He'd even asked if he could borrow some for gas.

Wow. I hadn't quite believed what the principal had told me. Now I did. Fiorenze and me, we didn't speak to each other; instead we warmed up as diligently as we could. I'd promised the principal I wouldn't rack up any more demerits. I imagined Fiorenze had made the same promise. I was desperate to be good; the basketball tryouts were just around the corner.

My first bout was against Steffi. He smiled and a tingle shot through me. But the smile didn't stay very long, and he didn't kiss me, or even slip his arm around me. I wondered where we stood now that my fairy was gone.

We plugged in and stepped onto the piste and were about to salute and put our masks on when Steffi said, "We have to talk."

"Oh," I said. According to Sandra people always say that before they tell you things you do not want to hear. In my experience—especially with my parents—she is entirely correct.

"Can't it wait till after the bout?" I asked, looking around nervously for Coach, even though I was pretty sure Steffi's fairy was protecting us.

"Why did you swap fairies with Fiorenze?" he asked. I wished he had the mask on, because the expression on his face was not tingly at all.

"Why?" I said, wishing I knew what the right thing to say was. "Because it was the easiest way to get rid of my parking fairy. It was driving me insane. Danders Anders kidnapped me! I didn't realize how horrible Fio's fairy would be. I stupidly thought nothing could be worse than a parking fairy. I was wrong."

"But why didn't you swap with someone else?"

"Fio was the only one who knew how. I mean her

mother was. Or, rather, the book. Whatever. It was just me and Fio. There wasn't anyone else."

"Hmm," Steffi said. I wished I knew what he was thinking. Was there a fairy for that?

"Swapping was the easiest way, Steffi. Much easier than nearly dying." My head still hurt. "And the bleaching thing looked just as dangerous. And to be honest I didn't really understand the flensing and grunching options."

"Huh?"

"Why are you asking, Steffi? I thought you didn't believe in fairies?"

"I didn't," he said. "I mean, I was agnostic."

"But you do now?"

He nodded very slowly. "Maybe. It's hard to explain swapping luck and scaring luck away. But tiny invisible luck-giving creatures? Well, it's still a stretch, you know?"

Not for me it wasn't. "You should come to Fio's house. Her mom has a mirror where you can see your fairy's aura. Maybe that will help you."

"Maybe. You didn't swap with Fio to get me to like you, did you?"

"No way!" I lied stoutly. Well, it wasn't entirely a lie. But him liking me wasn't my entire motivation. When Fio said swap, that's what I'd thought about finally knowing for sure that Steffi really liked me. No uncertainty. "Who told you that?"

"Heather Sandol."

"You can't believe anything she says. She *hates* the boy

fairy because it works on her boyfriend really strongly. You wouldn't believe how much she hated Fiorenze, and then when I got Fio's fairy her hatred went to me."

"So your swapping with Fio had nothing to do with me?" He pressed the tip of his foil into the piste, leaning into it so the thin blade bowed out in a half circle. If he leaned on it any harder it might snap.

"Fairy's honor," I said, even though that wasn't true. "You wouldn't believe how happy I am to be rid of that thing! It was worse than the parking fairy." Which was true. The fairy had made Steffi act as though he liked me, but that's all it was. Not one of his fairy-inspired kisses had been as good as when he'd kissed me in front of my house. That kiss had entirely come from him. No fairy involvement at all. (Well, except to keep us out of trouble.)

"A fairy like that shouldn't be allowed to exist," Steffi said, leaning harder on the foil.

"No," I said. The world would be much better off without it. "So you believe in the boy fairy now?"

"Whatever it was, I believe in it." He took a little of his weight off the foil and wiped his forehead. "I really kissed Fio, didn't I? A bunch of times. Even when she didn't want me to."

I could have done without hearing him say that.

"She's not my type. I'm not her type. It was horrible."

"Really?" I couldn't help asking.

"Completely horrible." He nodded emphatically. "Also I got into a fight with Heather Sandol and, well, she got a game suspension, but the teacher apologized to me for the disturbance, when I fought just as hard as Heather."

"Huh."

"Something keeps me out of trouble. It always has." He unbent the foil completely.

"Yes."

"I don't remember *ever* getting into trouble. But if I convince my 'fairy' that I'm about to die I'll get rid of it?" he asked.

"Or you could bleach or grunch your way out of it. But why would you want to, Steffi?"

"It's not right my having that kind of luck. Think of the things I could do with it," he said, stabbing his foil back into the piste.

"But you never do any of those things. Not on purpose." I thought about his set of lock picks. "Well, except for helping us with the luge thing. You just decided fairies were nonsense."

"You think I was a denier because I was scared of my own good fortune?" he asked, looking at me so intently I thought I would melt.

"Could be. Look, Tamsin says most people get their fairy for a reason. She also says that fairies don't die. If you flense or grunch a fairy away, someone else winds up with it. What if your fairy goes to someone who'll use it to do bad stuff?"

"Oh," he said. "I hadn't thought of that."

"In what way do you two think standing on the piste

274

gossiping will contribute to your foil skills?" Coach Van Dyck demanded.

"Sorry, Coach," I said.

"My fault," Steffi said.

We saluted each other and put our masks on. This bout I won.

CHAPTER 42
Monkey Knife Fight

Demerits: 10
Game suspensions: 3
Public service hours: 35
~~Luges~~ bobsleds dragged up the ice: 1
~~Luges~~ bobsleds ridden down the ice: 2
Near deaths: 1
Visits to the principal: 1

I decided to skip public service that night and see Monkey Knife Fight like Nettles wanted. I went straight home on the bus with Steffi. We teased each other the whole way—he called me an Avaloid, I called him a Raven Head, and he was pleased that I'd remembered he came from Ravenna—and I thought about asking him what I should do about testifying against Danders Anders. But I'd promised the principal I wouldn't talk to anyone about it.

It felt good to be friends again. He might not like me in a let's-get-linked way, but at least he still wanted to hang out.

"You really love the school, don't you?" Steffi asked.

"Of course. It's the best school in the world."

He was staring at me kind of funny. Then he shook his head. "I thought you were all brainwashed."

My turn to stare at him. "Brainwashed!"

"But you're not. None of you are. You really do love it. The long hours. All the work—"

"I'm doing what I've always wanted, poxbrain. Sports! Almost every minute of every day! What's not to love?" I pulled out my lucky cricket ball and spun it high. "Other than Accounting and PR and—"

"It's not what I'm used to, that's all."

"Nothing but slacker schools on the West Coast, eh?"

"Something like that."

"I'd like to visit Ravenna. A proper visit, not just for an away game."

Steffi smiled.

"You were right," I said.

"About what in particular?" he asked.

"My head hurts."

"Well, you had a mild concussion," Steffi pointed out. "Though it didn't stop you taking that bout from me today." He didn't lean forward to rub my temples or anything. When I had the fairy he would've done that. Not that I wanted it back. Friendship with Steffi was way better than his zombie love.

"It's only a mild concussion. And my head doesn't hurt from that." I searched for the words. These were new thoughts for me. "I've been thinking about some of the things you said. About us Avaloids and our blindness. We are a little bit—"

"Very. You are very self-obsessed. 'Self-obsessed' is too mild a word for how you people are."

I nodded, though it felt somewhat injured to be agreeing. "And the almost Ours at school like Danders get away with too much," I said, realizing that I was going to testify against him. "That isn't right."

"No, it isn't."

"Wanna hang out Sunday?" I asked. "We can scrimmage."

"Sure," Steffi said. "Sounds like fun. I can help you practice for the tryouts."

Even if he wasn't ever going to be my boyfriend I was pretty sure Steffi would support me while I did the whole scary courthouse thing. Rochelle and Fiorenze would too. Probably Sandra. And definitely my parents. I hoped the principal would too. I didn't think she was lying.

Maybe they'd even manage to protect me from the Water Polo Association.

◆ ◆ ◆

As soon as I got home I went straight up to Nettles's room. She was lying on her bed wearing the Monkey Knife Fight T-shirt, with her headphones on. I knocked on the door. She didn't stir. I signaled for her to take them off. She didn't.

I stood at the foot of her bed, spinning my lucky cricket ball back and forth from hand to hand. She hates that.

"What?" she asked at last.

"I skipped public service," I announced.

"What?" she asked louder.

"Turn the music down!"

She did, but kept the headphones on.

"I skipped public service. I'm coming to your concert."

"Really?" she asked.

"Really," I said.

"You're going to come see Monkey Knife Fight?"

"Yes."

"Will you put proper clothes on?" she asked, taking off her headphones. "Not your uniform, or training sweats, but actual proper clothes? Will you leave your cricket ball at home?"

"Yes," I said, catching the ball with my left hand and holding it behind my back. "I'll wear whatever you want me to wear."

"Really?" Nettles's eyes lit up.

I realized I might have been rash. "Unless it's shiny, or purple, or has a unicorn on it, or is in some other way injured."

"As if." Nettles jumped up and walked into my room, throwing open the wardrobe doors. I followed at the pace of someone with mild concussion.

"You're wearing this," she announced when I caught up with her. She was holding up the emerald green dress that Rochelle had bought for me at the fashion fair. It would be my first chance to wear it.

"With these," she said. She pointed out the black knee-high boots Rochelle had bullied me into buying last winter. I'd only worn them once.

"Okay," I said. As I looked up from the boots a flash went off. I blinked. "Nettles—"

"And you have to not complain about how many photos I take," she said, taking several more. "And let me do your hair."

"Sure," I said. "Whatever you want. Take photos! Steal my soul! Make me leave my lucky cricket ball at home! And, yes, you can do my hair." I said the last bit like it was a concession, but I was pleased. Nettles is gifted with hair.

"So how come you can make it tonight?" Nettles asked.

"I can't. Didn't you listen? I'm skipping public service to be there. I'm doing it for you."

"Well, don't expect me to kiss you or anything."

"Erk."

"What's that I hear?" Mom said, sticking her head into my bedroom. "You're coming tonight? Lovely! Now I can take the car!"

"I don't have a parking fairy anymore, Mom. I got rid of it."

"Yes, dear." Clearly she didn't believe me.

"Really, Mom. It's gone."

"But you got in the car with that sweet boy Andrew Rogers."

"Mom, he's not—"

"Just because he's a bit slow does not mean he's not sweet. He buried Nettles's dog for her."

"Mom," Nettles interjected. "That's because he accidentally—"

"Now hush, Nettles. Neither of you look even close to being ready. I want you both in the car in half an hour."

"Mom, we can't take the car. My parking fairy is truly gone."

"Darling, I know you want it to be gone. But everyone knows that the only effective way of getting rid of a fairy is to not do the things it wants you to do, and you've been providing it with parking spots."

"Mom, there are other ways."

"Half an hour," she said. "Charlie, I know you were in some trouble today. I could be asking you all about it. But I'm not. Now can you and your sister please get ready?"

"Yes, Mom," we chorused.

◆　◆　◆

Mom circled the New Avalon Stadium six times looking for a parking spot.

I didn't say a word.

"Why don't you just pay for the valet parking, love," Dad said.

"It's fifty dollars! That's an outrage. I've never paid for valet parking."

"I told you," Dad said. "This fairy business is nonsense.

Charlie does not have a parking fairy now, because she's never had a parking fairy."

Nettles rolled her eyes. "Mom! We're going to be late. Please can you valet park? Please! I've been looking forward to this concert since the beginning of time!"

Or two weeks. I guess when you're twelve that seems like forever. Actually even at fourteen a couple of weeks can seem vastly long. Like the last two for instance.

"Fine," Mom said between gritted teeth, pulling up beside the parking valet. She glanced at me in the rearview mirror and Nettles took a photo. Mom ignored her. "No parking fairy, eh?"

"No."

"This, I want to hear about."

We didn't see Danders Anders at the concert that night. Not that I missed him—I imagined I was going to see a lot of him when I testified against him—but I think he would have enjoyed it. Monkey Knife Fight were in fabulous form. They would have destroyed my butterflies within seconds.

CHAPTER 43

Reckoning

Demerits: 10 − 4 = 6
Game suspensions: 3
Public service hours: 39
~~Luges~~ bobsleds dragged up the ice: 1
~~Luges~~ bobsleds ridden down the ice: 2
Near deaths: 1
Visits to the principal: 1
Monkey Knife Fight concerts seen: 1

Saturday I had an inter-school tennis tournament. Except that I didn't on account of my game suspension. I tried not to think what the suspension would do to my rankings.

I spent the day doing public service. Six long hours, which, added to the four hours I'd done Thursday and Friday nights, left me with no demerits. I was free! I fell into bed knackered but happy, planning to sleep until noon, maybe catch up on homework, and best of all hang out with Steffi.

Instead Mom woke me just after nine. "Someone here to see you."

Steffi! I quickly forgave him for showing up so early on a Sunday morning. I threw on some clothes and dashed down the stairs.

Dr. Tamsin Burnham-Stone, not Steffi, was sitting in the living room chatting with my dad, all companionable and happy happy. Fiorenze sat next to her with her head bowed.

"Look," Dad said when he noticed me at the bottom of the stairs, "Dr. Burnham—"

"Tamsin," she said, looking at me with the opposite of a smile. The happy happy was only for Dad.

"Tamsin. Right. Sorry." He turned back to me. "Tamsin's offered to take you and Fiorenze to the beach for the day." Dad's voice sounded a little strained, like he knew something was up, but not what. "Isn't that kind of her? I know you have a lot of homework to catch up on, though."

"Huh," I said. It was so sweet of Dad to give me an out. "Sure," I said. I was in trouble. Best to get it over with. I tried not to think about how Sundays were my only day off, about how much I'd been looking forward to spending a whole day with Steffi. "The beach would be astral."

◆　◆　◆

It wasn't, of course. Not even slightly. And not just because we didn't go to the beach.

For the entire drive to the Burnham-Stones' house

Tamsin said nothing. But she said it loudly. The air around me felt tight and difficult to draw into my lungs. Like when you're running a marathon and close to meltdown—the air thickens.

Us two girls were quiet too. Not just on account of the gluggy air, but because I was in the backseat and she was in the front. I leaned back and closed my eyes. What was the worst thing she could do? Other than make the air too thick to breathe?

Well, let's see, on account of she's Dr. Tamsin Burnham-Stone, the person who knows more about fairies than anyone else in the entire world, she could take away my proto-fairy. She could give us boring fairies: a footpath fairy or a loose-change fairy. Or she could make sure we had no fairy at all.

She pulled into the garage and led us up through the house, the thick air traveling with her. I was starting to get a headache. Fiorenze kept her head down, so I couldn't even exchange eyebrow raises, or smiles of reassurance, or anything.

She opened the door to the fairy room and gestured to me and Fiorenze to go through. "Notice anything?" she said.

I did: I had no aura. I stared at my reflection. No fairy at all? Where was my proto-fairy?

Fiorenze had no aura either, but she hadn't had a proto-fairy.

"You frightened it away," she said. "Just like your parking fairy."

"I made it go away? But it was a proto-fairy. I thought the nearly dying thing only worked on real fairies!"

"You thought wrong." Tamsin looked at me. It was the same look Fiorenze gave me when she thought I was being slow. "Did you read the chapter on the dangers of fairy removal? Side effects? Contraindications? Or just the removal of fairies chapter?"

"Just that one." I looked at the locked metal box that contained *The Ultimate Fairy Book*. It was just where we'd left it.

"So you did get into my book?"

"Oh," I said. "Um." I glanced at Fio. Her chin was up, but she still wasn't making eye contact. "My fault. I bullied Fio into it."

"How did you know about my book?" Her tone of voice didn't sound cross, but then neither did my dad's when he was mad. Even when he was so furious his face was turning red. The air was thicker. I was pretty sure she was several varieties of angry. "How?"

I opened my mouth.

"I told her," Fiorenze said. She didn't sound afraid. She looked directly at her mother, who returned the stare.

I closed my mouth.

"You told her about the book," her mother said. "The book I expressly told you on more occasions than I care to recall that you must never tell anyone about? That you must never go near? You disobeyed me?"

"Yes."

"Knowing that I would punish you?" Tamsin's expression was scary. Her lips had thinned and her eyes looked hard.

"Yes," Fio said firmly.

"Why?"

And why didn't Fiorenze seem even a little bit intimidated by her mother? Maybe the thick air had broken her brain. Lack of oxygen and all that.

"Because I wanted to get rid of my fairy and you wouldn't help me." Fiorenze didn't sound sad; she was simply telling the truth.

"I told you how to get rid of it: stay away from boys."

"I did. It didn't work."

"Then you weren't trying hard enough," Tamsin said.

"Yes, she was!" I protested. Neither of them looked at me. I don't think they even heard me. They were staring at each other so intently that I shifted to watching them in the mirrors. It was gentler on my eyeballs that way.

I couldn't believe Fiorenze was talking to her mother like that. My parents had always treated me and Nettles like adults—well, not exactly—but not like we were little kids. They would let us say our bit, but eventually in an argument the I-am-your-parent boot would come down. Where was Dr. Burnham-Stone's boot?

"Did you give it enough time?" she asked, not sounding nearly as cranky as she had. Her lips were big again. "You're always so impatient, Fio. That method can take more than a year."

Fiorenze *impatient*? I'd only started to get to know her, but I had not noticed that. The opposite more like. Did Tamsin know *anything* about her daughter?

"I gave it oodles of time. I didn't say a word to any boy for more than a year! It *didn't* work!"

"Then you should have come to me."

"I did! You told me to go away. You don't listen to me."

"Of course I listen to you, darling. But sometimes I'm busy," Tamsin said, looking away from her daughter. Fiorenze was going to win this argument, I decided. Her mother had looked away first.

"You're *always* busy. I was sick of you being busy so I decided to look in your book and Charlie helped me and now we've gotten rid of our fairies and we're much happier. So I don't care what you think. I don't care if you send me to boarding school." Fio put her hands on her hips. For a second she looked like Nettles in her patented I-defy-you stance. Only Fiorenze wasn't sticking out her tongue. I had to look away to keep from giggling.

"We will discuss your punishment later. Your lack of remorse shocks me. You have jeopardized my career, exposing research I have been at great pains to keep secret—"

"Why?" I asked, turning from their reflections. Tamsin stared at me with a faintly surprised expression like she'd forgotten I was there.

"Yes, why?" Fiorenze asked. "Why does it have to be a secret?"

"Why?" her mother repeated. "That's obvious."

"No, it's not. Why don't you want people to know how to get rid of their fairies? Or attract new ones?"

"My research is incomplete. It's not ready."

"Tamsin, we saw your book. We read whole chapters," Fiorenze said. *Parts of whole chapters*, I amended in my head. "We tested some of your research and it worked exactly as you said. Both swapping and nearly dying. It's a great book."

"You didn't read all of it," Tamsin said. She was looking down now and her voice had gotten quieter. Almost like she didn't believe what she was saying. "Other parts are inconclusive. I need more evidence, more time. Fairies have only been with us for such a short amount of time. Only three or four generations.

"That's not a reason," Fiorenze objected. "Why don't you want to share the book?" She was staring at her mother so intently she reminded me of Coach Van Dyck.

Tamsin looked up quickly and her hand moved. For a second I thought she was going to hit her daughter. "I am not a sloppy scholar," she said at last.

"Why won't you share it?" Fiorenze asked again. She took a step closer to her mother.

"It's complicated," Tamsin said.

"Your book is brilliant," Fio said. "Waverly has five books and none of them are anywhere near yours."

"You read them all?" Tamsin asked.

"Well, I tried," Fiorenze said, "but they were kind of boring. Your book isn't boring at all. It's useful."

Had Fiorenze read the same book I did? The introduction had been vastly boring! All those endless examples and quotes.

"I *can't* publish it!" Tamsin exclaimed, crouching beside the metal box and putting her hand on it protectively, as if we were about to grab it and run off to a publisher, which I for one had no idea how to do. I didn't even know if there were any publishers in New Avalon. It occurred to me that Dr. Burnham-Stone simply did not want to share her baby.

"Yes, you can," Fiorenze said. "I bet there are publishers all over the world who would love to publish your book. I mean, if Dad could get his published. And that last one even paid him money."

"You'd be famous!" I added.

Fiorenze shot me a glance that said that wasn't the best argument to use.

"Think about all the people you'd be helping," I said.

"Yes. Wouldn't it be easier to have it available to everyone?" Fiorenze suggested. "Instead of feeling all choked up from being the only one who knows everything there is to know about fairies?"

Tamsin stood up, staring at her daughter.

"Maybe you're just afraid of finishing it," Fiorenze continued. "It's your life's work, isn't it? But you can keep researching and writing after it's published, you know. It will be so popular everyone will be clamoring for the next volume."

"How did you know?" Tamsin said. In the mirror her fairy aura was darker. I wondered what that meant.

Fiorenze sucked her teeth. I couldn't believe she'd just sucked her teeth at her mom! Mine would kill me if I ever did that. I'd be grounded forever!

"You can both go," her mother said. "I need to think about this."

Fiorenze walked toward the door, then turned to beckon me when I didn't follow. She was probably relieved her mom hadn't used the word "punishment" again.

"So, um, Tamsin, how do I get a new fairy?" I asked.

"What makes you think you deserve a new fairy?"

Because I'm going to testify against Danders Anders, I almost said out loud.

"Well?"

"Maybe I don't," I said. "But I'd like one. I'd hate to have gone through all that walking everywhere, getting all those demerits, almost dying, to wind up with nothing." Though as I said it I realized I hadn't ended up with nothing: I had Steffi and a brand-new friend in Fiorenze. "But it wouldn't kill me not to have one."

Fiorenze grinned. "That's the spirit!"

CHAPTER 44

Fairy Attracting

Demerits: 0
Game suspensions: 3
Public service hours: 45
~~Luges~~ bobsleds dragged up the ice: 1
~~Luges~~ bobsleds ridden down the ice: 2
Near deaths: 1
Visits to the principal: 1
Monkey Knife Fight concerts seen: 1
Friend acquired: Fiorenze Burnham-Stone

Tamsin took me up to the roof. Fiorenze didn't join us. She didn't want to be anywhere near someone getting a new fairy—just in case it accidentally wound up on her.

Tamsin made me lie on my back with dozens of red, yellow, green, blue, orange, and purple paper streamers tied around my arms and legs. The colors all clashed.

Then nothing.

She sat down in a comfy deck chair while I lay there. I would have fallen asleep but it wasn't even slightly comfortable and the sun was making my eyes water. I would have looked at my watch but Tamsin had made me take it off. She said it interfered with fairy energies. I tried to daydream about the tryouts and making it into B-stream basketball, but I kept getting distracted by the gravel under my back, and sore eyes.

After a while I started to suspect that this was Tamsin's revenge. "Am I allowed to talk?"

"If you want," she said, not looking at me. Not very encouraging. This really was my punishment: death by sunstroke and boredom.

"Does it matter what color the streamers are?" I asked. If this worked I was going to do it for Nettles. She'd always wanted a fairy.

"Yes."

"Or what they're made of?"

"Yes."

"Are the colors in any particular order?"

"Why do you ask?"

"Just curious. Would it work if you did it inside?"

"No."

"You know, Dr. Burnham-Stone—"

"Tamsin."

"Tamsin. I think you'll have to give more detailed answers when you turn *The Ultimate Fairy Book* into a real book."

"The what?" This time she looked at me.

"Your book. When it's a proper book with a pretty cover and everything. It will have to have detailed answers. You'll have to stop being vague."

"Is that what you call it? *The Ultimate Fairy Book?*"

"That's what Fio calls it." I paused. "Because she thinks it's so doos. It's the *ultimate* fairy book. The book which there is no book more ultimate than. I think it should have glitter on the cover."

"Not a very scholarly title. Maybe if I used a colon . . ."

Wasn't a colon part of your intestines? I decided not to ask. She'd gone back to her thinking place. At least the air wasn't thick anymore. I wondered how much longer I had to lie here sweating. The deck wasn't very clean. I could feel the grit under my hands and just to my right was a big pile of bird droppings. I hoped I wasn't lying on any. Erk! My stomach growled and I realized I hadn't had any breakfast and it was now well into lunchtime.

I wished the stupid fairy would hurry up.

Not that I meant that negative thought. I didn't want to attract a cranky fairy. Though Tamsin said they couldn't hear your thoughts or your words. If they did, then they would have known that we'd been planning to scare them and that we weren't going to die and they wouldn't have jumped off us. Or maybe there really had been a chance that we could've died? I wondered what Ravenna was like. Steffi said he used to surf a lot so it must have decent beaches too.

Tamsin stood up. "All done."

"You're sure?" I didn't feel any different. Well, hotter and sweatier, but I didn't feel particularly fairied. I couldn't feel an extra weight on me.

"There's one way to find out."

Back in the magic fairy room the mirrors reflected a dirty, sweaty me surrounded by a brilliant green aura. I squealed. "Fairy! I have a new fairy!"

"Congratulations," Fiorenze said. "I hope it's better than the last two."

I couldn't argue with that. "So what do you think it is, Tamsin?"

She shrugged. "Could be anything. You'll find out."

CHAPTER 45

True Best Fairy Ever

Demerits: 0
Game suspensions: 3
Public service hours: 45
~~Luges~~ bobsleds dragged up the ice: 1
~~Luges~~ bobsleds ridden down the ice: 2
Near deaths: 1
Visits to the principal: 1
Monkey Knife Fight concerts seen: 1
Friend acquired: Fiorenze Burnham-Stone
Good fairies acquired: 1?

The basketball tryouts passed by like a dream, except that my eyes were open, I remembered most of it, and my friends were there to cheer me on.

I made the team.

More than that: they zapped me past D- and C-stream and straight into B-stream basketball.

And I found out what my new fairy is.

I thought I would find out a lot sooner. I went shopping

with Rochelle, Sandra, and Fiorenze every day for a week, but the only time the shopping fairy worked for me, it also worked for Sandra and Fiorenze, but mostly it worked for Ro. I didn't have a loose-change-finding fairy either, my hair was as messy or tidy as I made it, and my demerit for being late to tennis ruled out a fairy as doos as Steffi's.

I was starting to think that Tamsin's mirror was lying or that my new fairy was the subtlest fairy in the known universe.

Until the basketball tryouts. Steffi watched with Rochelle, Sandra, and Fiorenze.

I shot twenty out of twenty free throws. And after the dribbling drills Rochelle gave me the thumbs-up. Then they paired us off with C- and B-stream players for a little defensive practice under the hoop. They shot and us wannabes had to stop them. Simple.

They paired me with Lucinda Hopkinson.

She turned to me and grinned. Evilly. Lucinda's even taller than Rochelle. Wider too. There's more of her in every possible direction.

Have I mentioned that I'm short? When Lucinda held the ball, just casually resting against her stomach, it was at my eye level. Barely.

I looked across at where my friends were sitting. They all waved. Steffi held up his hands so that I could see that his fingers were crossed for luck. I was going to need more than luck.

Coach Suravein threw Lucinda the ball and blew her whistle. I trotted over and looked up at Lucinda. Her head wasn't far from the basket. She was still grinning.

I stood in front of the basket with my arms out, bouncing on my toes ready to try and look like I had a chance of getting between her and scoring. Or at least trying to look as if I could stop someone if they happened to be considerably shorter than Lucinda. It was like a quokka trying to take down a dinosaur.

The coach blew her whistle again.

Lucinda dribbled the ball a few times lazily, like she didn't even have to try in the face of my underwhelming defense. She lofted it up, over my head—

—and off the tips of my fingers, the ball bouncing from the backboard, all momentum gone, glancing the outside of the rim as it fell.

I had blocked her shot.

Lucinda stared at me. I stared at her. Both of our mouths were open.

I looked at my fingers to see if they'd suddenly turned into meter-long snakes or something.

I'd blocked her shot. Tiny me had blocked gigantic Lucinda's shot. The first in my entire basketball career.

"Did you . . . ," Lucinda began and then trailed off.

"I saw it," Coach Suravein said. She shook her head. "Okay, let's go again." She tossed a ball to Lucinda.

This time she didn't mess around. She dribbled,

stepped back, and executed a fade-away rainbow shot, arcing high over my head.

I jumped. Straight up as if my legs were made of bouncy rubber. I smacked the ball away with the center of my left palm.

"No way," Lucinda said. "How is that even possible? How did you *do* that?"

I showed her my palms. The left one was still red. I had no idea how I'd done that.

"Is that usual for you?" Coach asked.

"Um," I said. It felt natural to leap up and smack the ball away, as if I'd been blocking shots all my life.

"Another try?" Coach said, looking at Lucinda.

"I guess so." She cracked her neck in both directions.

The whistle blew.

Lucinda dribbled to my left. I went with her, waving my hands at her chin. She switched right, then left, then back again. I stayed with her, kept my hands and feet moving. She bounced the ball between her legs, feinted left, and then shot.

I was already jumping, already swatting it away.

"Shot-blocking fairy," I thought as I landed.

"Shot-blocking fairy," Fiorenze said, coming over and holding out her hand.

We shook. Rochelle grabbed me in a bear hug. Then Sandra. And last of all Steffi.

He kissed me too. On the mouth. It made my head

throb and my heart swell and all sorts of strange feelings flood through me. Just like our first kiss and nothing like the fairy-driven ones.

"You are doosness personified," he told me when he finally let me go. "Awesome new fairy."

"Isn't it?" I said, smiling so hard it almost hurt. Steffi, Rochelle, Fiorenze, and Sandra grinned right back at me.

This fairy was a keeper.

DEMERITS AND SUSPENSIONS

Every time a teacher catches a student committing an infraction (doing something they're not supposed to) they issue them one or more demerits. Game suspensions mean that you have to miss your next game. Here's how you rack them up:

8 demerits = 1 game suspension
12 demerits = 2 game suspensions
16 demerits = 3 game suspensions
20 demerits = 4 game suspensions
25 demerits = 5 game suspensions = 1 school suspension

After that you're venturing into expulsion territory, and no one wants to go there.

LIST OF KNOWN FAIRIES

All boys will like you: Fiorenze's fairy.

Bacon: Ensures your bacon is always cooked just how you like it.

Bladder: You never need to go in the middle of a movie, and when you do need to go there's always a bathroom around.

Cat: All cats like you even if they bite or scratch everyone else.

Charisma: A fairy that seems to mostly hang out with Ours; or maybe they *become* Ours because they have this fairy.

Clean clothes: No one will ever spill ketchup on your white sweater again. Boring but useful.

Clothes shopping: Rochelle's fairy. I am *so* jealous.

Dog: All dogs like you even if they bite or pee on everyone else.

Ears like a fox: The existence of this fairy is only rumored. Oddly enough, only teachers and parents seem to have it.

Eyes in the back of the head: Another rumored fairy, which is also supposedly possessed only by teachers and parents.

Footpath: Your guess is as good as mine.

Getting out of trouble: Steffi's fairy.

Good hair: This would also be nice.

Good skin: As would this.

Good story: Even when bad things happen to you, this fairy turns them into an excellent story. When writers have this fairy, they always get great ideas—which is not that fabulous given that *writing* the good ideas is the hard part, not *getting* them.

Grip: Danders Anders's fairy: whatever he picks up stays in his hands until he decides to let it go.

Jukebox: Waverly Burnham-Stone's fairy.

Knowing what your children are up to: Charlie's mom's fairy.

Loose change finding: One of the most common fairies.

Monkey: All monkeys like you even if they bite or scratch or fling poo at everyone else.

Never being late: This sounds a bit more like a curse than a blessing.

Never getting cold: Another fairy I'd love to have.

Never getting lost: I've met a couple of people with this one. Dead useful.

Parking: Charlie's fairy. Something only crazy car-loving types would want.

Photogenic: The fairy that means you look great in every photo ever taken of you.

Serving (tennis): Sandra's fairy.

Setting students on fire: There's no proof this fairy actually exists.

Sleep: I'm not sure about this fairy. I really enjoy sleeping, but on the other hand, being able to get by with little or no sleep without being cranky or hallucinating or having accidents—that'd be good.

Stealing: The Burnham-Stone family fairy. Definitely dodgy.

Surfer: With this fairy you can catch any wave.

GLOSSARY

astral: excellent, wondrous, fabulous

benighted: horrible, bad, miserable

dirty on: cranky with

doos: cool, ace, brilliant

doxhead: an annoying person

doxy: crappy, irritating, terrible

fairy dung: a cranky expletive

hoick: to hoist abruptly, to pull sharply

injured: lame, uncool, the opposite of "doos"

knackered: tired, exhausted, drained

malodorous: hideous, wrong, dismal

Our: a celebrity from New Avalon. So called because New Avaloners think all celebrities belong to them, thus Our Zora-Anne

pox: exclamation of dismay

poxy: badly behaved, mischievous, exasperating

pulchritudinous, pulchy: beautiful, good-looking, attractive

spoffs: breasts

stellar: superlative, splendid

stoush: fight

torpid: boring, injured, sucktastic

XI: in cricket the team is called an "eleven," because there are eleven members on the team—only it is spelled in Roman numerals, as in the New Avalon XI. Charlie is a member of the New Avalon Sports High B Stream XI

ACKNOWLEDGMENTS

This book is a bit of a departure from my previous publications, so I was nervous about finding the right publisher. My fabulous agent, Jill Grinberg, never had any doubts. She gave me brilliant feedback and found it the perfect home at Bloomsbury. Thank you for everything, Jill. Thanks also to Katherine Cremeans and Kirsten Wolf. Not sure what I'd do without you three.

I don't want to think about what this book would have been without my editor, Melanie Cecka. She improved it in a million zillion different ways. She's a genius. I'd also like to thank everyone at Bloomsbury for being so welcoming and supportive. And Regina Castillo for doing such a great copyedit.

Stephen Gamble has a parking fairy, and it was he and Ron Serdiuk who gave me the idea for this book in the first place. Christine Alesich asked me to write a story for her Aussie Bites series and so I started writing, but what I thought would be a longish short story became a novel. Sorry, Christine!

Many of the first names of the characters in this book are borrowed from teenagers I met doing appearances in libraries, schools, and book shops in Australia and the USA. It's been a blast meeting you all. I hope you enjoy the little shout-out, and if I didn't borrow your name it doesn't mean I love you less!

Thank you so much to my first-draft readers: Holly Black, Gwenda Bond, Pamela Freeman, Maureen Johnson, Jan Larbalestier, Diana Peterfreund, Ron Serdiuk, Delia Sherman, Scott Westerfeld, and Lili Wilkinson. This book would be crap without you.

Thanks also to the New Bitches and all the folks at YA drinks night, especially David Levithan, who organizes it and keeps us all in touch with one another.

Maureen Johnson, Jennifer Laughran, Diana Peterfreund, Cherie Priest, John Scalzi, and many others came up with some great ideas for fairies. Bless. And thanks for all the procrastinatory online chats. Knowing there are others avoiding work is all that keeps me going.

Thank you so much, Libba Bray, for coming up with the title for this book. What would I do without you?

A million thanks to the readers of my blog for all their encouragement, conversation, and general fabulosity while I was writing this novel (or, as it used to be called, the Great Australian Elvis mangosteen cricket feminist monkey knife-fighting fairy book).

Five years of being a New York Liberty season ticket holder has completely transformed the way I think about women and sports and was a direct inspiration for this book. I'd like to thank the Liberty and the WNBA and all women athletes everywhere and at every level. Charlie would not exist without you.

This novel owes a huge debt to all the wonderful books on cricket I've read over the years. The books of Mike Coward, Ramachandra Guha, Gideon Haigh, and C. L. R. James in particular have been wonderfully inspiring. Thank you.

Lastly, all the love in the world to Jan, John, and Niki Bern and Scott Westerfeld.

Justine Larbalestier definitely has a novel-writing
fairy, and her next book is totally different, kind of
scary, and completely honest . . . *probably*.

Read on a for a sneak peek

PROMISE

I was born with a light covering of fur.

After three days it had all fallen off, but the damage was done. My mother stopped trusting my father because it was a family condition he had not told her about. One of many omissions and lies.

My father is a liar and so am I.

But I'm going to stop. I *have* to stop.

I will tell you my story and I will tell it straight. No lies, no omissions.

That's my promise.

This time I truly mean it.

———

BEFORE

The first two days of my freshman year I was a boy.

It started in the first class of my first day of high school. English. The teacher, Indira Gupta, reprimanded me for not paying attention. She called me Mr. Wilkins. No one calls anyone Mr. or Ms. or anything like that at our school. Gupta was pissed. I stopped staring out the window, turned to look at her, wondering if there was another Wilkins in the room.

"Yes, you, Mr. Micah Wilkins. When I am talking I expect your full and undivided attention. To me, not to the traffic outside."

No one giggled or said, "She's a girl."

I'd been mistaken for a boy before. Not often, but enough that I wasn't completely surprised. I have nappy hair. I wear it natural and short, cut close to my scalp. That way I don't have to bother with relaxing or straightening or combing it out. My chest is flat and my hips narrow. I don't wear makeup or jewelry. None of them—neither students nor teachers—had ever seen me before.

"Is that clear?" Gupta said, still glaring at me.

I nodded, and mumbled in as low a voice as I could, "Yes, ma'am." They were the first words I spoke at my new school. This time I wanted to keep a low profile, be invisible, not be the one everyone pointed at when I walked along the corridor: "See that one? That's Micah. She's a liar. No, seriously, she lies about *everything*." I'd never lied about *everything*. Just about my parents (Somali pirates, professional gamblers, drug dealers, spies), where I was from (Liechtenstein, Aruba, Australia, Zimbabwe), what I'd done (grifted, won bravery medals, been kidnapped). Stuff like that.

I'd never lied about what I was before.

Why not be a boy? A quiet sullen boy is hardly weird at all. A boy who runs, doesn't shop, isn't interested in clothes or shows on TV. A boy like that is normal. What could be more invisible than a normal boy?

I would be a better boy than I'd ever been a girl.

At lunch I sat at the same table as three boys I'd seen in class: Tayshawn Williams, Will Daniels, and Zachary Rubin. I'd love to say that one look at Zach and I knew but that would be a lie and I'm not doing that anymore. Remember? He was just another guy, an olive-skinned white boy, looking pale and weedy compared to Tayshawn, whose skin is darker than my dad's.

They nodded. I nodded. They already knew each other.

Their conversation was littered with names they all knew, places, teams.

I ate my meatballs and tomato sauce and decided that after school I'd run all the way to Central Park. I'd keep my sweatshirt on. It was baggy.

"You play ball?" Tayshawn asked me.

I nodded because it was safer than asking which kind. Boys always knew stuff like that.

"We got a pickup going after," he said.

I grunted as boyishly as I could. It came out lower than I'd expected, like a wolf had moved into my throat.

"You in?" Zach asked, punching me lightly on the shoulder.

"Sure," I said. "Where?"

"There." He jerked his thumb in the direction of the park next to the school. The one with a gravel basketball court and a stunted baseball diamond and a merry-go-round too close to be much use when a game was in progress. I'd run past it dozens of times. There was pretty much always a game going on.

The bell rang. Tayshawn stood up and slapped my back. "See you later."

I grinned at how easy it was.

Being a boy was fast becoming my favorite lie.

BEFORE

At the end of the second day of my freshman year, Sarah Washington found me out.

Nothing dramatic. I didn't slip up and go into the girls' room.

I laughed. Sarah heard me.

"You're not a boy," she said.

We were in the hall. Brandon Duncan slipped—I am not making this up—on a banana peel. I laughed. Lots of people laughed. But Sarah was walking past me. She heard me laugh. She turned.

"You're not a boy," she said again.

"Huh?" I repeated, continuing toward the exit.

"Boys don't laugh like that," she said, walking beside me, her voice rising.

"He what?" Tayshawn said, sliding across to join us, standing in front of me, blocking my escape. "We played hoops yesterday. He—" He was staring at me now, moving in close. I was forced toward the wall. "She?—shoots like a boy. You are a girl, aren't you? Look at her cheeks. No fluff."

"I'm only fourteen," I squeaked, my voice betraying me.

Now Lucy O'Hara was staring. Will Daniels, too. And Zach. All of them crowded around me.

"You're a girl," Sarah said. "Admit it."

"I'm a boy," I declared, wanting to push through them, to run.

"Let's pull off her clothes," Will said, laughing. "Know for sure that way."

I hugged my school bag to my chest.

"Girl!" Tayshawn shouted, laughing. "Boy would've guarded his nuts. Hah! You fooled us good, Micah." He nudged Will. "A girl beat you, man. A girl!"

Will looked down, saying nothing, and kicked his shoes into the floor.

I fought an urge to cry. I'd loved playing hoops with them. Tayshawn and Zach were so good. Especially Zach. When you play with the boys and they know you're a girl they either won't pass to you or treat you as if you're too fragile to breathe or they'll try to beat you down. Whatever way it goes it sucks. Playing as a guy had been so great. They'd passed to me, guarded me, blocked my shots, bodychecked me so hard my teeth rattled. But now Will wouldn't look at me. Zach had already gone.

"Freak," Lucy said, walking away. Sarah stared at me a second longer before walking after her.

Then there was me, alone, leaning against the wall, bag still clutched tight, as more and more students flooded by. I waited till they were all gone. Looking back, I saw the banana peel, trampled, broken into bits, but still identifiably a banana peel.

———

The first and second week of my freshman year were bad. Really bad. After Sarah Washington and the banana peel, everyone knew who I was: the girl who pretended to be a boy.

So much for being invisible.

I was called into Principal Paul's office and forced to explain.

"My English teacher thought I was a boy," I said. "I thought it would be funny to go along with it."

He said it most decidedly wasn't. Then lectured me about the danger of lies and erosion of trust and blah, blah, blah. I tuned him out, promised to be good, and wrote an essay on Why Lying Is Bad.

"So why's your name Micah then?" Tayshawn asked me. He was the only one who agreed that me pretending to be a boy was funny. He even asked me to play ball with him again. Will was less happy. Zach ignored me. I didn't go. Though I played H-O-R-S-E with Tayshawn a couple of times.

"It's a girl's name, too," I told him. "Just not as often."

"It's as if your parents knew you was going to look like a boy."

"Well." I paused, feeling the rush I always get when I begin to spin out a lie. "You can't tell anyone, okay?"

Tayshawn nodded, bracing himself.

"When I was born they didn't know if I was a girl or a boy."

Tayshawn looked confused. "How'd you mean?"

"They couldn't tell what I was. I was born a hermaphrodite."

"A what?"

"Half boy and half girl. You can look it up."

"No way." His eyes glided down my body, looking for evidence.

I nodded solemnly, figuring out how to play it. "I was a weird-looking baby." (Which is true. I like to thread my lies with truth.) "My parents totally freaked." (Also true.) "You won't tell anyone, right? You promised." In my experience those words are guaranteed to spread what you've said far and wide. I liked the idea of being a hermaphrodite.

"Not anyone. You're safe."

Tayshawn never told a soul. I know because days later there still wasn't a whisper about it. Turned out that he's good that way. Trustworthy.

I figure the rumor finally spread all over school because I told Lucy when she was hassling me in the locker room. I went for the sympathy card: "You keep calling me a freak. Well, guess what? I am!"

She looked more grossed out than sympathetic.

Or it could have been Brandon Duncan, who overheard me telling Chantal, who wanted to know how I managed to fool everyone on account of she wants to be an actress and thought it would be useful to know. She had me show her how to walk like a boy. I taught her how to spit, too.

Or maybe it was all three of them. Most likely. Hardly anyone's as tight-lipped as Tayshawn.

However it spread, it reached Principal Paul's ears, who contacted my parents, who told him it wasn't true, and there I was in his office again, explaining how I had no idea how the rumor got started and was hurt and upset that anyone would say anything so mean about me. "I'm a girl. Why would I want anyone to think I was some kind of a freak?"

Because I wanted them to pay attention to me.

Something like that.

Mostly it's the joy of convincing people that something that ain't so, is. It's hard to explain. But like I said at the beginning, I've quit the lying game now.

But that's now, back then it was:

"Why did you want everyone to think you were a boy, Micah Wilkins?" Principal Paul looked at me without blinking. I returned the favor.

"You don't know?" He sounded unsurprised. "Perhaps you will find out when you visit the school counselor."

I didn't let him see how much I hated that idea. There have been way too many counselors and shrinks and psychologists in my life. I mean, I know lying is bad, that's why I'm giving it up, but I've never understood why I had to see shrinks about it.

"You've been at this school less than two weeks, Micah Wilkins, and already you have a reputation for telling false-hoods and making mischief. My eye is on you."

I didn't ask him how that affected him seeing anything else.

My second essay for the principal was on the virtues of honesty. I ran out of things to say on the first page.

HISTORY OF ME

Being a liar is not an easy business. For starters, you have to keep track of your lies. Remember exactly what you've said and who you said it to. Because that first lie always leads to a second.

There's never ever just one lie.

That's why it's best to keep it simple—gives you a better chance of tracking all the threads, keeping them spinning, and hopefully not propagating too many more.

It's hard work keeping all those lies in the air. Imagine juggling a thousand torches that are all tied together with fine thread. Or running the world's most complicated machine with cogs on wheels on cogs on wheels on cogs.

Even the best liars, even the ones with the longest memories, the best eye for detail and the big picture, even they get caught eventually. Maybe not in all their lies, but in one or two or more. That's the way it is.

I hate when that happens. When people figure out that what you were saying wasn't true and your elaborate construction crumbles.

The lies stop spinning, there's no lubrication, gears grind on gears. That's the moment when Sarah stared at me after I laughed, and said, "You're a girl."

That moment could have lasted a week. A month. A year.

I was ashamed and angry and hating being caught and already spinning more lies to explain it all away.

But it was also a relief. It's *always* a relief.

Because the air is clear, now—*at last*—I can tell the truth. From this moment on everything will be true. A life lived true with no rotten foundations. Trust. Understanding. Everything shiny and new.

Except I can't, not ever. Because my truth is so unbelievable—lies will always be easier.

Spin, spin, spin.

I have been through the moment of being found out a hundred times, a thousand times, maybe even a million. I'm only seventeen, but I've already seen that look of shock—she lied to *me*—so many times I have lost count.

It never gets any better.

Yet that's not the worst danger of being a liar. Oh no. Much worse than discovery, than their sense of betrayal, is when you start to believe your own lies.

When it all blurs together.

You lose track of what's real and what's not. You start to feel as if you make the world with your words. Your lies get stranger and weirder and denser, get bigger than words, turn into worlds, become real.

You feel powerful, invincible.

"Oh sure," you say, completely believing it. "My family's an old family. Going way way way back. We work curse magic. Me, I can make your hand wither on your arm. I could turn you into a cat."

Once you start to believe you stop being compulsive and morph into pathological.

It happens a lot after something terrible has happened. The brain cracks, can't accept the truth, and makes its own. Invents a bigger and better world that explains the bad thing, makes it possible to keep living. When the world you're seeing doesn't line up with the world that is—you can wind up doing things—*terrible* things—without knowing it.

Not good.

Because that's when they lock you up and there's no coming back because you're *already* locked up: inside your own head. Where you're tall and strong and fast and magic and the ruler of all you survey.

I have never gone that far.

But there are moments. Tiny ones when I'm not entirely clear whether it happened or I made it up. Those moments scare me much more than getting caught. I've been caught. I know what that's like. I've never gone crazy. I don't want to know what that's like.

Weaving lies is one thing; having them weave you is another.

That's why I'm writing this. To keep me from going over the edge. I don't want to be a liar anymore. I want to tell my stories true.

But I haven't so far. Not entirely. I've tried. I've really, really tried. I've tried harder than I ever have. But, well, there's so much and it's so hard.

I slipped a little. Just a little.

I'll make it up to you, though.

From now on it's nothing but the truth.

Truly.

Guarina Lopez

JUSTINE LARBALESTIER is also the author of *Liar* and the Magic or Madness trilogy. She battles daily with an annoying procrastination fairy that will not go away, but she hopes that her good-boots fairy will stick around. She divides her time between Sydney, Australia, and New York City. Justine blogs daily at www.justinelarbalestier.com/blog.

Who's your fairy?

Enter this "doos" contest and add a little enchantment to your life!

In *How to Ditch Your Fairy*, just about everyone in New Avalon has a personal fairy.

But ditch the pixielike, flitting-about creature of legend from your mind—these fairies are from an entirely different realm. They're invisible but specialized good-luck charms, such as the:

- ✴Getting-out-of-trouble fairy
- ✴All-the-boys-like-you fairy
- ✴Good-hair fairy

If you lived in New Avalon, what fairy would you want as your lucky charm?

TO ENTER THE CONTEST, answer this question in 200 words or fewer, and you could win "astral" prizes, including a gift certificate to Forever 21 (and a clothes-shopping fairy) and a signed copy of *How to Ditch Your Fairy*.

HOW TO ENTER

NO PURCHASE NECESSARY. Contest begins October 1, 2009, and ends April 30, 2010. Enter by printing your name, date of birth, parent's/guardian's name if under the age of 18, full address, and phone number on an 8½ x 11 piece of paper or via e-mail and in 200 words or fewer let us know "Who's Your Fairy?" Mail to: How to Ditch Your Fairy Contest, Bloomsbury Children's Books, 175 Fifth Avenue, New York, NY 10010, or e-mail to children.publicity@bloomsburyusa.com. Entries must be received by Bloomsbury (Sponsor) no later than April 30, 2010. Partially completed or illegible entries will not be accepted. Sponsor will not be responsible for lost, late, mutilated, illegible, stolen, incomplete, or misdirected entries, or entries with postage due. All entries become the property of Sponsor and will not be returned, so please keep a copy for your records.

ELIGIBILITY

Contest is open to legal residents of the United States and Canada (excluding Quebec, Puerto Rico, Guam, the U.S. Virgin Islands, and where prohibited by law) to persons over eight (8) years of age. All federal, state, and local laws and regulations apply. Void wherever prohibited or restricted by law. Employees (and employees' immediate family and household members) of Sponsor, and its parent, affiliates, subsidiaries, suppliers, printers, distributors, advertising and promotional agencies, and prize suppliers, are not eligible to participate in the Contest.

PRIZES

There will be one (1) Grand-Prize winner selected and two (2) Second-Prize winners selected. One Grand-Prize winner will receive a phone call from Justine Larbalestier, a signed copy of her book, a $150 gift certificate to Forever 21, and a sneak peek at Justine's next book. Total approximate retail value of Grand Prize: $500.00 U.S. Two (2) Second-Prize winners will each receive a signed copy of How to Ditch Your Fairy, a $50 gift certificate to Forever 21, and a sneak peek at Justine's next book. Total approximate retail value of Second Prize: $200.00 U.S. No prize substitution except by Sponsor due to unavailability.

WINNERS

All eligible entries received by the end of the contest closing date will be judged by Justine Larbalestier and the Bloomsbury Marketing Department. All entries submitted in accordance with the submission guidelines contained in these Official Rules will be judged on the basis of creativity, clarity of presentation, and uniqueness of style. Winners will be notified by phone or e-mail on or about May 31, 2010. Any winner notification not responded to or returned as undeliverable may result in prize forfeiture and an alternate winner shall be selected. The potential prize winner and, if the potential prize winner is under the age of 18, the potential prize winner's parent or guardian will be required to sign and return an affidavit of eligibility and release of liability within fourteen (14) days of notification. In the event of noncompliance within this time period or if the prize is returned, refused, or returned as undeliverable, then an additional judging from eligible entries will be made to determine an alternate winner. No substitution or transfer of a prize is permitted except by Sponsor.

RESERVATIONS

By participating, Winner (and if under the age of 18, Winner's parent or legal guardian) agrees that Sponsor and its parent companies, assigns, subsidiaries or affiliates, advertising, promotion, fulfillment agencies, and suppliers will have no liability whatsoever, and will be held harmless by Winner (and Winner's parent or legal guardian) for any liability for any injuries, losses, or damages of any kind to person, including death, and property resulting in whole or in part, directly or indirectly, from the acceptance, possession, misuse, or use of the prize, or participation in the contest. By entering the contest, Winner (and if under the age of 18, Winner's parent or legal guardian) consents to the use of Winner's name, likeness, and biographical data for publicity and promotional purposes on behalf of Sponsor, with no additional compensation or further permission (except where prohibited by law). For the names of the winners, available after May 31, 2010, please send a stamped, self-addressed envelope to: How to Ditch Your Fairy Contest Winners, Bloomsbury Children's Books, 175 Fifth Avenue, New York, NY 10010.